# PROM THEORY

**Ann LaBar**



Srishti
Publishers & Distributors

**Srishti Publishers & Distributors**
A unit of AJR Publishing LLP
212A, Peacock Lane
Shahpur Jat, New Delhi – 110 049
editorial@srishtipublishers.com

First published in India by
Srishti Publishers & Distributors, 2023

First published by Simon & Schuster, New York



10 9 8 7 6 5 4 3 2 1



Published by arrangement with JABberwocky Literary Agency, Inc

Printed and bound in India

For sale in India only

*For Kaden*
*for the title and the inspiration.*

*Emma*
*for the enthusiastic support*
*and funny bits.*

*Karl*
*for everything.*

# CHAPTER ONE

## Monday

The fact that my mother and I were going to be only fifteen minutes early to school rather than my preferred twenty-five minutes had me noisily chewing gum. There was a standard rule against gum in school, but my mother, tired of my nervous habit of chewing my shirt sleeve cuffs and collars, had made a brilliant argument for granting me dispensation from that hard and fast rule. I no longer needed it every day for the anxiety relief it provided, but this morning had me reaching for the Juicy Fruit. It was going to be at least a three-pack day.

"We're going to be late," I said. It was imperative that I had some quiet time to get my books lined up in my locker in the order of my classes. My mother sighed and shook her head. Curls pulled free from her hasty attempt at a ponytail.

"Sorry, it's just I have an exam and—well, you know . . . ," I said.

Her frown quickly softened. "I forgot, I'm sorry. Trig, right? You work so hard in that class, I'm sure you'll do fine. Do you have everything you need? Calculator and, um, what's it called?"

"Protractor. You're an artist, you should know what they're called," I said as I crossed my arms and tried to keep my toes from tapping. If we were lucky, we'd make all the lights and save a few minutes of the lost time.

"I know what they are. I just never address them by name." She glanced at me with a grin.

"Please don't. You talk to the Roomba as it is. That's more than enough anthropomorphism to justify you considering the appliances family members."

"Your father travels for work, you're in school all day—who else am I supposed to talk to?"

I ignored that. She was trying to distract me from my worries. I would have none of it. I needed to stay on track. "Yes, I have everything."

"Be sure to request to take the test in the library. Oh, and remember your IEP gives you time and a half to take tests. Be sure you use all of it."

"I will, but the time and a half will cut into my lit class. I'll have to go in late . . . and everyone stares at me."

Talking about this was not making things better. My heart rate was approaching tachycardiac levels. Fight-or-flight instinct? My sympathetic nervous system was clearly preparing me to run as fast and as far as I could from the threat of awkward social situations that are broadly known as high school.

"Hey, we made great time! I don't think many of the buses are here yet," my mother said as we pulled up to the entrance of Hillcrest High.

She leaned over and gave me a quick kiss on the cheek. "You're going to have a wonderful day." I could hear the hope in her voice. She knew better.

"Yes. Well. Love you. Bye." I got out of the baby-blue vintage Volkswagen Beetle and closed the door before she could kiss me again. I sprinted up the steps and into school, not slowing down until my locker and Esther were in sight.

Esther Oplinger had been the resident of the locker to the right of mine since middle school. You could say she was one of my best friends. The truth of it was, I had only two friends. One lived next door to me, and the other had the locker next to mine. So as far as I was concerned, I had two best friends. That was enough for me, and some days it was too many.

Proximity and repeated meetings throughout the day, over many years, apparently made friendships not just easier, but possible. I wasn't comfortable with people, loud noise, wool socks, or much of anything, really. I certainly failed trying to engage in hallway exchanges that offered little more than gossip about people I didn't know or understand.

If people were talking about, for example, some new documentary series, I would enthusiastically step up and join in. The self-proclaimed cannibalistic Korowai tribe of Indonesian New Guinea? Absolutely. Sex, vaping, and decimating the football team one district over? Not so much.

Esther was frantically spinning her combination lock and then tugging on the latch. When it failed to open, she began quietly, but impressively, cursing. Not an unusual pattern of behavior for her. However, on the morning of the third-quarter cumulative trig exam, it was not conducive to my successfully preparing to conquer the Pythagorean theorem *or* Ptolemy's identities. Therefore, I needed to end her struggle or my morning was shot.

I elbowed her away from her much-abused locker. After spinning the dial two times and then to 24-6-17, I lifted the latch and pulled the door open.

"Gods, Iris Oxtabee, you are my very bestest Bee. I swear I'd be late for homeroom every freaking day if it wasn't for you."

"Yes, you would," I said. Moving past her, I reached for my

combination dial and stopped. Sloppily taped to my locker, at eye level, was a hot-pink sheet of letter-size paper.

**BAE OR NAY**

Only 19 days until Junior/Senior Prom!!
Tickets for sale during all lunch periods
from any Student Council representative.
😊 $75 per ticket 😊

I'd been vandalized. But in looking down the hallway for a perpetrator, I saw this was not a crime against my locker specifically, but instead the fallout of a propaganda campaign geared to force the student body into participating in clichéd adolescent activities. The postings were everywhere—on every other locker, littering the floor, and one even sailed through the air, as someone had folded it into an airplane.

Esther nudged me. "Hey! Have you heard any updates from Squeak about where he's going in the fall? He mentioned some little college in Oregon—do you think he'd really go that far away? I mean . . ."

Esther kept talking but I stopped listening. Not only was I surrounded with neon chaos, on edge and irritated from the now discernable tittering of nearly every female walking past or hovering in groups of three or four, not to mention a looming math test, Esther had to bring up the topic of my other best friend, Seth Fynne—otherwise known as Squeak—graduating and leaving. Something I was not going to address this early in the morning, or ever, if I could avoid it.

"Why is this on my locker?" I asked instead of acknowledging her question about Squeak. My stomach knotted. Squeak talking about Oregon, trig test, and now this. Before I could deal with the rest of my life, I had to deal with the flyer stuck to my locker. I couldn't leave it there, but if I took it down, the tape might leave a mark. And then I'd have to spend homeroom cleaning it off instead of reviewing my trig study guide.

"Same reason it was on mine. Because we're juniors, and time's running out to get prom tickets. You know, prom? That student dance you called—let me see if I remember—that's right, 'a barbaric mating ritual.'" Esther leaned toward me. "I can't wait!"

I looked away from the flyer. "For what?"

Esther rolled her eyes. As was often the case, I was missing what she thought was, as indicated by her eye roll, obvious.

"Prom!"

I looked back at the sign. Taking a deep breath, I took hold of it and carefully peeled away the tape. Nothing. Not a smear of adhesive left behind. It was like it had never been there. I exhaled, and some of the tension I'd been holding in my shoulders relaxed. Why was prom such a big deal? Trapped in a restaurant's overheated event room with loud music and forced to dance. I shuddered. "But why?"

"Well, for every reason I've been listing for the past month. Let's start over. If I had known it would take a pink flyer to get you on topic, we'd both have dresses and dates by now. But now that you've actually acknowledged there is a prom, let me repeat—it's important because we're juniors. We can go this year," Esther said. Even I could hear the excitement in her voice.

"You really want to go?" I asked. Of course she did. This was

Esther. She could dance in public without fearing humiliation.

"Oh, come on, even you said so, it's a rite of passage."

"I did?"

"Yes, but you might have been referring to something else. Anyway, what's not to love? A ridiculously expensive dress, cramming into a rented limo, the promise of romance, and, if you can get away with it, underage drinking."

"Oh." No. Nothing in that list sounded the least bit entertaining. Esther went on, talking about something concerning mermaid braids and disco buns. My attention shifted back to the blindingly bright paper. Where were the recycling containers? Who was going to pick all of this up? It was an accident waiting to happen. Someone could slip on the ones quickly gathering on the floor as they fell off lockers or were tossed there by uninterested students. These must be cleaned up and recycled.

"Iris? Yoo-hoo." Esther waved her hand in front of my face.

"Do you know where the recycling receptacles are on this floor?" I asked.

"No, why . . ." She looked down and saw I was still holding the flyer. She took it from me. And stuffed it into her locker.

"Don't worry about it. The janitor will clean up as soon as everyone is in class. We have more important things to discuss, like prom and . . ." Esther, *still* talking, reached into her locker, a motion immediately followed by the sounds of sliding textbooks, crumpling paper, and what sounded like a small jackpot win spilling onto the floor.

It took an effort, but I ignored the change gathering at Esther's feet and took the opportunity to open my own locker.

Where *was* Squeak? He jokingly referred to himself as my "book buddy," but he was just that. Organization did not come naturally to me. After years of learning methods and "tricks" to keep my things where I needed them, when I needed them, I managed on my own fairly well. But having Squeak around helped me relax, and that made getting through the day much easier. I really needed him this morning. I took a deep breath and pulled out my trig notes to put in the front of my backpack for easy access.

Since he started a tutoring job a few weeks ago, I hadn't seen him as much as usual. At least we'd been able to hang out yesterday, if only for a little while. His father pulled him away to mow the lawn before my mother even had the chance to feed him—one of her favorite things to do.

The rustling stopped, one last coin pinged as it hit the tiled floor, and then it was quiet. Until, that was, Esther squealed and slapped her hand to her mouth. It wasn't out of the ordinary, so I continued emptying my backpack and putting my homework folders next to the appropriate textbooks.

Esther reached around my open locker and tugged my arm. I leaned back and peered around the long, thin metal door between us.

She appeared to be attempting to conceal herself behind said door.

"If you are trying to hide from something, don't take this wrong, but you are not nearly thin enough to hide behind this." I tapped the door with one finger.

She was peering intently past me and down the hallway.

I started to turn away from her to see what she was staring at.

"Don't look."

"Okay." I shrugged and went back to my books.

"No, I mean—look. Just don't be so obvious like you usually are," Esther said.

"How am I supposed to look but not look like I'm looking?"

Esther pointed emphatically down the hall. I looked, as casually as I could manage. A group of males stood together several lockers away. I assumed she was referring to one of them I'd seen her talk to a few times. Darren something? She had mentioned him in the past, but as I didn't know him, I hadn't paid much attention.

"And?" I asked.

"What do you mean, 'And?' I mean, look at him. That sweet messy brown hair. Those cheekbones. That tan. Those rock-hard biceps. The way his Levi's lovingly cup his . . ." She bit her bottom lip, cupped one hand, and lifted it like she was cupping his—well, I assumed she was referring to his buttocks.

I gave her a little push, hoping to break the hormone-induced trance triggered by seeing Darren. "I had no idea you were so interested in anatomy."

"Oh, come on! You can't tell me he's not one of the hottest guys we have around here."

"I'll admit he has symmetrical features and a square jaw. Generally speaking, females are naturally attracted to strong, successful males. They can't help themselves. Such males have the greatest potential for superior genetics," I said.

"Well, no, yeah, whatever. He's hot," Esther said, still staring at him. "And really nice," she added, her voice quieter now.

I followed Esther's gaze to Darren. The small group he stood with wore Hillcrest High track sweatshirts. They were laughing, throwing mock punches and such—commonplace young male physical bonding behavior.

Watching them wasn't very interesting. I turned back to Esther. "Why do you get so worked up about the male species? You know being attracted to the buttocks of possible mates is just chemical, right? A subconscious response to the environmental and physical signals that say, 'Hey, over here—I'm good breeding stock, a good protector, and all that.'" She wasn't paying attention. Nothing new. She was, however, still watching Darren.

"Man, he's got the nicest ass from Cincinnati to Cleveland."

I took another look. "Guess so. However, his physical build is a bit unusual. His legs are extraordinarily long."

"He's a hurdler," Esther said.

"Oh. That must be beneficial. But as I was saying— it's all chemical. Did you know, when they put drug users and people who are newly infatuated or in 'love'—I made the necessary air quotations—"into an fMRI scanner, the same reward centers light up like a slot machine?" I pointed to Darren's butt. "That, right there? That's your brain on drugs."

Esther finally looked away from Darren. She had one hand on her hip; with the other she pointed at me. "Back up. What is an fM-whatever scanner?"

"Functional magnetic resonance imaging. It's an essential tool in the study of brain activity and function. It actually looks at a brain in real time while a person performs cognitive tasks. It's helping researchers discover which areas of the brain are responsible for our emotions, reasoning, and animal instincts—those that make us more than primates. Though not much more, if you ask me." I was onto something and seriously warming to my topic. I could feel it. Literally.

My feet tingled and I felt like hopping. But I didn't. I'd learned not to do that. People tended to look at me strangely when I did.

"What's got you in wiki mode this morning?"

"I do not have a wiki mode," I said. That was what Esther had labeled my somewhat lengthy monologues on the various topics I was interested in. I absorbed verbal information in detail and retained it, I suspected, forever.

"Maybe I update and correct Wikipedia entries when I see a need or an error, but who doesn't?" I was about to launch into a sound explanatory defense of my choice of topic for the morning's conversation when I noticed Darren walking away from his group and toward us.

"Hey, Esther!" he called out as he approached. I wasn't sure if he was going to stop or if he was just saying "hey" in place of a generic greeting. Why didn't anyone just say "hello" or "good morning" anymore? Ambiguous language was the bane of society, not to mention politics.

Esther turned toward him as he walked by. "Hey, Darren!"

He smiled and, still continuing down the hall, spun so he walked backward to maintain eye contact with her as he passed. How did he do that without tripping? Not being able to see where I was going was a recipe for disaster. I was not, as Esther put it, on good terms with gravity.

When he turned back around and proceeded on his way, I glanced back at Esther. Her face was bright red. And so was her chest.

It was then I noticed there was something different about her. She had on a low-cut, stretchy, tight-fitting top and—was she wearing a push-up bra? Before I could stop, my so-called wiki self took over.

"Did you know we evolved to hide signs of ovulation? Other apes' and monkeys' buttocks swell up and turn bright red, pink, or, in some cases, blue when they're in estrus."

Esther didn't react, other than to look at me stone-faced.

"It's a visible advertisement for the availability of the female. But humans don't, or I should say, our bodies no longer exhibit those signs of fertility. So women, feeling the rush of hormones, suddenly feel 'sexy' and therefore enhance and expose more of their breasts. Heterosexual men can't resist cleavage because it basically looks the same as a butt crack and swollen cheeks. Men's primal brains respond because of the visual cues, just as their primate cousins do. It naturally catches their attention, and the sight of such a display"—I opened my hand, palm up, to indicate her chest—"can increase the level of testosterone, which in pubescent boys is already off the charts. It makes most of them that much more susceptible to a female in mate-seeking mode."

Her stone-faced stare became a serious frown. "Why do you know these things? And why do you need to tell me about them?"

"Because you're my friend and you listen to me?" I said uncertainly.

Esther rolled her eyes, shook her head, and then smiled. "I don't care if my boobs look like a baboon's butt to a boy's brain. If it gets me a prom date, that's awesome. I'll buy Darwin a drink."

"You're not old enough to buy anyone a drink, much less a dead Victorian. Besides, Darwin didn't come up with that . . . well, not completely, anyway. You know, there's a good argument for our mating and mate-seeking behavior in Jared Diamond's book *The Third Chimpanzee*—oh wait, I see, you are *very* attracted to Darren! That explains your sudden flushing," I said, pleased with myself for so accurately reading her physical responses to the social contact with Darren.

"You think? Besides, it's only nineteen days till prom, and I've dropped enough hints about asking me, I'm surprised he hasn't tripped over them."

I looked back down the hallway, but he was no longer in view. "He seems very coordinated."

Esther sighed. "Never mind. Have you thought about who you might go to prom with?"

"Huh?"

Esther turned toward me full on, with one hand resting on the side of her locker and the other on her hip. "You heard me. You should go . . . even if . . ." She smiled slightly. "Well, even if you go with a friend."

"I thought you just indicated you wanted to go with Darren," I said.

"I don't mean with me. You goof . . ." She then glanced up and down the hallway, face scrunched in a way that made me think she was confused or suspicious. I sometimes had trouble deciphering Esther's moods. They could change very quickly.

"Speaking of Squeak, where the hell is he? He's going to be actually, for real, late today."

"Squeak? We weren't talking about Squeak, we were talking about Darren."

"Darren? Who's Darren?" Squeak said, suddenly appearing behind me.

# CHAPTER TWO

"Who's Darren and what about him?" Squeak repeated when I turned to find him looking peeved about something, as his squinting glare and half frown indicated.

Esther stepped up. "Darren Havercamp, and we were talking about him because of prom."

He looked at Esther and then at me. "Prom? Are you going to prom with this guy?"

"She better not be. He's mine, or at least I hope he will be. Oh, and you're late, by the way," Esther said.

Squeak relaxed, as did his expression. One corner of his lips quirked up in its more familiar friendly and slightly amused state.

He wasn't officially late, but since fifth grade he and Esther had tried to arrive early to help me deal with the noisy and confusing school mornings. I'd gotten completely lost the first day of middle school in the building's mazelike hallways. Ever since then, as they'd told the guidance counselor and my mom, they'd "had my back." Although recently he had been late more frequently than ever before. Was he trying to spend less time with me so I would become accustomed to handling things on my own before he left? My chest tightened, and I realized, while I probably would do fine without him, I would miss him.

It was to be expected. Primates have shown behavior that suggests they grieve over the loss of a family member or even the death or capture by poachers of a troop mate. I wasn't sure how that was an evolutionary tool for survival, but it was probably for an obvious reason, and the pain in my chest was just making it difficult to think logically. So I did what I always do when I feel uncomfortable in a social context. I opened my mouth.

"You must be staying up too late and your body is trying to avoid sleep deprivation by sleeping later into the morning. Most Americans get only seven hours of sleep. Research indicates we should get around nine to ten. Other primates sleep up to fifteen. That also includes monkeys—"

"Are you calling me a monkey?" Squeak raised his eyebrows and tilted his head in such a way that indicated he was joking rather than feeling insulted. Sometimes I inadvertently insulted people. It was always a relief to know Squeak knew me well enough not to take offense at anything I might blurt out.

"No, and I wouldn't, because we're descended from old-world apes, whereas monkeys—"

"Stop!" Esther said with a laugh.

"Ah, are we in wiki mode this morning?" Squeak grinned. He tilted his head downward to look at me. He'd had a growth spurt in the fall. Common enough among late-adolescent males. Females stop growing around the time of menses. Males, however, can keep growing until they are almost twenty. I had assumed he'd reached his adult height, but I didn't remember having to bend my head so far back to assess his expression. Maybe I was slouching. I straightened so I stood at my true height of 5 feet 6¾ inches. His head was bent; his hazel eyes were fixed on me. His crooked grin was the same as it had always been, and yet—Esther smacked my arm with the back of her hand.

"Ow," I said, and Esther laughed. She was, indeed, looking very bright and healthy this morning. Her full lips and bright complexion might be signs of the estrogen surge women have right before ovulation. The close proximity of a male, even Squeak, would probably set off her need to be the alpha female. "What's with the dominance display?" I asked, rubbing the back of my arm.

"I'm just trying to keep you on topic. We're supposed to be talking about prom and Darren, not eyeing up Squeak."

Eyeing up Squeak? I wasn't eyeing up anyone. I certainly wasn't objectifying my oldest friend. I grabbed what I needed for the first three periods from my locker. Squeak's expression turned odd.

I had studied microexpressions for years and what they indicated about a person's emotions or mood, but this was new. Ever since I could remember, not understanding what people were thinking or feeling had made me anxious. I'd never seen him make that particular face. I was stumped and I didn't like it.

Behind me, Esther coughed. I slammed my locker shut and frowned at her. She laughed again.

My hand shot out and quickly closed her locker. I gave her combination lock a quick spin.

"Hey! You suck, you know that?" Esther's face screwed up in a way that said, *This is going to take all day*. She set to work on the combination wheel.

"Ouch. You're in a mood," Squeak said, before giving my ponytail a quick tug. I swatted his hand away. It was pretty much a twice-a-day—or more—incident between us. Had been since kindergarten. Most days I barely noticed it. This morning, however, I must have been hyperaware due to the rare cup of coffee I'd had before leaving for school. I seemed to be noticing all sorts of new things about him.

Squeak and I had lived next door to each other since preschool. His mother used to take us to school and mine picked us up after school, and snow days had mostly been spent at my house due to his parents' work schedules. When he was twelve and his mother became ill and soon after died from breast cancer—well, we were already his second home. All that time together had likely wired our brains to recognize each other as siblings. Brothers pulled their little sisters' hair. It was the way of our species.

Esther was making a valiant third try to open her locker when she finally succeeded.

"Aha!" she shouted, and grinned, obviously pleased with herself.

I could almost see the dopamine, the pleasure enzyme, race to her basal ganglia via her ventral striatum, directly to the reward center of the brain. Life is really about the small victories. The occasional win creates intermittent reward cycles that ensure future attempts despite successive failures. She must be wired for exaggerated pleasure rewards. It must be why she kept dating, and why I didn't bother. Come to think of it, Squeak didn't bother dating either. That just confirmed my opinion that he was one of the few people not as susceptible to such illogical impulses as most. He was an extraordinary person in many ways.

"Well done. It took only three tries, not your usual five. You might have this down by June," I said.

"I don't know, sounds like wishful thinking. It's May," Squeak said.

Esther stuck her tongue out and then said, "You two are lucky you're my friends, otherwise I'd hate you both."

Esther reached into her locker and started to pull out her Algebra

II textbook, when loose paper, a couple of lipsticks, and several worn, nearly mangled novels tumbled out into the hallway.

Squeak rushed to the rescue. He was like that.

"She'll never clean out her locker if you keep helping her stuff it all back in," I said. "It's a classic example of operant conditioning. You're setting up a positive outcome for a negative behavior. You're just going to reinforce her sloppy habits."

"Bee, you're going to make me regret talking you into taking a psych elective with me this year—wait, I already do." Squeak gathered the change into a small pile and then lifted his head to hand Esther a well-worn paperback of *The Curious Incident of the Dog in the Night-Time*. He froze, book in hand. He was no doubt mesmerized, being nose to breasts with Esther as he was. So predictable, and not just because I'd known him since we were three. He was a heterosexual adolescent male, and therefore certain visual stimuli short-circuited his ability to speak.

"Words, Squeak, use your words." I gave him a soft boot in the back with the toe of my sneaker.

Squeak coughed and stammered once or twice before he got out, "Uh, here." He stood quickly and handed Esther the remaining books, while trying to look away from her prominent cleavage. He was failing.

"Humph." I was beginning to get annoyed by Squeak's uncharacteristic show of primitive behavior. But I wasn't sure how much more I could tolerate.

"Thanks," she mumbled, and they both looked away, blushing and obviously embarrassed. Such things were bound to happen occasionally, even among friends. If only they knew that their brains were awash in phenylethylamine, which triggers the production of norepinephrine and dopamine. Those neurotransmitters were causing them to flirt, however subtly. But for some reason Squeak and Esther being susceptible to each other annoyed me.

"Watch out. She's trying to get a date for prom," I warned Squeak.

"You know," Squeak said, turning back to me, "I'm not surprised Esther is getting worked up about prom, but I didn't expect you to be interested. You thinking about going? Think you could get a date?" He grinned and reached for my ponytail. I caught his wrist and held it. If I let go, he'd mess with my hair again. Usually it didn't bother me. At that moment it did.

"I could get a date. If I wanted to, which I don't. Attraction is chemical and easy to trigger in someone if you know what you're doing." I pushed his hand away, and he abandoned his attempt.

"It's not chem lab. Man, you really know how to take the mystery out of everything," Squeak said.

I pulled my phone out of my pocket to check the time. We had to break up our little morning meeting of the minds soon or we'd be late for homeroom.

"Using what I know about human behavior and neurochemistry makes inducing attraction, like I said, easy-peasy. There are some exceptions, of course, and there are several conditions that need to work in agreement. It's not entirely clear which are fail-proof."

"Then I guess there's some mystery left after all. But I can say, as a representative for the straight male species, a little boobage works wonders." This time Squeak's eyes went straight to Daun Doyle—otherwise known as Double D—and her breasts as she walked past us. I poked him. Hard. "Wipe the drool off your chin, monkey boy."

Squeak turned his head toward me. He winked. He caught my

gaze and held it. I assumed it was because he was about to make further "boobage" comments. But he didn't. He was just . . . looking at me. Why? His eyes held my gaze, and I was momentarily distracted by them. Had his eyes always been more green than brown? Interesting. Did everyone's eye color appear to shift due to, perhaps, the color spectrum of the new, more energy-efficient LED lighting?

"Iris, don't take this wrong or anything, but I don't think you know more about the secrets of love than anyone else," Esther said.

Squeak's attention shifted away from me to Esther. I released a breath I hadn't realized I was holding. It was strange how Squeak was affecting my ability to breathe. So much so that it took me a moment to replay what Esther had said and respond. "I know more about neurology and what triggers chemical reactions in the human brain than anyone in this school. Actually, most likely much more than anyone in this and several adjoining counties."

"You know, she's probably right. Hillcrest isn't exactly a hotbed of neurological research," Squeak said.

Nice of him to back me up. I nodded in acknowledgment of his support. He bent his head toward me, a clear gesture that said, *You're welcome.*

"Although, I have to agree with Esther on this. Love is one of those things you can't explain away with science, or logic. It isn't logical. The only thing that makes any kind of sense is that it *is* out of our control." Squeak tilted his head and gave me a sidelong glance. "'There are more things in heaven and earth . . . than are dreamt of in your philosophy.'"

I scrunched up my nose. "Shakespeare is not an authority who can argue for your side. A poet is not a reliable source for sound scientific hypotheses."

"You can't deny that people have turned to poets for thousands of years to express and explain love," Squeak insisted, taking a step closer to me.

"Yes, people often put their faith in all sorts of pseudoscience and use faulty sources to explain the seemingly unexplainable. Take the Roman god Cupid, for example. How long have poets kept that myth alive?" I said, pointing and leaning closer to him. I tapped his chest for emphasis.

"Hey, some of my best friends are poets," Esther said.

At her comment Squeak looked up as if startled. It was as if we both had lost track of where we were and that Esther was with us.

"Just sayin'." Esther smirked, as if she was teasing us. And she must have been. After all, we were her best friends. Did she even know anyone who wrote poetry? Could Darren be a poet? "Jocks" weren't seen as having an aptitude for language, but stereotypes were just a broad generalization for a group of people. They never truly reflected the individual.

She finished loading her backpack for morning classes and closed her locker. She motioned for us to follow her and then began walking toward the stairs that led to the junior-class homerooms.

Squeak turned his full focus on me once again. "Poets are, however, experts in love."

I snorted dismissively.

"Oh, come on, Bee. Against all odds some people find themselves together." He paused and held my gaze with his. It became awkward almost immediately. It felt as if he were trying to get me to answer a question. But he hadn't asked me anything. I looked away.

Squeak took my arm and pulled me down the hallway, quickly

catching up with Esther.

"Forget it, Iris. Even if what you're saying about neuroscience is spot on—" Esther started.

"It is," I said.

"There's a bit of cosmic chance and chaos and a butterfly flapping its wings in Paducah that you can't account for. No matter how hard we try to be in control, some things are a mystery, and I like that," Squeak said.

But that was science's purpose, taking the mystery out of life. There were some mysteries left, but this was only a half mystery at most. All the more reason for scientists to continue to test and confirm findings. Half mysteries had one foot in fact. The other foot would follow. It didn't always follow quickly. That was science. You asked the same question repeatedly until you found the answer that always worked. Or you found the right question.

"We aren't in control because we don't know enough. Everything we do is explainable. Maybe it doesn't seem logical, but we can track it back to a survival strategy in our evolutionary past. The world has changed so fast our brain's wiring hasn't had time to catch up with our modern environment. Once you have all the right information, people make sense. They have to." After all, I'd been working on understanding people since I first realized I was surrounded.

"Bee, no they don't. . . ." Squeak was now walking so close to me our shoulders touched. I needed a little space. I took a few quick steps to get slightly ahead of him.

I was starting to exhibit unusual signs of awkwardness around and because of Squeak, no less. Something had triggered my stress response, and Squeak was right there. Therefore, he must be the source of my increasing sense of unbalance. Or maybe I was dehydrated. That could explain my odd mood. I just needed to drink more water and get more sleep. And Squeak, his pituitary had to knock it off as well. His newly matured masculine traits were unnerving. Too much change too soon always put me on edge.

As we headed up the staircase, I noticed his T-shirt, the kind colleges send you when you've been accepted and they're hoping for a commitment. Lewis and Clark. A small private college—in Oregon.

"Oh." My mouth went dry. I forced myself to focus on Esther. "Well, like I said, it's simple chemistry. Studies prove adrenaline and oxytocin spikes in the brain create not only attraction to a person, but also a deep bond between two people, if done right. One that can be easily translated to love." As I looked at Esther, her eagerness about prom this morning prompted an exciting, a toe-tinglingly exciting, idea. One that took my focus far away from Squeak's shirt. "Hey, what if I helped you use my knowledge of the proven ways to enhance attraction to help you subtly persuade Darren to ask you to prom?" Inspiration didn't come often, but when it did, it really did.

Squeak barked a laugh. I glared at him. He stopped, but the deep wrinkling around his eyes told me he was sincerely amused, which also meant he thought it was a ridiculous proposal. He thought I couldn't do it.

Esther's eyes widened and she grinned. As she looked back and forth between Squeak and me, her excitement was so evident that even I had no doubt she was thrilled.

"Oh, come on. You can't possibly believe you'd be able to set up situations that could automatically release hormones, much less have him fall instantly into pop-the-prom-question mode," he said to me, and then turned to Esther. "Besides, even if you did whatever Bee dreams up and he does ask you to prom, it wouldn't prove anything. If I know you at all, you've been working on the poor guy for a while now. He's probably going to ask you as soon as he gets up the nerve. Hell, better yet, you could ask him."

Esther stopped a few yards from our homeroom. "I can't," Esther said, alarm clear in her voice.

"Why not?" Squeak asked.

"What if he says no? I mean—I can't."

"It would be fascinating to try some of these theories out. They are sure to increase his interest in you so much he'll be driven to ask you," I said. This would be awesome. Real life as a laboratory. How exciting was that? The tingling left my feet and was now making my fingers tap against my backpack strap.

"It would be a waste of time, and who knows, whatever you two pull might freak him out. Then Esther totally blows her chance," Squeak protested.

"So much of the research I've read indicates it wouldn't take much. Induce a little adrenaline, add some extended eye contact along with proven mating readiness cues, and she can't lose," I insisted. Squeak enjoyed a good debate, but denying flat-out solid research was not like him at all.

"Whoa, missy, I didn't say anything about looking to mate, at least not yet," Esther said. She punctuated the last bit with a smirk and a waggle of her eyebrows.

Squeak took a step closer to me. He glanced at Esther, and they traded some look I didn't get a chance to decipher before he lightly took my arm and pulled me a few steps away.

"Listen, Bee, can we please just drop this? I wanted to talk to you this morning about some stuff. I'm not around tonight, and I won't be free again until sometime this weekend. We should focus on just hanging together, you know, before graduation stuff starts eating up even more of my time. Why bother with something that isn't going to do anything anyway?"

Esther slid over and began to lean into the space between us. She was just about to insert herself into Squeak's new topic of conversation when something distracted her. Her whole body turned as her eyes followed the student who was walking toward us down the hall.

I followed her gaze. As he passed, I saw that it was Theo Grant, the school's track-and-field star and captain of the team. He was undeniably strong, tall, and blond, with noticeable ice-blue eyes. He was the quintessential popular male.

It was unusual for Squeak to be dismissing something I could easily do to help Esther in her dateless predicament. Well, if he didn't think it would do anything . . .

"Fine, I'll prove it to you. Not only will Esther get the prom date of her choice, but I'll convince Theo Grant by scientific means to ask me to prom." I tapped my foot. This was far more interesting than the looming threat of school ending and having to think and, much worse, talk about Squeak leaving, perhaps forever. I rocked back on my heels and then caught myself.

"Oh, come on! There's no way in hell that would work," Squeak said. His lowered brows and wide eyes were clear signs of exasperation.

Esther hooked a thumb in Squeak's direction. "I hate to agree with him, but Theo is way out of our league. Not only is he a superstar around here, but he is seriously hot."

"Prom is a little more than two weeks away. There's no chance he doesn't have a date. Plus, he's got a girlfriend," Squeak said. His disdain for this alpha male was more than obvious.

"Um, Princess Pom-Pom *just* dumped him, like, over-the-weekend dumped him," Esther said as she crossed her arms under her breasts and thrust her chest out, more likely in indignation than exhibition.

"I didn't hear about that. How do you know about it?" Squeak said.

"Well, of course you didn't hear about it, why would you? And don't forget, I'm Esther the Pester, I see all and know all."

Squeak frowned thoughtfully. "She hasn't said anything about it."

"Why would she tell you?" Esther asked. Her disbelief was evident in her tone.

"I see her for an hour after her cheer squad practice most days. We talk every day," he said.

Esther and I asked in unison, "Why?"

"She hired me to be her physics tutor to the sweet tune of thirty-five bucks an hour, cash. That's why."

"And you didn't tell us this?" Esther asked, her voice climbing in pitch.

"Why would you care who I'm tutoring?"

"Any intel on the power brokers in high school is good to have. When it has to do with someone like the captain of the cheerleading squad, yes we care."

Squeak looked at me. "Do you?" His tone was quiet and hesitant.

"Not really," I said. Because it was true. I had no reason to care about the cheerleading squad or if Squeak was spending the time he normally spent with me with some athletic, and attractive, socially significant female. Why would I?

Squeak sighed. "No, of course not."

"Well, I say you go for it. It's a subject you haven't really thought about—prom, I mean. So you don't know much about it, the social customs and all. I would think you might find it fascinating, plus I can see what works best before trying it out on Darren," Esther said. Her enthusiastic smile replaced her expression of shock at Squeak's failure to inform her of his possible source for insider gossip.

"This is a bad idea." Squeak seemed more resigned than upset, like he had been a few minutes ago. I really didn't know what was prompting his change in mood and attitude.

He reached out and gently tugged my ponytail. I let him. "Nothing I say will change your mind about this, will it? You're really excited about helping Esther and this . . . experiment, aren't you?"

"I am," I said.

"And I've never been able to talk you out of something you're this excited about. But—keep me in the loop, okay? If nothing else, I can be there to help you out if and when things go wrong. Who knows, this experiment might finally convince you that science isn't always the answer. Plus, it could help *everyone* get the prom date they really want," he said.

Esther's eyes grew wide, and Squeak gave her an intent look before his eyes came back to rest on me. Then he backed up, saluted, and slipped off into the now-thick morning crowd.

The first bell rang, signaling the three minutes we had to get to homeroom and start the school day. "You know, this is going to be *very* interesting," Esther said in a thoughtful and serious tone. "Come on, let's get to homeroom." She headed to the door of the classroom.

I followed her. I needed to get to my desk; I had a hypothesis to formulate.

# CHAPTER THREE

Squeak's preconceived conclusions were wrong. There wasn't anything that couldn't be explained in terms of science given enough time and data. No, I wouldn't live in a world where Squeak's thinking was in any way correct. It was crucial to show him that romantic feelings could be controlled, and that by doing so, we would be less vulnerable to our randomly evolved systems of fallibility. I seriously suspected he assumed his theories or lack thereof would be proven correct. And they wouldn't be. He needed to understand how endocrinology and our basic wiring put us at risk for—well, at risk of someone like Pom-Pom, who might have ulterior motives for hiring him. Such as gaining his affections so he would take her to prom, thereby saving her social status. Someone of her position in the hierarchy of high school couldn't risk being seen as not worthy of a prom date.

The importance of the experiment hit me with such clarity that I was unable to stop myself. "That's it!" I said louder than I should have, considering I was talking to myself and sitting in homeroom. Jenna Pratt, the girl behind me, rolled her eyes and expelled a puff of air that sounded a bit like "ugh."

"She's so weird," Paris, sitting next to Jenna, said.

"Weird and Aspie," Jenna replied.

I didn't respond. It wasn't an unusual situation, but I had managed to keep a low enough profile for the past few years that I didn't often evoke such reactions with my social faux pas. Especially since autism spectrum disorders had gotten so much attention in the media and education that most students knew something about them. Some people were now more understanding of neurodiversity, but in my experience, it had given some students new vocabulary to use to tease and bully. In the long scheme of life, their lack of understanding and tact didn't matter. But Esther thought it did, and as usual, she jumped to my defense.

"She's not on the autism spectrum. She has nonverbal learning disability. At least get it right. Oh, and by the way, 'Aspie' isn't an insult. It's an honor and a gift, as is NVLD. She can do stuff you can't even imagine with your so-called normal brain. She's going to change the world. But don't worry, she'll still tip you when you deliver her pizza." She turned back around again, very pleased with herself.

I knew the dead silence behind us was an indication of the two either being confused by what Esther had just dumped on them or not wanting to deal with her.

Esther smiled at me. "She shoots, she scores," she said, and pantomimed tossing a basketball. Though I didn't like drawing that much attention to myself, her actions made me grin.

"All right, Miss Oplinger, while I don't have a rule about talking quietly during homeroom after morning announcements, I do discourage shouting."

"Sorry, Ms. Jensen."

She smiled at us and winked. I moved my chair closer to Esther so we could talk softly.

"'Aspie' doesn't fall that far off the mark. It's actually a good shorthand for some of my social difficulties and anxiety. Thanks for trying."

Esther was very smart about people.

She and Squeak were my best friends and the people, other than my parents, who understood me best. We have evolved to take care of our blood relatives and close friends. It pays off in a myriad of ways: better chance to be protected when the need arises, which in turn, betters your chances of continuing to be included in the gene pool.

And sometimes she and Squeak operated with less than logical thinking. Their occasional purchase of scratch-off lottery tickets was a prime example. They were certain of a win every time one of them came out of the mini-mart clutching one. The dopamine rush was short lived, immediately followed by disappointment.

My father, a man who made his living with numbers and statistics, had tried to explain how their chances were one in ten; they might never win. For example, if you had nine white marbles and one black marble and you randomly picked a marble, you might never pick a black one. Plus, if you did win once in a while—which just fed the reward system, making you want more—the lottery didn't indicate what the real chances of the big win were. More likely one in tens of thousands. The one-dollar wins were often just enough to keep the uninformed feeling lucky. If they were so easily susceptible to such blatant scams, who knew what else they could fall for?

Which was why it was so important to show them how our brains and bodies could blind us—literally in some cases—to others' social manipulation.

It was so clear. Why hadn't I recognized the real reason I had to prove those theories earlier that morning? It was this: Friends don't let friends date drunk. If I could prove this and get the outcome I expected, it would show them how easy it was for unscrupulous individuals to take advantage of them. This would be my chance to protect them.

For me, going to kindergarten and suddenly being surrounded by people who weren't family, I had realized that one mind was forever locked away from every other mind. It had been terrifying. There was no way to know everything about a person, or predict his or her reactions to random stimuli. You can never truly know another person.

But if *I* could understand human behavior with science, then it was a puzzle that could be solved for everyone. If I could save them from being fooled by some chemically enhanced submissiveness brought on by spending too much time with the likes of Princess Pom-Pom, not to mention sycophantic salespeople at cosmetics counters and clothing stores, it was my duty to do so.

If I failed, Squeak would be unbearable, and worse, he'd probably be conned into going to prom with Pom-Pom, as I suspected might have been part of her plan when she hired Squeak as a tutor. Not that whom he took to prom mattered, but Pom-Pom just wasn't a suitable date for Squeak. She just—she just wasn't. He deserved someone who could match his intellect and hold her own in conversation or debate, much like, say, I could.

I needed to decide where to start. What exactly did I want to prove? I'd need to keep the parameters narrow. The more specific and focused my theory and hypotheses were, the greater chance I had of success. Tapping my toes, I started writing.

It was nearly the end of homeroom, and I had filled two pages with differently worded hypotheses. The bell rang, announcing the start of the first academic period. It surprised me, and I stood up so fast my chair fell backward, hitting the floor with a bang. No one paid much attention, since everyone else in the room had just woken up from their morning nap and were pushing between desks to leave.

Esther bent down and quickly righted the chair. "Hey, sorry to take off like this, but I need to catch Susan Schilling before Animal Studies starts. I need to nab her notes."

Esther was at the door before I had the chance to respond. In fact, most people were already out of the classroom. A teeming mass of adolescent humanity clogged the hallways. As I pushed the chair in under the desk, I was starting to panic at the thought of having to maneuver through the crowd. I scrambled to get my notebooks and papers gathered.

Sometimes, when I needed to stay calm, I ran through the periodic table. It's similar to when people count to ten when they're angry. It takes the mind's focus off the offending stimulus long enough for the fight-or-flight response to diminish.

I glanced at the doorway. I really did not like crowds. The noise of indistinguishable loud voices, people running into me and shoving past, made it impossible to think. Sometimes I froze and couldn't move until things quieted down. However, it had been a long time since I'd had to hide in a stall in the girls' bathroom until it was over. Just thinking about it—hydrogen, helium, lithium, beryllium . . .

"I'll write you a note for first period if you want to wait here until the halls clear," Ms. Jensen said. She was a good teacher. I'd had her my freshman year for study support. I didn't need the academic help but, the school counselor had explained to me, having a quiet place to go during the school day would benefit my studies and reduce my stress level. Ms. Jensen understood.

"Thank you." I was still organizing my colored highlighters—

yellow for urgent, green for factual information, blue for theoretical speculation on the part of the textbook's author, and orange for things to dispute in the next class. I lifted my head and managed a smile. "I have Intro to Psych with Mr. Boyer," I said.

"He won't have any issues with you coming in late, especially since you've been on time all year." She began filling out the hall pass. I put my highlighters in their case.

Thanks to Ms. Jensen, I would have a chance to recover my focus. That was crucial, since I needed to come up with distinct test situations that could be carried out without Theo becoming suspicious. If this experiment was going to run smoothly, I needed to brainstorm ideas as soon as possible. For that, I needed to include Squeak. His input was always invaluable no matter what the situation. After all, he did say he wanted to be kept "in the loop." I slipped my phone out of my bag and tried to unobtrusively text Squeak and Esther. **Meet up in Library tomorrow 4th period.**

# CHAPTER FOUR

## Tuesday
## Days to Prom: 18

**Possible Hypothesis: Feelings of romantic love are unconscious physical, neurochemical, and hormonal reactions to external stimuli.**

I was the first one in the library. I arranged my notebook and the handout I'd prepared neatly in front of me on the table.

Squeak arrived soon after. When he saw me, he spread his arms wide, indicating the empty space, and asked, "Esther?"

"Not yet," I said, relieved he'd come. I hadn't been entirely certain he would after his negative response to most of what I proposed yesterday. I hadn't heard from him last night nor seen him this morning. I had thought he was absent and perhaps ill, until I walked into psych and felt the familiar tug on my ponytail. However, I didn't get a chance to speak to him then, either, and spent second and third periods anticipating our planned meeting and seeing him, or not.

He sat, and after a few moments he reached across the table to place his hand on mine, stilling my fussing with my handouts. "Hey, look at me."

I did. Meeting his eyes was difficult today because I wasn't sure he'd be supportive. So for some reason I was staring at his lips. I forced myself to look instead at his forehead.

He sighed. I was sure he recognized my old coping mechanism, but he didn't say anything. "Okay, listen. It was a fun verbal volley yesterday, but I think you're taking this idea too far." He looked at me like he did when he was trying to explain someone's reaction to something I'd said that was unintentionally hurtful or insulting.

It happened sometimes. Had I done so? I didn't know how to respond, worried I'd say something wrong.

I thought of yesterday morning and the strange reactions I'd been having to Squeak. It was unusual for me to be concerned about what he thought of me or what I said. Mostly because he was always so understanding despite my bluntness and lack of social grace. But I was nervous.

Perhaps his absence was making me less accustomed to him, and therefore I needed time to "get used to" him again. I looked down at his hand, which was still on mine. At least his touch wasn't setting me off. He was one of the few who could touch me without all my sensory alarms going off. Again, that was because I'd become desensitized to it over the fourteen or so years I'd been in nearly daily contact with him. At least that was still comfortable for me. The idea of it no longer being pleasant gave me a sinking feeling.

"Why are you so set on doing this?" he asked as he pulled his hand away and sat back in his chair.

I stood and started pacing and kept my eyes glued to the floor rather than look at him. I needed to focus and explain so he understood I wasn't doing this just to prove him wrong. Of course, I was, but . . . "I'm doing this because I need to prove that things, like attraction, can be out of our conscious control. If we understand the fact that the endocrine system can hijack the rational brain, we're more likely to recognize when we're vulnerable to being used or hurt. We'll all benefit from this. You'll be better able to make genuinely logical choices." I paused and looked up. "You'll be safer. You'll be able to better understand other people and what's driving them and you." And so would I.

He had to remember the mixed-year phys ed classes we had in middle school and when they covered the dance section of the curriculum. How Donnie Howell had smiled at me, talked to me, gotten the whole class to make a circle around me to clap and cheer while I danced. At the time I hadn't understood that he and the rest of the class weren't impressed by my dancing. Instead they were making fun of me. I was the entertainment.

Squeak and Esther had listened patiently for days while I recounted the story about how popular I had been that day, how well I had danced, and how everyone had said so.

It wasn't until a few years later, when I was better at recognizing social cues and understood what humiliation meant, that I felt the pain and the shame of my ignorance. I wasn't mad at Esther and Squeak for not saying anything; my only friends had tried to protect me and my feelings. I had been more vulnerable than them then, but now I felt it was my chance to be the protector, as they were now clouded by the suppression of logic by romantic and physical attraction. I'd learned a lot from my less-than-positive peer interactions, but there was so much more to learn. Part of learning was putting things into practice. The best way to see things in others was to first discover how they manifested in yourself.

Squeak didn't respond right away. We had discussed in psych that morning how people are uncomfortable with silence during a conversation and especially during an argument. Rather than launch into some additional list of physiological symptoms of, well, everything I could think of, I resisted the urge to fill the silence.

Squeak leaned close again and held his hands open and faceup. It was a posture that indicated he was about to be honest and open. That made me more uncertain about what he was going to say than if he'd stepped back and crossed his arms, effectively closing himself off.

"Bee, that's really sweet. But love doesn't make us vulnerable. It makes us human, and being human means we're vulnerable. Nobody is ever safe from anything. It's called being alive. Most people do fine relying on their instincts about this sort of stuff." Squeak's brows pulled together in a visible sign of concern as he sat back and clasped his hands. Signaling the end of the conversation.

Instincts? The only instincts we still had were of the fight-or-flight variety and, of course, the drive to reproduce. Any other instincts we might have had in our more primitive evolutionary past were lost when we left the cave and planted beans. That couldn't be his real reason for telling me not to move forward on this.

"I am doing this. It's important."

"Then why am I here, if not to be the voice of reason?"

"Because when you said you wanted to know what I was going to do, I assumed you meant the specifics," I said, picking up the paper with my hypothesis outlined for emphasis.

"And do you know why I want to know what's going on? It's not about prom. That's not the issue. The issue is that I know you. And some of this"—he indicated the paper I still held—"will probably work in ways you can't predict. One way or another, I don't see how this ends well . . . for you or for me," said Squeak. Not understanding what he meant by the last bit—"for me"?—I chose to ignore it.

Esther arrived at that moment, saving me from the uncomfortable and increasingly confusing conversation. Rushing up to our table, she said, "Let the games begin!" Squeak shushed her and smiled. He put his feet up, stacking them on the table while simultaneously tipping his chair back and lacing his fingers behind his head. "All present and accounted for. I move to start this meeting," he said.

"I second that," Esther said. I was still standing across the table from them.

"I can't stay much longer. So to get things rolling and therefore wrapped up sooner than later, is that your plan?" he asked, looking pointedly at my papers.

"Of course. The hypothesis and the theory—"

"A prom theory?" Esther asked.

"Prom theory. That's excellent! Good work," I said. This meeting was off to a promising start.

"May I move to add to the meeting notes that I'm pointing out that a theory is just that—a theory? And 'theory' is defined as 'an assumption, an idea formed by speculation or conjecture,'" said Squeak, reading the last from his phone. Sometimes I wished he'd never learned to Google.

"It's a scientific principle to explain phenomena," I corrected.

"It's a guess," Squeak insisted.

"Fine. It's an educated guess," I said.

Squeak crossed his arms and nodded. "That works."

"Good. Now here's my hypothesis. Romantic feelings of love are simply a neurochemical and hormonal response to the environment and situational stimuli. The triggers of mate-seeking behavior are increased when the senses, in particular sight, but also including smell, touch, taste, and feel."

"Taste?" Esther asked.

"Yes." I nodded.

Esther put her elbows on the table and leaned forward. "This is going to be fascinating."

"As I was saying, when the senses encounter stimuli, as in this case another person, the brain interprets that individual's traits as signs of healthy and successful mate material." I paused, waiting for their response. They said nothing, just looked at me. "Well, what do you think? Is it specific enough?"

"I'm not the one to ask, but it sounds good to me," Esther said.

"It's a guess," said Squeak.

I ignored him.

"I've prepared a handout." I slid them each a copy. "On the front is a list of the experimental categories and general procedures. On the back is the list of possible materials needed."

Squeak immediately flipped the page. He scanned it and, incredulous, asked, "Fresh baked bread? Wobbly ladder? Closet with an external lock?"

"Well, they're possibilities. There may be more easily attainable and manageable materials that will suit the purposes of the experiment."

"Okay, I might know why you want a wobbly ladder, and, God help me, I'm pretty sure I know why the closet is on the list, but fresh baked bread? Are you going to make him a sandwich?" Squeak asked.

"Well, if she's going to lock him in a closet, the least she can do is set him up with a good sandwich while he's in there," Esther said. "Hey! I love to bake—want to come over tomorrow to make bread?" She scanned the list again. "High heels? Have you ever worn high heels?"

"Well, no, but that's not important right now. What's important is that we consider what increases the modern sense of attractiveness." So much for a good start.

"Hmm, healthy, well-groomed physical appearance. We can give each other mani-pedis," Esther said. "Hey, wait. You're going in a seriously girly direction. Are you sure you don't just want an excuse to get a makeover? And what about Squeak?" I wasn't sure if she was teasing or not.

"What about me?" Squeak asked.

"Are you going to be part of the makeover? Wouldn't be such a bad idea—you getting a manicure," Esther said as she peered down at his hands, which still held the papers I'd passed out.

Squeak ignored her and started in on the list again. "Facial feature analysis software?"

"It would be useful in determining my facial symmetry. Symmetrical faces are universally seen as beautiful and are good indicators of physical health and healthy genetics," I said, trying to sound authoritative. Both of them were being extremely frustrating. With the software I could create a photo with minor adjustments to my features and then figure out how to use makeup to help my face appear more symmetrical.

"It's just an idea. Remember, I have only two weeks to complete these experiments in time for prom. I need all the ideas I can get so I can choose the best ones. So can we talk about the materials section later? I need your help coming up with a schedule to best carry out these experiments. Please, turn the list over so I can explain the order of experiments listed that would optimize the results," I pleaded.

Squeak did so with a roll of his eyes and an exasperated "Okay."

Esther flipped it over. Her eyes grew wide. "Wait a minute, how did you get into the office to use the double-sided copier?"

"I have connections," I said.

"I guess so! Mr. Grabner sits guard in the printing center," she said.

"Can we not talk about this right now?"

"Okay, but this isn't over," she said.

"Nothing ever is," Squeak said under his breath as he tipped his chair back onto two legs. Esther shot a foot out from under the table and kicked one of the back legs of his chair. Squeak flailed a little to keep from falling off as it lurched forward onto all four legs.

She bit her bottom lip to keep from laughing.

What did I expect? It was spring. The entire student body was excited by the warm weather and increasing daylight, which resulted in higher levels of vitamin D and serotonin. Both of which were energy and mood enhancers. I was never going to get them to focus. "Please," I begged again.

Squeak put his hands on the table and pushed himself to standing. "Bee, you've obviously put a lot of work into this. But I'm sorry, I'm having real trouble supporting you. To be honest, I don't think I want to be around when both of you are acting, well, let's face it, a little desperate." He picked up his backpack and pushed his chair in.

*He was leaving?*

"Is Pom-Pom waiting for you? I know how *important* your time is with her." I was surprised by the words that had come out of my mouth. What was wrong with me? This was his job. It was important to him. He did need the money. But I was irritated and angry that he was leaving so soon. During such times my "filter" didn't always function well. It was one thing to think something. It was another thing to actually say it.

I could tell he was taken aback by my comment. But strangely, he also looked a little . . . was that smug? Or pleased? He and Esther exchanged a look. They both reacted like they had passed some crucial information between them, and Esther nodded in a way that clearly affirmed whatever Squeak was "saying." They obviously understood each other at a glance. There was so much to learn about the mind—maybe telepathic communication really was a thing.

Squeak glanced up at the industrial-style clock above the doors of the bathrooms. "Speaking of tutoring."

"But . . . ," I started, but didn't go on because I didn't know how to convince him to stay. What I did know was that I had to get this endeavor on the fast track.

And I was about to introduce and discuss engaging the other person's senses. The more senses I could appeal to, the more immediate and, hopefully, successful the results would be. I needed to start with sight. The only way forward was to be in Theo's line of sight as often as possible. Nearly every time he looked up, if I could manage it. And for that I needed Squeak's help.

Theo Grant was a senior, I was a junior, and our paths rarely, if ever, crossed. Like most of Hillcrest High, he didn't know I existed. Only Squeak would be able to get the information I needed before I could get started. Unfortunately, it involved him talking to Pom-Pom. The time to ask him was now.

"Bee, I have to go. I'll see you guys later." He waved good-bye and headed to the large double doors.

"I'll be right back. Stay here," I said to Esther. Before she could assure me she would be there when I returned—I knew she would—I walked quickly after him, following him out into the hallway.

# CHAPTER FIVE

"Squeak, wait. I just need to ask a favor," I said to his back as I exited the library and saw that he was already a few yards away.

He stopped, turned, and walked back to me. "Is this about prom theory?"

"Yes," I said.

His shoulders slumped, and he sighed, shaking his head in a dramatic manner. "I know you are doing a lot of this to help Esther. She doesn't need much help, but she could use a little. Most people would never guess it, but we both know she can be shy and not as confident as she acts."

"Yes and no. This is more about Theo," I said.

The muscles in his jaw twitched. He was not pleased with my response. "Seriously? This whole thing sounds less like science and more like testing out flirting methods. Something I obviously know so little about. So I can't see what kind of favor you need from me."

"You seem to be doing fine flirting with Pom-Pom," I muttered.

Squeak laughed. "You think I'm flirting with Taylor? Wow, you need Esther's help more than she needs yours. Hey, wait, are you jealous?" He grinned, and a lighter demeanor replaced his attitude of seconds before.

"What? No! Where did that even come from?" I frowned up at him—was he even taller than he was yesterday? He should really get his pituitary checked. Too much was changing too fast. And his teasing wasn't making any of this easier. He raised a questioning eyebrow and smirked.

"I'm not jealous. Well, maybe I am, but only because you are wasting what little time is left of the school year with her. Instead of with me—me and Esther. I don't trust her. I get why you are tutoring, but why her? Not that it matters who you tutor. I just mean . . ." I shrugged and looked away. How had the conversation turned to this? This could end up about only one thing—the one thing I didn't want to talk about. His leaving for good.

He reached out and loosely took my hand. "Look, I've got a chance to do some easy work for some serious cash. Something I need more than getting you, or even Esther, a prom date. I hate to be a downer, but I have some real-life decisions to start thinking about." He dropped my hand and shrugged. He stuffed his hands into his pockets and looked away from me, staring at nothing somewhere in the distance.

I couldn't think of anything to say.

He looked back and sighed. "I kind of owe her. If her parents hadn't paid me up front for a bunch of sessions, I would've never been able to get my college applications out at all. They were late enough as it was."

As much as I disliked this whole situation with Pom-Pom, I did need his connection to her to start my experiments. And the money the job provided him would greatly aid his college plans. So we both needed her help in the short term. However, though I wasn't sure why, every time the Pom-Pom subject came up—which since yesterday morning felt like all the time—I became more committed to proving my theory of human attraction. I needed to get this over with. "Please, I just need one favor," I said.

"What?" he asked warily.

"Get Theo Grant's daily routine and class schedule from Princess Pom-Pom."

He straightened away from the wall. "And how am I—why would I—"

"Shush." I put my hand on his chest as the door to the library swung open. One of the teachers stepped out and, closing the door behind him, turned left without looking our way and went down the back stairwell. His footsteps echoed as they faded.

Squeak watched him walk away before turning his attention back to me. "How am I supposed to do that? 'Oh, by the way, my friend wants to stalk your ex. Could you tell me where he goes from the time he wakes up until he passes out after the track party?'"

His chest was unusually warm, hot even, and his complexion appeared reddish. Maybe he was getting ill. I dropped my hand from his chest and then placed it across his forehead.

"What the hell?" He pulled my hand away.

"I was just checking to see if you had a fever." I was mumbling and suddenly unable to concentrate. I looked at my hand.

"Why?" He looked stupefied.

"I just—well, your chest seemed really hot."

"I'm a mammal, Bee. Mammals have a nice toasty body temperature. See?" He took my hands, wrapping both of his around mine. "You, however, have cold hands. You always do. Maybe you need a little more time on your rock under the heat lamp."

"Stop it." I yanked my hands out from between his.

"Bee?"

I turned away. I could feel my face getting hot. I never blushed.

Ever. Certainly not when Squeak teased me. Something was definitely wrong with me. It felt like someone was changing the rules.

He placed his hands lightly on my shoulders and gently urged me to turn back to face him. "Bee, your face is bright red. Oh my God." He laughed a little. "I've never seen you blush. It's cute. Did I embarrass you? I didn't know I could." His grin was huge.

"You didn't embarrass me. I do not get embarrassed, especially not by anything you say or do," I said. I knew it made sense due to our upbringing, but why did he *always* have to act like a sibling?

He crossed his arms and leaned back against the wall. "I think she doth protest too much," he said. My mother would say his teasing grin and mussed, dark, wavy hair were charming. It made me want to pinch him and tell him to get a haircut.

"I'm going to regret Esther getting you to take drama club with her two years ago. Look it, are you going to ask Pom-Pom for his schedule or not?"

"Quizzing Taylor about her ex is going to look a bit obvious and make both of us look like stalkers," he said.

"I guess it is a bit obvious. It would really undermine the results if word got back to Theo about what we're doing," I said. But how else would I get the information I needed?

"What *you're* doing. And yeah, it wouldn't help much." He unfolded his arms and pushed away from the wall. His grin was gone.

"Okay. Let me think. You said she was chatty, right?" I asked.

"Yeah. I get paid by the hour, so it's like overtime for me. It feels like overtime."

That was good news. If he got tired of listening to her constantly talk about herself and gossip about everyone else, he'd be more receptive to helping me. Plus, he'd realize this tutoring job was far more trouble than it was worth. And then we could get back to normal.

"So you get her talking. Say things like, 'I heard you broke up with Theo.' That alone should set her off. Let her gather up some momentum, and then slip in comments like, 'I bet track really keeps him busy. He probably didn't have time for you.' Or, 'That's got to be rough—you're probably together in a bunch of classes.'"

Squeak rolled his eyes. "Bee, come on—"

"Use offhand suggestions and subtly point out something that will stick in her subconscious. Then when you set her up with a question or a choice, you've already influenced her to do what you want! I know you can do it."

"You really ought to go into marketing. There's the making of a grand manipulator in you, or at least a prosecuting attorney." He was back in teasing mode. His easy smile, the one I knew and expected from Squeak, lightened his features.

I suddenly realized I'd been holding my breath waiting for his response. Of all people, Squeak shouldn't make me anxious. I relaxed, and the air rushed from my lungs. I smiled up at him. "It's nice to know you're thinking about my future. But I need you to stay focused on this right now."

He gave an exasperated sigh. "This will make you happy?" he asked with a slight tilt to his head. "I won't have to do anything else?"

I nodded. While body language can be misinterpreted, nodding means yes in every culture. "Nothing else, except admit defeat when the time comes."

"Oh, Bee, damn it. Fine. I can't say no to you when you look at me like that."

Like what? I wasn't sure what I was doing to influence him, I was just glad that whatever it was had worked.

"I can do this one thing for you, since I'll be getting paid. But I won't be able to get the information to you until later tonight. If she does what you say she will, it's going to take at least a couple of hours to get through the stuff I need to so she'll be ready for tomorrow's quiz."

If he wasn't able to get it to me before the end of the school day, I would lose a day when I could otherwise have been making progress. I'm sure my concern over the time lag was apparent, because he sighed before saying, "Enough already, knock it off. I already said I'd do it."

"Knock what off?" I asked.

"Looking at me like I just broke your balloon."

I wasn't quite sure what he meant, since I had an aversion to balloons and their potential for high, squeaky sounds when rubbed. Not to mention, a balloon popping close to me was painfully loud and, I admit it, scary.

Before I could ask him to clarify, a high-pitched squeal sounded from somewhere in the hallway behind Squeak. He dropped his hand and spun around, both of us peering down the hallway to see who or what had made the noise. Speaking of painful sounds . . .

Princess Pom-Pom.

Now? Maybe this interruption wasn't so bad. The sooner he could get the information, the sooner he'd be able to get back to me. She raced up and took his arm.

"I found you! I've been looking everywhere," she said. "Where were you? I've been waiting." She tilted her head down, looking at him with upturned eyes. Her bottom lip puffed out in a pout. A clear indication of submissiveness mixed with disappointment. That was a posture and look that was intended to incite not only a protective response from the male, but also guilt. Pom-Pom was obviously trying not only to make him care about her, but also to induce enough guilt so that he would be driven to act in ways that would please her and relieve said feelings of guilt.

Still holding his arm, she placed her other hand on his chest. I had to stop myself from asking her if he felt unusually hot. No need to call attention to Squeak's body; it would just make her notice him more and might even increase her interest in him. I didn't have time to deal with any additional Squeak unavailability. I certainly didn't want to have to lose his companionship any sooner than necessary, and that would be inevitable with the addition of a girlfriend to his remaining time at school and in town. Though there was really nothing to be concerned about in that department, because honestly, if and when Squeak did get a girlfriend, it certainly wouldn't be someone who couldn't pass physics without a tutor.

"I got permission for us to use the first-floor conference room next to guidance. Cool?"

"Sure," he said. He was smiling, but his hands were stuffed, once again, deeply into his front pockets. A clear sign of reluctance. I was a little shocked to realize his reaction toward her pleased me.

Her soft laughter in response to his agreement wasn't a grating sound and shouldn't have made me reflexively cringe—but it did.

She touched her hair, tucking it behind one ear. Squeak had to know what she was doing, even if she didn't. I'd told him about contact readiness cues the very first time I read about them. Maybe I shouldn't have. If he recognized she was interested in him as more than just a tutor, it might not bode well for our friendship.

Pom-Pom leaned into him, pressing her breasts against his arm. “You’re such a lifesaver.” She leaned back and jumped up and down in small, quick movements. She had Squeak’s full attention now. Everything about him suddenly seemed more masculine, more flexed. He was my oldest and best friend, but that didn’t mean I wanted to see his primal male responses kick in the minute some female started to wiggle in front of him with what appeared to be great enthusiasm.

Did she really think hanging all over him would get her what she wanted? Well, she was wasting her time, I hoped. I realized she had yet to acknowledge my presence.

“So,” I said loudly, interrupting their flirting.

She turned her head and glared at me with narrowed eyes. A clear sign of suspicion. So that’s what they meant when they said, “If looks could kill.” Thank goodness they didn’t. I’d be sprawled facedown, heart stopped, right there in the middle of the hallway.

Ignoring her, I smiled sweetly at Squeak. “See you tonight. I’ll let my mom know you’re staying for dinner.”

Squeak had been looking down Princess Pom-Pom’s V-neck sweater. I mean, he was only human. And how could he possibly avoid it? She was a good deal shorter than him, and when he looked down at her, they were just right there.

He looked up, met my eyes, and smiled a Duchenne smile. It’s the kind of smile you can’t fake. The orbicularis oculi, the muscles around the eyes that lift your cheeks and wrinkle the skin around the eyes, aren’t under our conscious control. We control only the muscles nearest to the eye. That I had elicited an honest smile and Pom-Pom hadn’t made me irrationally pleased. But maybe it wasn’t such a silly reaction. She hadn't won him over entirely, and that meant he was still mine—my best friend, that is.

"Yeah, I'd like that. I missed your mom's cooking last week." His voice softened, and he was talking to me and only me. It was obvious she'd been left out of this conversation whether she knew it or not. Given her popularity and success as a team leader, she must be in tune with social cues and would quickly realize she'd been left out. I moved closer to Squeak.

"My dad is still on a business trip, and my mom would love the extra mouth to feed. Besides, your dad's working tonight, right?" When Squeak's mother died, his father began working late shifts at the automotive plant where he worked on the assembly line. He had become and still was a depressed and distant man. Squeak tried to make dinner for his dad on the nights he was home, but it didn't do much to bring his father closer to him, despite the connection between food and a feeling of closeness and affection.

Squeak had developed the survival strategy of showing up at my house close enough to dinnertime that my mother would ask him to stay and eat with us. He would stay late into the evening on those nights. Later when we were in middle school and Esther became our friend, she would usually join us after dinner to do homework or convince us to watch some movie with little or no educational value.

Squeak's playful mood dampened a bit. "Yeah, he is. Thanks, Bee."

"Come on." The princess was unhappy with not having Squeak's full attention. She urged him back down the hallway toward the stairwell, presumably to head to their quiet, private room.

"See you later." I emphasized every word and raised my voice to be sure he heard me.

He gave me a little wave, then turned around and let Princess Pom-Pom drag him away. The thought of him not enjoying being with her lifted my mood.

I'd have preferred it if there were something I could begin with that didn't involve Squeak spending even more time with Pom-Pom. But given that she would have some crucial insight into Theo's movements and even his preferences that I could then appeal to . . .

Maybe Squeak tutoring Pom-Pom wasn't such a bad thing after all. Maybe.

I headed back into the library, where Esther and our plans were waiting.

# CHAPTER SIX

The ability to understand what is going on in other people's heads is called theory of mind. It's important for survival and navigating society. We developed the skill as soon as our brains had evolved to be large enough to handle more than finding food, sleeping, and mating. Rather than only focusing on the wants and needs of our own minds, we began to consider what was going on in others'. As social animals, it was a necessary survival tactic.

But like in all things, some humans are better at theorizing someone else's thoughts than others. Esther was particularly good. To be honest, sometimes it was a little creepy, considering I *never* knew what she was thinking.

"Okay," I said as I moved to the other end of the table to sit next to her. More than ready to get started, I pulled out the leather-bound notebook I used as a journal. Unlike many, I had no need to call this book a diary, as if it were a pen-and-paper confessional. I entered only observations that might prove to be important for one reason or another, as well as questions that needed further exploration and research. Sometimes Squeak got hold of it, but Esther never had, which explained her persistent curiosity.

"Oh my, that's your little black book you never let me snoop through," she said.

"Because you'll say it's boring."

"There's nothing boring about this. Show me!"

"Not a chance. Okay, so basically, the experiments are going to fall under four main categories. We'll begin with priming, and then elements and methods of enhancing attraction. Then the role of adrenaline in the misattribution of arousal will follow, along with methods of increasing suggestibility. The overall goal is to create an attraction and emotional attachment between Theo Grant and me, resulting in him inviting me to prom."

Esther chewed her lip. "I mean, that's cool if it works between Darren and me, but between you and Theo? Do you mean you'll fall for Theo if these experiments work?"

"No." Would I? In the course of this would I unintentionally become awash in a wave of neurochemicals? Would these situations, these experiments, cause my lizard brain to react despite my logical mind? "Of course not. I don't have any sort of instinctual reaction of attraction to him now, do I?"

"Do you?"

Definitely not. "No."

Esther shifted in her seat and stared at me. It made me uncomfortable, so I looked away. "Maybe we need to think this through some more, so that we can catch anything that goes wrong early," she said.

"Now you sound like Squeak. I have thought this through. The only thing that can go wrong is that he becomes attracted to me but doesn't ask me to prom, thus giving Squeak enough ammunition to say I failed completely and that he was right all along."

"You're sure?" Esther asked, obviously starting to have second thoughts.

"I am. Completely confident. The science is too solid." Solid enough, anyway.

"Okay, in that case." Esther held out her arms in a grand gesture. "Let's go for it."

"Great. I'll need you to help me set up the experiments and make observations. Maybe you can take notes if we can figure out how you can observe the experiment without being noticed. You can try it out on Darren. Then we can write up an analysis and make plans for the next step based on what we learned."

"No prob! I'm not part of Theo's cheerleader groupies, so he has no reason to notice me. It also means you're going to really have to stand out to get his attention." Esther took my outline from the table and began to study it.

I reached around and pointed to the first heading on the page. "Here. Priming. You know what priming is, right?"

"It's when you push the little button on the lawn mower three times before you start it," she said.

I looked from the outline to her. "Huh?"

She laughed. "I know what priming is. You talked about it nonstop when you guys covered it in psych."

"Oh, okay," I said.

"Although, you should probably come over soon so I can show you how to use a lawn mower."

"Sure," I said. Esther had many odd preoccupations. Obviously, lawn care was one of them.

"Would you feel better if you explained what *you* mean by priming?" Esther asked.

"Yes, please." I was relieved to have her back on topic. "The best definition I've found so far is from the Wikipedia entry."

"Of course," Esther said. "And how much did you correct the Wikipedia definition?"

"Oh, not much. It was quite succinct as it was. Just needed a little tweaking." I skimmed down to the bottom of the page, where I'd listed a few terms I thought might need clarification. "Strictly speaking, it's 'an implicit memory effect in which exposure to one stimulus influences the response to another stimulus.'"

"And that means?"

"Let me back up a little so you can get a better picture of the different types of priming and how we can use it to get the desired outcome. There's a region in the midbrain that's called the substantia nigra/ventral tegmental area."

Esther coughed.

I scowled at her, and she made a rolling-wheel gesture with one hand, which meant, *Get to the point.*

"Fine. Okay, basically when we see things that remind us of something we are previously familiar with and, perhaps, that is important to us, we transfer that importance to the new things that remind us of the old thing."

Esther tapped her fingers on the table before pointing at me. "So if you do something that reminds him of Pom-Pom, he'll pay more attention to you because you remind him of her. That could really backfire, since she dumped him."

"That's an important point. You're right. But that wasn't my plan. I need to do things or take on attributes he will notice. We're hardwired to get excited by new things. We're drawn to novelty without even knowing that's what's happening. So I need to be the new thing that catches his attention. Then we can set up other things that will grab his attention by causing him to recall me and all my unique newness."

"Makes sense, but I could have told you that. No need to be poking around in the middle of your brain," Esther said.

"Also, novel things motivate us to find out more about that thing. Each new stimulus gives you a little rush of motivation to explore, because it makes you anticipate a reward."

"'Cause chemicals and the brain."

I nodded. "Exactly."

"So you need to run into him a lot and catch his attention. Once he sees you a bunch of times, he'll want to know more about you. So he starts looking for you and maybe talks to you." Esther considered me. "I know you've got all kinds of crazy science to back you up on this, but you can get this kind of advice from a magazine."

"They get it second-, third-, or fourth-hand from science articles in real publications."

"Don't be a snob."

"Are we working together here or not?" I asked. Esther waved a hand, and I took that as a sign of agreement. "The problem is that I don't know what visual stimuli I can use that will be unique and make me stand out."

Esther sat up straight and slapped her hands on the table. "You came to the right place. Oh, this could be fun! You should definitely have a signature color, something bright but not ugly, or neon. After the first few times he sees you, that color will *prime* him to think of you whenever he sees it. Or maybe you keep changing things up after a day or two of running into him, then that change will stand out as something new. He'd be all like, 'Whoa, what happened to the fluorescent orange cape you always wear?'"

"Fluorescent orange is really bright. It would feel like wearing a loud noise. I'd be on edge all day. And a cape is kind of silly, don't you think?" Esther had good ideas, but sometimes . . .

"I'm joking. Fluorescent orange doesn't look good on anyone. The only good thing about it is it keeps you from being mistaken for a doe during hunting season. But I'm serious, let's figure out your signature color. Can't be white." Esther scrunched her lips to one side and tapped her fingers on the table.

"Why not? It's bright. A surprising percentage of the student body wears black, so it would stand out," I said. Seemed like a perfect choice. I had lots of white shirts. I might even still have the white dress my mother made me wear to some concert in the park last summer.

"No, white would make you look like a ghost or a bride," Esther said, shaking her head.

"Good point. Not the image I'm going for," I said. I was glad Esther was helping me. I would have shown up to school dressed in all white.

"How about red? It brings out your rosy complexion. It looks very pretty on you. . . . Squeak always says so."

"Really? Um, then I guess that would be a good choice." Not that it made any difference what Squeak thought. I was surprised that he had any opinion at all about my appearance. I suddenly felt hot and uncomfortable. The air conditioning must not have been working properly. Air conditioning . . . oh!

"Wait." I got up to get my backpack from where I had left it near the head of the table. I pulled out the red sweater I kept on hand in case the janitor turned the air conditioning all the way up. He did that when he was angry at the administration.

"This is perfect because red can carry a sexual message. It especially attracts mate-seeking males. Humans in general pay more attention to the color red when it comes to dating. It all goes back to what I was talking about yesterday morning about primates' bright red—"

"Are we back to swollen asses?"

"Yes." This was going swimmingly. Esther had great instincts.

"Well then, red it is. Now we need to find something else that will make Theo notice you. Maybe you could wear something with flowers on it so he can remember your name when he sees you." Esther was moving right past any more conversations that involved swollen genitals and evolutionary biology.

"Like a headband or a hat with a flower on it?"

"Oh. God. No. He'll look at you, but it won't be in a good way. I was thinking about a necklace my aunt has. It's really expensive looking, and the kicker is, wait for it, it's an enameled iris. He sees that—it's pretty and shiny, so he'll notice it—and he'll remember your name."

That had some interesting possibilities. "I like it, but will she loan it to us?"

"Sure, that's why I brought it up. A very ex-boyfriend gave it to her a long time ago. Doesn't wear it much. When she does, she just complains, says it reminds her what an asshole he was."

"Why does she still have it?"

"Sentimental reasons."

"Oh. Can you get it tonight? The sooner, the better," I said.

"She lives really close to us. I'll have my mom pick it up later." Esther started to stand and reached for her backpack.

I was so caught up in Esther's excitement that I'd forgotten one of the reasons I hadn't wanted to do this without Squeak. "Wait. We have a major strategic problem."

Esther stopped, her hand resting on her backpack. "I could probably come up with a list of strategic problems if I wanted to. Which I don't, 'cause that would just suck the fun out of this. But if you must, what is it?"

"Well, we don't exactly travel in the same social circles as he does, we don't have any classes with him, and we don't even have the same lunch. So I asked Squeak to ask Pom-Pom for Theo's schedule while he is tutoring her today."

"Wow, that was a really good idea. You won't have it to be able to start today, though. But we do know where his locker is," Esther said.

"It's a start," I said.

"Oh hey, I almost forgot. There's a boys' track practice right after school today."

"How do you know?" If she was right, I could get started right away.

"It was on morning announcements," she said.

"Oh. I never pay attention to those."

Esther's mouth turned up at one corner in a half grin. "I know." Esther reached for her bag and stood up. We walked out of the library into a day now rich with possibilities, and ready to test the adolescent male mind and its so-called mysteries of the heart.

## HANDS OFF

Iris Oxtabee's Very Scientific Journal

***

Prom Theory

### Introduction

*The expectation of this research is to prove that the emotion of romantic love can be clearly explained by the effects of the release of enzymes and chemicals in the brain such as oxytocin, adrenaline, dopamine, and norepinephrine in response to specific external stimuli.*

*In addition, this researcher hopes to prove that responses to* specific external stimuli are predictable and consistent.

## Hypothesis

By employing previously proven research, the researcher (me) can use prearranged and accidental situations to activate the unconscious and involuntary release of neurochemicals and enzymes in the subject (Theo Grant, hereinafter known as TG). Affecting the body's physiological response—such as rapid heartbeat, sweating or chills, and enhanced senses—will result in the misattribution of said responses to feelings of love and the excitement of new love.

Further, using psychological techniques, such as priming and increasing suggestibility, TG will be compelled to ask the researcher to prom.

## Materials Needed

Subject's class and track schedule. Tutor (Squeak) will obtain from subject's former girlfriend (Princess Pom-Pom).

Once familiar with TG's schedule, this researcher will be able to encounter the subject, ideally several times a day.

Note: It may take some time to learn certain specifics about his personality and taste in order to tailor stimuli to his particular preferences.

# CHAPTER SEVEN

## Tuesday After School
## Days to Prom: 18

**Step One: Repeated Exposure and Priming**

*Novel stimulus creates motivation to further explore the novelty in anticipation of reward.*

**Method one:** *the use of novel stimuli to trigger motivation in subject (TG).*

**Notes:**

- *Intermittent reward is a strong motivation for action, possibly the strongest.*
- *It is important to keep in mind that the reward is not the exciting payoff for an action. Instead, it is the anticipation of the reward that is so compelling.*

"I'm glad you came with me. With you here I won't look like I'm a stalker. Plus, I know you know some of the guys on the track team," I said as I peered down at the field from where Esther and I sat halfway up the bleachers.

"Yeah, I know some of these guys." Esther grinned. She paused for a moment and then put the back of her hand against her forehead. She sighed heavily. It was very forced and very dramatic. Which meant she was about to tease me. "And here I thought you just wanted to do something I enjoyed for a change. You know, like maybe you were just looking to hang out with Esther, thinking of me first. Alas, I should have known better. You're just here for you."

"Well, I suppose I am," I said. I was only half-serious and fairly confident that Esther knew that I was teasing in return. But in case she didn't, I grinned.

"Hello, ladies!" Squeak said loudly as he dropped onto the metal bench behind us. The sudden clang and rattle of the vibrating aluminum added to the element of surprise. It also made me clench my jaw, and a shudder ran through me.

Both Esther and I jumped. Esther instinctually clutched her heart and panted. With adrenaline most likely still coursing through her, she enthusiastically swatted at him with both hands. He must have tiptoed all along the top bleacher until he reached us and could pounce. He reached over and tugged my ponytail.

"Since when did you start calling us ladies? It's sexist. And stop sneaking up like that! You know it freaks me out." Esther dismissed him quickly after that and resumed scanning the field, holding her hand above her eyes to reduce the glare from the sun reflecting off the bleachers.

Squeak pulled his sunglasses out from where he had hung them by one temple in the neckline of his shirt. He lightly tapped Esther's shoulder with them. With the barest hint of acknowledgment, she glanced back, took the sunglasses, and put them on. With that, she turned her gaze back to the field. The three of us had been spending time together for so long that such gestures were basic habits between us. No need for thank-yous or any other social conventions. I found it comforting. No pressure on me to make sure I was saying or doing the proper niceties.

I'd previously gone to the field only during pep rallies, so it was comforting to have them both with me, especially in a place I'd been to so rarely. It made it easier to ignore the unfamiliar people and noises. They created something of a buffer. Without them I would have to find something else to focus on in order to try and tune out everything around me. Such efforts for me were exhausting.

"I almost called you poseurs, but I didn't think that was very nice." Squeak's face was flushed from running up the bleachers. The exertion highlighted his obviously strong legs and good cardiac health, as he wasn't breathing heavily. He appeared energetic but calm.

"Poseurs? That isn't something in your usual repertoire of descriptive language," I said. He turned his smile toward me, and it proved to be contagious.

I looked away, but not before something about it—our shared look, maybe, or the unexpectedness of his being there—set my toes to tingling. Probably because my resulting smile was positive proof of mirror neurons' effect on facial expression. Real-world proof of neurobiological theory always gave me a sense of discovery, even something as simple as *I smile because he smiles, and he smiles because I smile*—hence the tingling toes. I tapped them lightly on the metal footboards despite the soft ringing of the bleachers.

"I got a college admissions ad from some school in Illinois that said 'poseurs need not apply,'" he said.

Esther snorted. "Which means poseurs go there. Hope you tossed it."

"Straight into recycling."

"Why are you here?" I turned to look at his relaxed smile and his barely noticeable crooked nose. I was pleased that he had shortened his session with Pom-Pom to spend time with us. However, that meant he likely hadn't gotten the intel I needed. "Did you get Theo Grant's schedule?"

"Not yet." He leaned back, resting his elbows on the bench behind him.

"But—"

"Relax. Taylor had a cheer squad emergency and had to go to a quick meeting. I'm just waiting for her. We're headed to the library near her house." He leaned forward and briefly waggled his fingers in my ponytail.

Esther smirked at us and shook her head. Squeak pulled his hand back. He looked down at the athletic fields, squinting against the sun.

His eyebrows raised slightly, and his eyelids slid half-closed. He looked bored, perhaps uninterested in the track practice. Esther handed his sunglasses back to him. He took them with a nod of thanks and slipped them on.

"Oh, um, okay. I mean, that's good. You'll still be able to quiz her for me," I said.

He wasn't staying. I was disappointed. His not being with Esther and me nearly every day after school these past few weeks was a significant change to our daily schedule. I didn't like change very much. In fact, I didn't like it at all.

We all sat in silence for a moment. A whistle cut through the low murmur of voices, the occasional shouts, and loud laughing coming from the boys below. None of the action taking place in front of us inspired conversation. Suddenly Esther's eyes widened and she quickly twisted around. "So, Squeak, you've known Iris for, like, ever."

"Yeah." Squeak narrowed his eyes. Normally, such a facial expression would suggest suspicion, but that didn't make sense, since there wasn't anything suspicious in Esther's observation. It was a simple statement of fact. So much so, it didn't make any sense that she would be bringing it up.

"What are some things that make you think of Iris? I mean in a good way, not annoying things like long explanations and useless information," Esther said.

"No information is useless information," I pointed out.

Esther and Squeak spoke over each other, and I wasn't certain which one said what.

"The sun makes twenty-five percent of people sneeze."

"An average human loses two hundred head hairs per day."

"What's your point?" I said. Why was Esther starting this line of inquiry? For whatever reason, I didn't like it much.

"What do you mean?" said Squeak.

"Well, like are there things you see or run into that make you think of Iris?"

"You mean like ponytails, sharpened pencils, sticky notes, microtip pens—"

Esther laughed. "Sort of, but what are some things that might have the potential to move Iris out of the smart-girl zone to the hot-must-have zone?"

Squeak hesitated, opened his mouth, and then closed it. I thought his reddened face was due to the direct sunlight and his propensity to burn, but it started to fade as quickly as it had appeared. He was likely embarrassed by the question. Though why it was embarrassing was beyond me.

Suddenly her inquiry made sense. Of course. Highlighting and enhancing my most attractive features and personal traits would make getting Theo's attention that much easier.

"I see where you are going with this," I said to Esther. I turned my attention to Squeak, who was looking down at his shoes. Information of all types excited me. Information about myself was something often difficult for me to recognize. This project was becoming more and more intriguing.

"There must be something you can think of," I said to Squeak.

He continued to look at his shoes. "Can't help with that data set. I've known you so long that everything reminds me of you. I mean, you're everywhere I look."

I moved up a row and sat next to Squeak in order to look at his shoes. There must be something wrong with them to have caught his attention so completely. "Is something wrong?"

I glanced up to see Esther make an odd face. "No, nothing's wrong. Squeak's just being honest." Then she turned to Squeak, an intent and determined look on her face. "At least with what he is saying. Anything else you might want to add? What about it? Now's a great time to speak up. Especially if you have any good suggestions or, say, questions you want to ask."

"Pester." There was warning in his voice indicated by the way he used and then dragged out the pronunciation of her less-than-complimentary nickname.

I glanced at Squeak. He was staring at Esther now.

"Enough. Just drop it," he said.

"Drop what?" I looked back and forth between them. "Are you guys still talking about what I could do to be more noticeable?"

"Yeah, you know Squeak. He knows how much you like office supplies and doesn't want to tell you that sticky notes aren't sexy," Esther said.

Esther glared at Squeak, but he was pretending not to notice. If they were having some sort of silent conversation, I was unable to guess what it was about. The only thing I could infer was that sticky notes were somehow front and center in my bid for Theo's attention. Or not. It was frustrating.

"Why is that important? Really, I doubt my liking such things would have any benefit to executing the testing of my prom theory." Neither of them responded. Just continued to glare at each other. However, they turned their attention to me when I sighed loudly and then said, "Well, of course sticky notes aren't sexy!"

The corner of Esther's mouth quirked as she looked at me and then glanced at Squeak.

"It's all in how you wear them," she said.

Squeak slapped his hands on his thighs and sat up straight. "So, track and field—Bee what's up with that?"

"Did you know most of the events originally held in Olympia are still the same? Footraces, discus, javelin, long jump." I ticked them off on my fingers and then turned to Esther to continue my explanation, but she was already gone—racing down the bleachers to a nearby area where the hurdles were set up.

"Darren! Hey, Darren!" Esther was yelling and waving her arms above her head while she ran. I had no idea just how unsubtle she could be. No, that wasn't true. I did. There were many reasons we called her Esther the Pester.

"So, you think Esther knows that guy?" Squeak asked as we watched her bound away. Her long brown hair floated behind her as she raced toward the hurdles.

One boy looked up from stretching, a leg slung up on a hurdle. "Darren Havercamp. Senior class secretary and hurdle jumper. Mr. Prospective Prom Date," I said.

"Thought so," Squeak said with a grin.

I glanced around and saw that Pom-Pom was heading up the bleachers toward us. Squeak stood and waved to her. She motioned for him to come down.

"Well, Bee, it's been real, but I've got to go to work." He hopped nimbly between people, bleacher benches, and randomly scattered backpacks. With a field filled with young males who were aspiring to the Greek ideal, Squeak was easily as physically graceful as anyone on the track team.

Squeak was more capable than all of them put together. He had physical adeptness and brains.

Suddenly alone on the bleachers, I had the urge to call him back. But he had work to do on prom theory, so instead I shouted, "Don't forget."

"I won't," he said over his shoulder as he left.

# CHAPTER EIGHT

When Darren spotted Esther headed his way, a huge smile broke out across his face. He waved enthusiastically.

Glancing back to see Pom-Pom take Squeak's hand as they walked to the parking lot, I almost missed seeing Esther nearly bowl Darren over. This was my chance to use Esther's connections to get close to Theo Grant.

I trotted down the bleachers and tried to run. I don't normally run by choice, and I remembered why. I suck at it. Why was I running? She certainly wasn't going anywhere when she had him cornered. I slowed my pace to a brisk walk. Nothing to see here. No desperate, out-of-shape honors student racing so she wouldn't be left behind at a school activity she had no reason to be attending.

Esther was laughing. It sounded like her real laugh, not some put-on fake laugh to make a boy feel clever. She honestly liked him. I was smiling. Breathing hard, but smiling. Blame my mirror neurons. Her happy moment was making my moment happy. No wonder we like people who enjoy life. We watch them enjoying it, and our mirror neurons imagine what it would be like to be someone else and feel what they're feeling. I didn't have a lot of friends. But the ones I had were good, happy ones to have.

"Hi, Esther," I said, trying to sound casual and not like I was gasping for breath.

"Iris, this is Darren." It was amazing she could still manage to speak with her lips stretched into such a wide smile.

"Hi." I gave him the obligatory smile and head lift in his direction.

"Hey. Esther said you talked her into hanging out during practice. Thanks!" he said.

"I did?"

Esther jabbed my side with her elbow.

"Oh, right, um, you're welcome." I was pleased at my quick understanding of and response to Esther's physical hint to back up her story. I assumed she was trying to appear casual in front of Darren, rather than broadcasting that she was intentionally seeking him out. It was a wise move on her part. Many of our actions can easily repel rather than attract if we are too obvious about our intentions.

He turned a little so he was facing Esther more than me. "I meant to tell you about practice, but I totally spaced when we didn't have lunch together."

Esther's laugh in response was light and airy. "We've never had lunch together."

He grinned sheepishly. "I know, but it would be cool if we did. Senior-year lunchtimes are so screwed, though. Half the time I miss it. I never know where I'm supposed to be. Ten forty-five? I'm not even hungry yet."

"I'm not looking forward to that next year, but early dismissal will make up for it." Esther was looking at him as if he were her next meal. I felt like I was intruding when all we were really doing was hanging around the track.

I pinched Esther in an attempt to get her attention without having to insert myself into their mindless chatter.

"Ow! What?" Esther hissed.

“So, Darren, what’s the schedule of events?” I asked.

“Well, I mean, it’s just practice.” He shrugged and gave me a weak smile. Then he looked to Esther as if for help.

I waved my hand a little. “I mean, I know, I was just wondering—”

“So, how long are you stuck here? Because I think I might need some help with my homework,” Esther said quickly to Darren.

“Esther, I can—” I began. Esther stepped firmly onto my big toe. I had to bite my lip to not verbally express my pain.

“Oh, yeah? Oh, yeah! Hey, there’s only a little more than an hour left of practice. I bet I could help you after.” Darren grinned. Esther smiled sweetly while her hand reached up to curl a length of her brown hair around one finger.

Two juniors who I thought I recognized from assemblies trotted up behind Darren. They were obviously teammates, since they wore running shorts and the purple-and-white tank that had the team name and logo on the front. The Hillcrest Hilltoppers.

“Hey, Darren, Coach wants us to run some intervals,” one of them said.

“Yeah, sure. Hey, guys, this is Esther and . . .” Darren fumbled around trying to remember my name.

“Iris,” I said, stepping in.

“Hey,” said the first boy with a small salute.

“Hey,” said the second boy, and he sort of, kind of, waved to me.

Heys all around.

“So . . . what time is practice over?” Esther asked.

“We have about forty-five minutes of warm-up and working out a bit, then about half an hour working on our weak spots. Got a big meet coming up next week over in Lycoming County,” Darren said.

"Awesome," Esther said.

"You gonna stay and watch?" Darren asked.

"That's why I'm here." Esther smiled, and Darren's face lit up.

"See you later," he said, giving her a small wave, and then all three trotted off, landing lightly with each step.

Esther watched Darren as he jumped over a hurdle with ease on the way to the inner track, where the rest of the team was lining up to run sprints. "Wow" was all she said. It came out as a sigh.

"His mannerisms are gentle and expressions seem kind. I think I like him. He doesn't make me uncomfortable. I'm glad I had a chance to meet him. Good choice," I said when she didn't say anything more.

"You think so?" she asked.

"I do. Now help me get in Theo's line of sight. You seem to know your way around better than I do. Oh, and take if from an expert, you are well on your way to securing a prom date," I said.

"Expert?" She lifted one eyebrow. I wondered if that ability was a genetic trait, like being able to roll your tongue or having detached earlobes. A Punnett square was already beginning to form in my mind. Just as I was about to ask if either of her parents could do that, Esther started walking in the direction of the far end of the outer track.

"Okay, come on, let's get this party started." Esther looked back at me and shouted, "Race you!" She sprinted off with impressive speed.

"Esther! You know I don't run!" I started to jog. This was a hazard I'd failed to predict or plan for. Really? I just wanted to attract the alpha male, not join the team.

When I finally caught up with Esther, it occurred to me this might already be a complete failure. I hadn't run far, but it felt like I'd never catch my breath. At this rate, I'd be dead before Theo even had a chance to meet me. She turned away from a woman she'd been talking to who appeared to be a coach.

She held up her hand to her brow, shading her eyes. "There," she said, pointing to the pole vault pit. "There's Theo." She turned to me and lowered her hand. "Jesus, walk it off. You don't want him to see you looking like you're about to have a heart attack."

I nodded because I couldn't talk, and turned around to walk along the front bleachers. After a few up-and-backs my heart began to slow. I was just about to sit down to rest for a minute and make sure I'd regained the ability to speak without gasping when Esther slipped her arm through mine.

"I have a brilliant idea," she said.

"What?" I wheezed.

"Well, other than the one where I take you on a jog every night to build up your endurance. It seems the regular volunteers haven't shown up," she said.

"So?" I managed to ask without gasping for air. Much better.

"So I asked if we could help hand out water to the team." Esther looked very pleased with herself.

"Hand out water? Why?"

"Come with me. There are some things they don't tell you about on Wikipedia."

The team was taking a break and moving to different areas of the track and field to do drills. A couple of tables were set up near the entrance and the snack stand. Big orange and yellow tubs filled with water and sports drink were lined up next to stacks of cups. Scantily clad, long-legged boys with bright red faces and sweat-drenched tank T-shirts swarmed the tables. I was so busy trying to fill the little paper cups that I almost missed Theo in the rush.

Oddly enough, he was the one who was trying to get my attention. When he did, he held up two fingers. I barely stopped myself from breaking into a lecture concerning the fact that no one else was getting two drinks at a time, and why did he think he should? Then I remembered he was the alpha male in the group. I caught myself before my expression gave away my initial thoughts. Picking up two small cups of sports drink, I met his eyes again. I gave him my best slow smile and tilted my chin slightly up, accompanied by a brow ridge lift that said, *I recognize you. We know each other.*

A look of confusion crossed his face, but he quickly changed course, puffed out his chest, and said, "Hey." With a wink, he took the first cup and downed it.

"Hey yourself," I said, voice half an octave higher than normal. Estrogen gives women rounder faces and smaller chins than men. It also raises the pitch of a woman's voice. Many males tend to find that sort of thing attractive.

When I handed him the next cup, I hesitated. He'd been looking down at the cup as he was taking it, but at the slight resistance he looked up at me. His gaze met mine, and I held it for a second longer than a normal glance before letting go of the cup. Widening my smile and breaking the gaze added just a touch of shyness.

I had to admit the last bit had been genuine. He was handsome and appeared somewhat more physically mature than most of the boys on the track team. He was the sparkly thing that catches your eye, and it surprised me that it—he—had caught mine.

As I went back to the other table to start filling cups and lining them up for the guys to grab and go, I heard him ask someone, “Hey, who’s the little blonde?”

I couldn’t help it. I knew I was smiling. Even if the “little blonde” comment was demeaning given my slightly taller-than-average height. This was going to be easier than I had anticipated.

## Prom Theory Notes

### Esther’s Observations

*Theo is self-centered and conceited. But he’s hot. Oh, and two cups of sports drink at the same time? He’s selfish, too. Couldn’t you have picked a better guinea pig, I mean, subject?*

### My Observations

*Need to review with Esther what constitutes useful observations in order to apply the scientific method.*

*TG is not necessarily observant of the people around him unless they are actively trying to gain his attention. He does, however, seem to be more aware of the females in his immediate area than the males. This is beneficial to the experiment. When researcher made eye contact and indicated that she knew him, it seemed he recognized her as someone new. Therefore, he was motivated to seek out additional information about her.*

*Overall, being conspicuously present at the practice, in addition to the use of eye gaze and minor physical contact, seemed to be quite effective.*

### Plan

*Continue to cross TG’s path and be noticed. Wear color (red) to* help prime TG to connect the researcher with the color and be easily seen in a crowd. Make brief physical contact to increase TG's attention to novelty (me) and pique curiosity. Will continue in this manner utilizing the information of his class schedule.

# CHAPTER NINE

## Tuesday Evening
## Days to Prom: 18

"You know, there are studies that show that stuff is as addictive as heroin. Why would you choose to bring something into this house that could result in neurochemical changes in our brains that could leave us trapped in a serious addiction?"

"Iris, these are chocolate chip cookies, freshly baked by me, your mother, with all organic ingredients. If you continue to berate the little things that give me great pleasure, and are, for now, legal, I will not share them with you." Little bells on her embroidered slippers chimed as she crossed her ankles and leaned forward on the kitchen stool, resting her elbows on the island.

She licked the chocolate off her fingers and then broke the cookie into pieces and tossed them one by one into her mouth.

"Oh, Iris, these are amazing. Soft and gooey. And warm—I love them right out of the oven, don't you?" She spoke around the mass of fat, sugar, and chocolate that now filled her mouth. She raised her eyebrows at me and reached for another cookie.

"Mom, chocolate is the worst. It has all kinds of things that affect opioids in the brain." I held my hand up and ticked the culprits off one by one. "There is tryptophan, an amino acid related to serotonin. High levels can actually make you high. Phenylethylamine is a neurotransmitter and is used to derive amphetamines. Its nickname is 'chocolate speed' and can totally derail you—send you spiraling off into an overblown thrill. If that doesn't spell addiction, I don't know what does." I walked over to the back door, looked out the window and down the path that connected Squeak's and our backyards. Where was he?

My mother shrugged, nibbled a cookie, and shook her ankle chimes at me. "They're just cookies to me, and that's all I need to know." The oven beeped, and she hopped down from her seat. She pulled the sheet of cookies out of the oven and shimmied over to me.

My mother dances into a room. I usually stumble into one. She was a beautiful, noisy mess, and I was nothing like her.

Her curly hair tumbled over her eyes as she bent with the spatula to lift the cookies off the sheet and place them on the cooling rack. I hadn't inherited her wild hair, either. Mine was thick and straight, like my dad's. Curly hair was a dominant trait. Maybe I was adopted. That would answer a few questions.

"Hey, Mom, was my hair curly at all when I was a baby?" I couldn't remember any pictures where I had curls.

"It was! But not for long." She sounded wistful. "Your hair is so thick and heavy that the minute it started to get long, the curls went away. But thinking about it now, I would say your hair was wavy more than curly."

Curly hair was a complicated trait. It wasn't possible to have a straight-haired baby if one parent had curly hair. But it was possible for the child to have wavy hair. So, not adopted.

She went to work dropping more dough onto a clean baking sheet. She hummed and rolled her hips in a figure-eight movement she'd recently learned from a Middle Eastern dance class.

"Really, Mom? The bells, and the scarf tied around your waist?"

"What about it? It's fun. You know, there's a mother-daughter class next weekend. Want to come with me?"

"No."

She stood back and folded her arms, considering me carefully. "You really are in a mood today, aren't you?"

"You sound like Squeak," I said as I leaned forward on the table. I was getting tired of waiting for him. He'd been so different lately. I looked at the clock and sighed.

"Poor Seth. If you haven't noticed, let me point out that his voice doesn't squeak anymore. In fact, he's growing into quite the fine tenor," she said with a smile. I guess it made sense. If his being around all the time made him seem like my brother, my mother probably considered him the son she'd never had.

"He'll always be Squeak," I said.

My mother gave me a sly glance as she began to pull out containers to store the cookies. "He's really becoming quite handsome."

"Squeak?" His name came out as a squeak. It was more from surprise than trying to insult him.

My mother gave me a half smile and then sighed. "Iris, my flower, you can be so smart about some things and so not smart about others."

I didn't know what bothered me most: her calling me her little flower or her saying I wasn't smart.

"I'm smart about what matters," I told her.

She went back to the island after putting another sheet of cookies in the oven and setting the timer. "He needs to get out of that house and this town. He's so bright and so kind. You're very lucky, you know. I don't think I've ever met a kinder boy. And he seems very devoted to you."

"Please, can we not sing Squeak's praises right now?" Devoted? Where had that come from? If he was so devoted to me, he'd be making the most of our remaining time together. I didn't need to be constantly reminded how wonderful he was, especially when it looked like he might be standing me up. I leaned back and looked out the glass patio door to see if he was on his way. But the path leading to the back patio was empty. Damn it, where was he? I walked to the island, leaned forward against it, and laid my head down on my hands.

A bell jingled, and jingled, and kept jingling. This whole new obsession with Middle Eastern dance was starting to annoy me. "Mom, please stop shaking your foot. It's making all of my sensory issues surface. Besides, there were small groups of women who belly danced as temple prostitutes, right? There are all sorts of spiritual meanings inherent in the dance, but it can also be meant to be highly erotic."

The skin around her eyes was scrunched into deep crow's-feet—and she was laughing.

"What?" I asked her as I sat up and straightened in my seat.

"I'm glad you're home, that's all. I've been stuck here alone, all day, baking for the Arts Association's bake sale. I tried to get your father to come home a day or two early from San Francisco, but he's in the middle of an audit." She reached out and took one of the smaller cookies off the plate she'd just refilled. Three was usually her limit, and although I hadn't been counting, I guessed she was heading into her fourth cookie of the evening. If this kept up, I'd have to cut her off.

"Dad will be very sad if there aren't any left for him when he gets back," I warned.

She made a little wagging gesture with her finger. "Tish tosh, pish posh. Besides, you know I always save him something when I bake." She put the cookie back onto the plate and pulled a baggie out of the drawer underneath the island. After putting five cookies in, she looked at me, eyebrows raised in question. I held up a finger. She laughed and dropped in one more before sealing it. With a smile, she held the bag out to me. "Here, these will stay fresh until he gets back in a few days. Go put these in his desk before I eat them. Put them in the bottom—"

"Left-hand drawer, I know." It's where he kept his "secret" stash of candy. I took the bag of cookies and headed toward the stairs that led up to his home office.

My father was an actuary for a large insurance firm. When I was in grade school, he told me his job was predicting the future. True, sort of. He took mind-boggling amounts of data and a few of his favorite "bits of wizardry," as he liked to say, such as the Pearson product-moment correlation coefficient (PPMCC) and bam! Life insurance premiums and world investment futures for your wonderment and fiscal health. My father loved numbers.

I, however, understood numbers well enough but did not love them. Nor was I interested in what they could be manipulated into telling us. I was more interested in why, despite what the numbers said, people insisted on ignoring logic, and when given the choice between having another cookie and living to one hundred, they choose the cookie. The answer to that sort of question was in the brain.

I slipped the cookies into the drawer, setting them on top of a bag of miniature candy bars, before heading back down to the kitchen.

"It's not like baking isn't a science—'cause it is and you're a genius." I heard Squeak buttering up my mother as I came down the stairs from my father's office. He was here, finally. I quickened my steps. Jogging into the kitchen, I saw Squeak perched on a stool, and I hopped up onto the stool beside him.

"You are too kind, Seth," my mother said just as the timer beeped.

"No, I'm just deeply interested in having more cookies," Squeak replied.

"Well then, you are in luck, because I happen to have more." She smiled at me as she held out a spatula, atop which sat a rather large, steaming-hot cookie. Squeak carefully took the cookie and made a smooch sound with his lips. I automatically held out my hand as he broke it and passed half to me. We both simultaneously blew on it to cool it off and began to eat without even saying hello. The day was looking much better than it had just a few minutes ago.

I caught a momentary glance and amused smile pass between my mom and Squeak. They were always doing that sort of thing. I never knew what was going on, but I had a sense it was about me. Not that they would confess to it.

"So, Seth, it's almost graduation. Anything exciting coming up? Prom is soon, isn't it?" my mother said, turning away from us to finish putting the latest batch of cookies on a cooling rack. She glanced over her shoulder and gave him a questioning look. Squeak shook his head and reached for another cookie.

What was she getting at? She hadn't asked me about prom. Well, maybe because she knew I avoided crowded social events. I did and didn't want to hear what he said. Was he going? Did he have a date? Who would he even take? I glanced at him, quietly and intently studying his cookie. Pom-Pom was the only other female in his life besides Esther and me. That I knew about, anyway.

I needed to move, to do something other than sit there staring at Squeak, waiting for his answers to my mother's completely random questions. I got up, took the milk out of the refrigerator, and poured us each a glass. Once I was sitting next to him again, Squeak held his hand out to me while still focused on my mother, as if carefully considering a response. He knew my mother well and probably understood that if he admitted to not having a date or any intention of going, she would be disappointed. She loved events and any excuse for anyone to get dressed up. At least she hadn't asked him to go to belly dancing class. Although, that would be a much more entertaining conversation.

This topic was making me nervous; any talk about prom would eventually come around to me and my involvement in what she certainly viewed as one of the high school experiences not to be missed. Besides, I wasn't ready to confess to my current experiment, especially since I wasn't going to go when Theo asked me. Getting asked and then not going would definitely disappoint my mother.

I put the glass in Squeak's hand. He took a sip before placing it on the counter. I tossed him a napkin. He caught it without looking. After performing this routine countless times since we were in grade school, his reflexes were flawless.

"Well, I was thinking about prom. Made plans even, but—well, it's complicated. I'm not sure I'll go."

My mother took a few steps closer to the counter. She crossed her arms, and I knew her mom voice was about to come out of her mouth. "What do you mean by 'complicated'?"

Who cared about complicated? What about him having a plan for prom? He hadn't mentioned any plans to me *at all*. I'd been prepared for him to say he wasn't going.

I pushed the remainder of my cookie away. Despite its mood-enhancing qualities, I knew not only that I had lost what appetite I might have had, but also that it wouldn't help the sinking feeling that had lodged itself in my chest and stomach.

But what if by "complicated" he'd meant that Pom-Pom had turned him down? I picked my cookie back up and took a bite before I looked at Squeak. There was a nudge from my unconscious that tried to make me consider just why that thought had made me feel better. I ignored it. The sugar from my earlier consumption of cookie was probably just spiking my blood sugar.

"I—well, it seems like the person I was going to ask might have other plans," he said.

My mother looked at me with narrowed eyes and a half frown—in other words, suspiciously. As if I had anything to do with this. He certainly hadn't involved me or thought to share his plans with me in any way. Since he usually told me everything, my mother probably thought I was involved somehow. But what could I have possibly done?

"Have you asked this person?" my mother asked.

"No."

"Then how do you know? You don't know if you don't ask, and besides, the worst thing they can do is say no." My mother shot me another not-so-pleased look. I opened my hands and lifted my shoulders and mouthed, "What?"

"I'd rather get some things sorted out first, then I'll ask."

"Promise?"

He lowered his head a little in a submissive gesture. "I promise."

I couldn't hold back anymore. "Promise what? You never said you were going to prom."

Squeak turned to me, not smiling. “You never asked.”

“When would I? You’re sooo busy.” The mocking voice I used surprised me more than it surprised my mother, who looked at me with wide eyes and a slightly opened mouth.

“Bee, hello, I’m here. I was at the library today when you asked me to come. You’ve been a little preoccupied, so I’m surprised you even noticed I’ve been *sooo* busy.”

I wasn’t sure I’d ever felt like I wanted to fight with Squeak. We never argued. Not like petty kids, anyway. I had definitely started this, and in front of my mother, no less.

“Iris,” my mother said in a soft but scolding tone. I knew that it meant, *Say you’re sorry*.

“I’m sorry. I know you’ve been working.” I glanced at Squeak as I said it and then turned to look at my mother to make sure she thought my apology was adequate. She nodded to me.

“All right, both of you obviously need some time together. Seth, would you stay for dinner?”

He nodded. “If it’s all right—I’d like to.”

My mother leaned on the plastic lid of the container she’d just packed with cookies.

“On one condition,” she said. “You take these with you when you go home later so I do not fall prey to the irresistible urges that Iris assures me are caused by ingesting these potentially addictive home-baked goods.”

“Okay. Thank you.” He smiled.

“All right, you two, out of my kitchen so I can get dinner started,” she said, and pointed to the backyard. The old picnic table had our names on it. Literally, we’d carved them there in third grade. I picked up a cookie and made for the kitchen door.

"Iris?"

"Yes, Mother?" I paused, waiting.

"Be careful, that cookie will spoil your dinner," my mother said.

I frowned at her before opening the door and heading into the yard.

Squeak was already at the picnic table.

"I know you came over for food, but did you get *it*?" I asked

"You're in a snappy mood for someone who may or may not have put her best friend in an awkward position with his tutee. I think you owe me an apology," he said, trying hard not to smile at me, the rather large stash of cookies from my mother obviously having a positive effect on his mood. I had been inappropriately argumentative with him, but I could tell he wasn't all that upset about it.

"All right, I'm sorry, again. Now hand it over," I said.

He tried to look innocent. "Hand what over?"

"Knock it off. You have intel for me. Hand it over," I said. Actual data that would get this project rolling! My toes tapped under the table.

"Patience, Ms. Evil Scientist. Yes, I have intel for you. I thought you were doing serious scientific research. You're starting to sound like you're playing secret agent. Iris Oxtabee, larping for love," Squeak said.

"You think you are so funny." I scowled at him.

"I do not think. I know. Get your notebook. You need to get started on this prom activity you got going. You need to wrap it up as soon as possible, before your mother starts quizzing both of us about our plans. And nobody wants that. Am I right?" He pulled a slip of paper out of his pocket.

I hesitated before I took it from him. "Are you going to prom?"

"We'll see," he said

"Are you going to ask Pom-Pom?" That slipped out. I winced even as I asked it.

"Wasn't planning on it. To be honest, she is hinting pretty hard. Though I'm sure she has a list of candidates. Why? Are you worried? Not that it matters, I'm not likely a top contender."

So not only was he planning on prom, but he was also in the sights of the stereotypical popular girl. The thought of being forced to wear clothes that would have me crawling out of my skin was enough to make me say with confidence that I wasn't going. Besides, if I didn't go *and* Squeak wasn't "a top contender" like he claimed, we would have a little more time to spend together before he was gone.

"Well, I'm not going," I said.

He handed me the paper with a general outline of Theo's schedule. "We'll see," he said.

## Prom Theory Notes

*Squeak scored. Researcher has Theo's class schedule.*

# CHAPTER TEN

## Wednesday
## Days to Prom: 17

"Hey, Iris, you're gonna be late for lunch," Esther said as she jogged up the hallway, catching up with me. The morning had flown by, and I hadn't had a chance to fill her in on my plans for the day.

"Not going. Sorry I didn't catch you earlier. I offered Mrs. Sanderson my help in the library this period," I said.

Esther narrowed her eyes at me. "Oh yeah, and why did you do that?"

"So I had an excuse to go to senior lunch this morning and spend sixth period in the library."

"And why would you want to do that?" she asked.

"Face time," I said, and then shrugged.

"Face time," she repeated with a deadpan expression. "That's a video call. Your lingo is out of date."

"Okay. Eye time. Just putting myself in his line of sight," I said.

"And by 'his,' I'm guessing you mean Theo. And I'm also guessing he has study hall in the library?" she asked.

"Of course. This is prime priming time."

Esther nodded. "Gotcha. Nice red sweater, by the way. And what a beautiful necklace . . . Iris. It's Iris, right?" She winked conspiratorially—tilted head, open half grin. "Tell me what happens in the library so I can make some notes. Oh, and you're gonna be starving by last period. Good-bye, cutie pie." She wiggled her fingers in a farewell wave. Esther's laughter floated above the rush of students pushing their way to the cafeteria.

She was right, however. It was only 11:40 a.m. and my stomach was growling. Although, I reminded myself that rumbling didn't mean I was hungry. When the stomach becomes programmed to the times you eat, it prepares itself by churning and starting the digestion process, whether there is food in there or not. I shut my locker door and rested my forehead against the cool metal. Someone help me, I was wikiing myself.

The bell rang, and I rushed towards the library. If I got there before him, I wouldn't look so obvious when I walked past him in the stacks.

I slipped in. Thanks to some of the schedule information Squeak had gotten from Pom-Pom, I knew that Theo had study hall in the library. I also knew that the Western Civ sections had a paper coming due. All except the honors class. I never understood why the other sections didn't cover the same time periods, but the teachers had to cover the basics, and most didn't want to spend time in the years B.C. if they could help it. I guess we can't all be fans of Heraclitus of Ephesus, although I didn't understand how you couldn't be.

I put my head down as I walked back to the history section, and there he was. A tall, broad-shouldered, fair-haired boy. Who was in the entirely wrong section. This late in the semester they would be up to the seventeenth and eighteenth centuries, and he was hanging out in the seventh century.

I wanted him to notice me only a couple of times today, but I couldn't help myself. He was in the *entirely* wrong section. When he started moving into the sixth century, I made straight for him.

Trying to be subtle, I squeezed past him in the fifth-century section, headed for the Renaissance. My shoulder brushed him, just enough to make him look up.

"Sorry," I said, trying to be cute and deferential, but all I wanted to do was drag him by his sleeve and deposit him between Newton and Catherine the Great.

"Huh? Yeah, no worries," he said.

"What are you looking for? I mean, if you need help, I know where a lot of stuff is," I said.

"You do?" he asked, looking somehow disbelieving but hopeful.

"Yeah." I did my best to look embarrassed. "Whenever I get into trouble, they send me back here to shelve stuff."

He laughed a little. "Man, that's got to suck."

"Yeah." I shrugged, not knowing what else to say. Actually, it wouldn't suck at all.

"Hey, I saw you yesterday. You were at track practice!"

He'd noticed me. This was good. Even better, he remembered me. This was working. I nodded. "I was helping at the water table."

He nodded. I remembered I was supposed to be priming him for the color red and making my flower name memorable. I pushed up my sleeves and, pretending to be looking at something past his shoulder, moved just enough so my incredibly soft red cashmere sweater brushed his bare arm. He looked down briefly at the sweater and then smiled.

"I don't know your name." His voice deepened, just a touch, and his lips crooked up at one end, giving him a sly expression. I played with the necklace so that the flower swung just under my chin.

"Iris, like the flower," I said, trying to have the pendant catch his eye but not be too conspicuous about it. He gave it a glance. Good. Now enough of the mindless banter. "What are you working on?"

"Some dumb senior project thing for Western Civ." His top lip curled in disdain.

I could do this, I told myself. It would be a true challenge, but I could. It was for science, after all. Besides, it wasn't like I wanted to engage him in deep debate about the rise of science as a model for society versus the rule of religion over science. I had Squeak for that.

"Who do you have?" I asked.

"Bobo the Clown," he said with a roll of his eyes.

"Mr. Bobinsky—wait, I think somebody was talking about that yesterday. Here, the books he wants you to use are down this aisle." I motioned for him to follow me. If he questioned me on how I knew, I would tell him I'd been shelving them for the past two weeks. He didn't ask. He probably just wanted to grab a book and bolt. Projects were due in a couple of days. Nothing like waiting until the twelfth hour to write a paper that might be instrumental in whether or not you graduated. He probably had library fines too, but it was none of my business. All I needed was for him to ask me to prom.

"This shelf is pretty much where people are grabbing stuff." I pointed to a series of books concerning George Washington. He would at least have a head start if he was writing about someone he had some previous knowledge of. I hoped he knew something, *anything*, about George Washington. If not, I might have to abandon this project—

"Oh, hey, George Washington. He'd be easy." He snatched the first book, only glancing at the title to make sure Washington was mentioned.

Thank God.

"Huh?" He turned his head to look at me.

"What?" I asked. I must have spoken out loud. "Oh, nothing, I just looked at the clock. I get to leave in ten minutes." I made a little *yay* fist pump as I scrambled to explain my unintentional giveaway.

"Awesome." He flashed me a grin. "I am out of here before the bell. Got things to see, people to do."

People to do? Did he get the colloquialism wrong, or was it a joke? A joke, I decided, and giggled. He smiled and was gone. He moved quickly. But then again, he was captain of the track team.

That had gone exceedingly well. I was the girl who saved his grade point average. He was sure to remember me.

I glanced up at the section from where he had taken the book. Whoever had shelved these did a horrific job. It took me fifteen minutes just to straighten out two shelves. I almost missed the second bell, but I still made it to trig in time.

## Prom Theory Notes

### Esther's Observations

*Lunch is boring without Iris. My guess is that Theo doesn't read very much. A couple of possible outcomes of helping him in the library could be (1) he could remember that cute girl who helped him out in a time of need, or (2) he will forget where the book came from, won't read it, and will threaten some sophomore's place on the track team unless they write it for him.*

### IMPORTANT ESTHER EXPERIMENT UPDATE

*I managed to "run into" Darren at least five times today. By the end of the day he was actually looking for me, and not in an I'm-avoiding-the-stalker-chick way. It's working!*

## My Observations

While not purely evidence based, Esther's conclusions may lend some insight into TG's character. This could help the researcher to choose tests that are more likely to be successful.

The use of the red sweater and iris necklace was successful in grabbing TG's attention for a moment. It remains to be seen if it has been recorded in any way in the hypothalamus or if the amygdala has attached any meaning to the items as associated with the researcher.

## Plan

Tomorrow is the "healthy long hair test," while beginning to wear subtle makeup, eye-catching red, and the iris necklace. Need to take every advantage to walk by or, even better, run into TG.

Need to consider the possibility of adding a signature scent as well. Need to discuss this further with Esther. Research into the efficacy of human pheromones might be needed.

## Personal Note

Esther had to take a shift at the animal shelter because someone called in sick and the Chihuahua-Pomeranian mix puppies were vomiting in their crates. I tried to pay attention but I can't remember what she said about the blind cat.

I'll fill her in on the upcoming test in the morning.

# CHAPTER ELEVEN

## Thursday
## Days to Prom: 16

**Step Two: Elements of Attraction—Part One**

*Long, shiny hair is an indicator of good health and youth. It is one of the strongest signals of a desirable mate.*

I couldn't see anything when I looked down to open my locker. While I was getting ready for school, it had seemed like such a brilliant yet simple plan. I mean, really, half or more of the girls at school did this sort of thing every day. Tossing my head back and to the side to get my hair out of my face, I almost hit my head on my locker door.

"Dammit." Using both hands, I pushed my hair out of my face, as if I'd just walked into a spider web. If I did go to prom, I would definitely wear my hair up and out of my face. The thought made me stumble where I stood. Where had that come from? I had no real intention to go to prom.

When I caught my balance and looked up, Esther was standing there, staring at me, her mouth hanging open.

"Good morning, Esther," I said. "Curling iron got your tongue?" I pulled a face and went back to getting my things together for my first-period psych class, with Squeak.

"What happened to you?" Esther asked.

The question made me stop organizing my locker. I peered around the door at Esther. "Is it okay? I mean, does it look—um—long and healthy? Do you think it will make me stand out? I mean, I'm blond, and blonds used to be so rare in populations that they were fought over. Did you know that's why Scandinavians are so blond? The trait was so desired that blonds of both sexes had the reproductive advantage. But I suppose now there are so many because of hair dye. I guess Europe had so many plagues it never took hold quite as much. I wonder—"

"It's gorgeous. I mean really gorgeous. You look amazing." Esther actually squealed.

"Honestly?" I was ready to reach for the familiar security of my hair band.

"Are you kidding? Oh. My. God. Is your hair naturally wavy, or did you curl it?" Esther was walking around me, playing with my hair.

"Oh. My. God. Stop touching me . . . but I guess if it's working on you—"

"Yo, Esther, you seen Bee?" Squeak was coming up the hallway behind us. Behind me. Esther could see him, but I was facing Esther.

Fear. I felt actual fear. He was going to be such an idiot about this. He messed with my hair as it was. This was just asking him to tease me. I needed to avoid him all day if I wanted any peace. Maybe this hadn't been such a good idea after all. Not if it was going to get a shocked response rather than an attracted stare.

"Here's your chance to try it out on a member of the male species," said Esther.

"Who, Squeak? Why would I want—" I hissed.

Esther spun me around and gave me a little push. I stumbled forward and collided with Squeak as he walked toward us. My hair was tossed back and over my shoulders by the sheer force of impact.

Kinetic energy. Movable and unmovable forces.

He reflexively grabbed me around the waist to stop us both from falling. He said, "Whoa." And then he said, "Whoooa." And then he stared.

And stared.

"What?" I pushed him away and he let go of my waist.

"Your hair. What did you do?" Squeak reached out, and before I could duck to avoid his hand reaching for my absent ponytail, he ran his fingers through my loose hair. My breath caught. We were both silent. I couldn't move or talk. Something replaced the fear. But I couldn't begin to describe the feeling. It was . . . odd. And uncomfortable. Or maybe it felt awkward . . . in a tingly-warm kind of way. Whatever it was, it needed to stop. I took a step back and away from him.

"Nothing—just curled it this morning." I brushed back the hair he'd just fondled. That had to stop. I'd hoped to catch Theo's eye, not get mauled in the hallway, and certainly not by Squeak.

His forehead furrowed as he frowned. "Is this part of your experiment?"

"Part of it, yes. Long, shiny hair signals health. The brain registers it as a sign of a good breeding partner. So it's interpreted as attractive, and being blond makes me a shiny rare object even though—"

"Wiki morning," he said, looking past me to Esther. He was trying to be his usual obnoxious self, but he was still frowning.

I blurted out the question before I knew what I was saying. "You don't like it?" I immediately regretted it. His answer certainly didn't matter. This was Squeak, and as far as I could tell, he was not susceptible to overly made-up females. Except maybe the ever-popular Princess Pom-Pom.

There were a few logical reasons why he would be attracted to her. She had olive-toned skin, light brown hair, and big brown eyes, whereas he had the "dark Irish about him," as my mom would say. Pale skin, dark hair, and hazel eyes. So he and Pom-Pom obviously had different genetic backgrounds, and that made passing on recessive genes unlikely. It also made for a likely unconscious interest in each other.

"Forget it. I don't care if you like it, it's not for you." I was getting angry he hadn't responded reassuringly to my weak moment of seeking his approval. Wasn't that something friends did for one another? He was always going on about why those little white lies—like saying, "These musical socks were just what I wanted"—were important to keeping society and relationships functioning smoothly. What was wrong with me? Whatever, it didn't matter what he thought.

He looked surprised, as if my response to his nonresponse had caught him off guard. "Hey, don't snarl at me."

"I wasn't snarling," I snapped.

"Sounded like a snarl to me," Esther said.

I turned toward her and poked her shoulder with my finger. "I wasn't snarling."

I looked back at Squeak and made a *So?* gesture with my hands. I was not going to be accused of snarling again.

"I mean, it's nice, but it's not . . . you." Squeak's furrowed brow was back.

"I agree, but a ponytail doesn't make much of a display." Something about his comment made me less—*snarly*. If blow-drying and styling my hair resulted in my having radical mood swings, it was going to produce the opposite effect than the one I intended. No one, male or female, wants to spend much time with someone who is emotionally unpredictable. It doesn't bode well for a long-term partnership and successful child-rearing, much less any level of friendship.

"Display?" Esther asked.

"You know, like a peacock's feathers or a bowerbird's colorful nest."

Esther and Squeak exchanged a look that said, *Wiki*. That stopped me from continuing on and telling them everything I knew about bowerbirds. Fascinating animals. Their loss.

"That might be true, but personally, I'd rather have a ponytail to pull." He reached out and squeezed my nose.

Esther laughed. I rubbed my nose and looked at Squeak in horror. I'd rather him pull my ponytail than injure my nose. My scalp had grown accustomed to the torment, whereas my nose—

"Seth," a voice singsonged with way too much emphasis on the *e*. All three of us turned to look at the approaching interloper.

It was Pom-Pom—and she had her hair in a ponytail. That was new. She waved and stopped at his side, her ponytail swinging.

I could feel my eyes narrow as I stared at her. What was she doing? Why had she suddenly changed the way she wore her hair? I supposed it was obvious—for the same reason I had. Squeak glanced at me and, seeing my expression of general annoyance and irritation, grinned. I scowled at him and turned away. I was developing a low tolerance for all things Pom-Pom.

"Hey," she chirped.

"Hey," said Squeak, a little chirpy himself.

*Hey.* If the conversation was going to continue in this manner, I needed to make better use of my time, immediately. I was sure his seemingly unconscious manner of matching his tone of voice to hers was a simple case of mirror neurons kicking in. Mimicking a person's greeting simply makes you more approachable. It might have made sense in terms of survival and social bonds, but it didn't suit him.

"Sit with me at lunch today? I need some help before my lab quiz," Pom-Pom cooed.

"I would, but I have the later lunch period." Squeak actually looked sad. He couldn't possibly want to have lunch with her, could he? Then I remembered his need for money and decided that was what he was really sad about.

"You do? How come?" she asked.

"I managed to avoid my last elective until this year, and it was the only time the class was held." He shrugged.

"He has to take shop," I added in a confiding tone.

"Industrial arts," he corrected.

"Tuh-may-toe, tuh-mah-toe," I said.

Pom-Pom gave me a little eye roll and a *pfft*. But I noticed she never actually addressed or directly acknowledged me in any way.

"Okay, I'll just go to lunch with you." She smiled up at him, clearly satisfied she'd bypassed his reason not to be with her.

I'd never thought Squeak could be so blind to such obvious machinations. This little episode only clarified the need for this project, the proof of my prom theory. These were desperate times, and Squeak needed to see how wrong he was about the magical love fairy. Before the said fairy tried to affect him any further. Plus, this was seriously cutting into the few lunch periods we had together.

"You will? Okay. Cool, we can do that," he said.

Why *was* her hair in a ponytail? With a head toss, I sent my hair drifting over my shoulders and walked off, late for class.

In my first class every female oohed and aahed over my hair, but all the males seemed oblivious or not interested. I'd known this was going to be something of a subtle move on my part, but I'd expected the males of the class to at least spare me a glance. If any had, they were good at doing so on the sly.

Squeak stared at me for the entire class, but he was likely trying to come up with new ways to tease me. Couldn't he just be a friend and give me a compliment at least? I did my best to slip away quickly so he wouldn't have the opportunity to make me regret what was a scientifically proven method of attracting attention.

In the hallway I all but ran into Theo going in the opposite direction. I nearly tripped when I realized it was him. I tried to look like nothing had happened when he glanced my way. *Everything is fine. I'm attractive and cool.* I remembered to toss my hair to one side and reached down to touch the iris pendant. As I did, I met his eyes for a couple of seconds. I knew he saw me, but I had no idea if he recognized me from yesterday's encounter in the library. I held the iris pendant between my fingers and rubbed my thumb along the enameled petals. He might not consciously notice my hair and eyes, or my red, lightweight button-front shirt, but I was certain his right orbitofrontal cortex and hippocampus were making note of them and tucked them away as motivation to pursue in the future.

I was so busy trying to look confident that I walked past the cafeteria doors. My cool demeanor crumbled as I tried to turn against the flow of traffic in the hallway. I managed to squeeze between people and push my way through the caf doors without turning my ankle or falling down. Despite the near miss on the encounter with Theo, I had managed to pull it off. That and the lack of injuries counted as a win.

"You know, I'm not sure you should do it," Esther said.

"Do what?" I hadn't been paying attention to whatever she'd been talking about. I'd been preoccupied watching Squeak, two tables over, supposedly tutoring Pom-Pom. She was basically climbing onto his lap. He barely noticed. He was too intent on explaining whatever physics problem she was paying him to teach her how to do. On her own. By herself. As soon as possible.

"Theo Grant, Mr. Track and Field, stick tosser extraordinaire. I don't think you should be messing with his dope mixture—"

"Dopamine."

"Whatever. Taylor says he's kind of a dick," Esther said in the way she does when she wants me to take the bait and ask her for the rest of the juicy gossip. I normally would have, but . . .

"Who's Taylor?" I asked.

"Taylor—the one you're staring at," she said with an exasperated sigh.

"Pom-Pom? Pom-Pom's name is Taylor?" I forced myself to stop watching Squeak's completely clueless nonresponse to Pom-Pom's obvious lack of interest in physics.

"Yes, you know that, and she says Theo's a dick. At least, that's what I heard her say to her minions the other day."

I glanced over at the two of them. Squeak's face was animated with pure joy. He really, truly loved physics. Just seeing him work on a problem with some basic principles in play was like watching someone incredibly talented and dedicated to music play an instrument. It was one of the things I admired about Squeak. How could I not?

"Has Squeak been working out?" I asked.

"What?" Esther looked over at Squeak and squinted.

"Squeak—has he been working out? He looks different. Larger maybe. I don't know—it's weird." I didn't like this new, confused version of me. It was like I'd lost the ability to think straight and stay focused on anything. Maybe I hadn't been getting enough sleep. I made a mental note to get to bed earlier. Especially if I was going to continue getting up early to do anything other than put my hair into a ponytail.

"I don't think Squeak has ever stepped foot inside a gym unless it was a required class. But you're right, skinny Squeak is looking good. Working those weekend jobs for the construction guy your dad hooked him up with during the winter is probably where he got his manly biceps," Esther said, lowering her voice and flexing her arms.

"Oh right."

Esther considered the cup of chocolate pudding she'd managed to nab. That hadn't been an option when I made my way through the line.

"I don't understand why he can't find other students to tutor. I mean, how can he stand that?" I waved a hand in their direction, where Pom-Pom had rested her head on his shoulder. I was certain she was acting as if she needed to be that close to see the physics textbook Squeak was holding.

"I know he needs a bunch more money than he's been able to save. You know, for college and prom." Esther had been too intent on eating her pudding and had not looked up at the PDA Pom-Pom was forcing on *her tutor*. Esther licked her spoon clean and laid it down next to the empty container. She considered it thoughtfully, and with a last sad glance she sighed and turned her attention to me.

"Do you think he needs money so he can take her to prom?" I couldn't look away from Pom-Pom, who was now playing with her newly adopted ponytail, and then touching her face before touching his shoulder when she spoke to him. I could almost believe she was hanging on every word he said, the way she leaned into him. She probably didn't understand a word of it.

Personal space. That was a girl who didn't have a grasp of the concept. Even I had that figured out by seventh grade.

"He hasn't asked her or anyone else. But will he? I don't know. Does it bother you?" She leaned in close and gave me a wry smile.

"No, why should it?" I took a long drink from my water bottle so I wouldn't have to respond. Esther was being her usual ridiculous self.

"You look pretty bothered," she said as she sat back.

I carefully put my water on the table and considered how to put my concern into words without Esther turning it into something it wasn't.

"Okay, maybe it bothers me a little. But only because she's obviously trying to manipulate him into asking her to prom. She can't possibly maintain her social standing if she doesn't have a date."

"About prom—" Esther started.

"What about it?" I asked.

"Well, if you are worried about him being conned into asking her, you should talk to Squeak about it. You know, tell him to be careful or whatever," Esther said.

She gave me an odd look but nevertheless continued. "I mean, if your prom theory works for you, it certainly would work for Pom-Pom. I think you're right to be worried. She is definitely on the hunt. I mean, I can't believe she broke up with Theo, dick or not, so close to prom. I mean, who does that?"

I spun around on the orange plastic cafeteria stool and waved my hand at her dismissively. "Who knows why people break up, especially in high school? She probably caught him measuring the mating readiness of some other female on the squad. As my mother would say, 'Pish posh, tish tosh.'" Hopefully this would end the conversation. I'd had enough of my time taken up with having to think about Pom-Pom. I had more important things to do, primarily having to do with affecting the brain chemistry of her ex. Something I needed to speed up if I was going to have the evidence I needed to convince Squeak that if he was feeling anything for her, it was only because she'd manipulated his baser male brain.

Esther stood and picked up her lunch tray. "Your mother would say, 'Keep calm and carry a condom.'"

She was right. But I had no wish to encourage her to continue on the awkward topic. Instead of responding, I dug in my pocket for a hair band. I quickly pulled my hair back and twisted the band around it with a snap. I took my still-full lunch tray, dumped it in the garbage bin, tossed the now-empty tray onto the rack, and followed Esther out.

## Prom Theory Notes

### Esther's Observations

*Theo was looking at you when you didn't know he was around. That hair was like flying a sexy blond flag. Oh, and really, I'm getting tired of Pom-Pom being so obviously into Squeak. You need to hurry up and do something about that before it's too late.*

### My Observations

*The attention from TG wasn't quite as obvious as this researcher had hoped. This researcher has concluded that the "big strategy" is not as effective as, perhaps, other methods.*

In response to the above comments: I will prove the science of this to Squeak. It's obvious that he is vulnerable and lacks self-awareness of his instinctual responses. I do take issue with the above statement about doing something "before it's too late."

## Plan

Tomorrow will explore the potential of holding eye gaze. There are studies that show holding someone's gaze for more than nine seconds can increase feelings of intimacy and attraction. Squeak is the perfect guinea pig: He's safe and won't be misled by any reaction in the moment that could lead to the physical sensations that can be mistaken for "love."

## Personal Note

This researcher admits to feeling uncomfortable holding someone's gaze for more than a few seconds at a time.

When I was younger, my mother made a game out of it. She'd have us have staring contests when Squeak and Esther came over. The method is a proven one. More exposure to something fearful or uncomfortable desensitizes the subject to it. Thus reducing a person's fear and anxiety associated with whatever activity poses problems.

It seemed to work. While not entirely comfortable, I have been, somewhat, successfully desensitized, if only to a few people. Also, I know a few tricks to get through it as well, such as shifting my gaze to the bridge of the person's nose. However, I believe the eye gaze will be successful only if I am actually gazing into the subject's eyes.

# CHAPTER TWELVE

## Saturday
## Days to Prom: 14

### Eye Gaze and Attraction—the Squeak Test Run

I needed to prepare for the eye gaze test with Theo. The best way I could think of to do that was to practice on Squeak. So I texted him, gave him a brief rundown of what I needed him for, and then bribed him with his favorite lollipops.

He texted back saying he'd be right over. While waiting for him, I unwrapped a small red lollipop and rolled it around on my tongue. Lollipops all have the same five ingredients: sugar, corn syrup, citric acid, artificial color, and artificial flavor. There are no strawberries in a red lollipop. There is no such thing as a strawberry lollipop, just a red lollipop. And red was my favorite flavor. But I'd learned a long time ago not to waste time and research on lollipops. There were things that, in fact, did not matter.

I sat on my front porch with my arm wrapped around my bent legs, my free hand twirling the pop across my tongue. The citric acid was doing a good job of giving my tongue a chemical burn, but not a very good job of making me any less nervous about testing a few things out on Squeak before I utilized them in the study.

I needed to, at least, try this out on a male with whom I was familiar. That way I could easily determine if his responses to me during the eye gaze differed from our everyday interactions. Squeak was the only male of the appropriate age I had available.

I was trying not to think of Theo as a guinea pig. He was an animal by definition, but he was also a human, after all, and there were the parameters of ethical research that needed to be respected. Squeak, however, didn't pose as much concern to my conscience, as he knew I meant to experiment on him. He'd seemed oddly positive about being part of it. . . .

Squeak was approaching through the alleyway between our houses. I could hear his Chucks slapping against the old brick walkway. Without a word, he turned the corner of the house, threw himself down beside me on the porch, and held his hand out. Without looking at him, I slapped a lollipop into his hand. Green. His favorite flavor. He tore the little waxed paper wrapper off and stuffed it into his pocket. After quietly sucking on the pop for a few seconds, he pulled it out from between his lips with a loud slurp.

"So, what are you working on now?" Squeak asked.

"Eye gaze and attraction," I said.

"Yeah? And what do you think about that?" he asked, his words sloppily formed around the lollipop, now back in his mouth.

"We think it's our next move."

Squeak took the lollipop out of his mouth and pointed it at me. "You mean your next move. I'm not staring at anyone. Except you." He leaned back, resting on his elbows.

"Okay, fine, *my* next move. So?" I asked him.

"So, what? How is staring at the stick tosser going to get him to ask you to prom?" He was frowning at me. He was doing a lot of that lately.

"Come here." I turned my body to fully face him, then grabbed the back of his arm and pulled him upright.

He made a face and rolled his eyes. “Give me a minute before you get all pushy and clinical.” He carefully took the wrapper out of his pocket and began to slowly put it back on the remains of the candy. He held it close to his eyes and was squinting, as if he were taking precise measure of the fit and the proper twist around the stick.

I swatted at him and snatched the lollipop out of his hand. “This is serious.”

He laughed lightly, and I realized he seemed more relaxed than he had the past few days. I was relieved to see it, since it would make this a lot easier for me. He’d be more engaged in the experiment if he wasn’t distracted by some worry.

“Of course it is,” he said—and then his hand shot out and tugged my ponytail. “Glad to see you’re back to normal. I missed your rockin’ ponytail.”

“Why? Pom-Pom has one now. You could just assault hers. Come on, I need your help. Just for a couple of minutes.” I repositioned myself and sat up a little straighter. I smoothed my hair and curled my ponytail around my hand before laying it across one shoulder so it hung down in front.

“Fine.” He shifted so that he was resting against the porch post. “Now what?”

“Okay.” Leaning forward, I put the lollipop back into my mouth. I rolled it—what was left of it—around a couple more times to finish it and clear my thoughts. I held up a finger, telling him to wait. Since glucose molecules are rapidly absorbed through the moist tissue of the mouth, I wanted to make sure I made the most of the blood sugar rush to help me focus on this potentially awkward and nerve-racking activity. He was my best friend; I wasn't sure why I was hesitating.

I removed the now-candy-free stick from my mouth and set it next to me on the porch.

Squeak pointed at it. "Don't forget to throw that away."

"I won't." I looked away from him for a minute and watched a car pull out of a driveway down the street and drive past us. I took a deep breath. I was ready for the trial run. I could do this.

I looked at Squeak. He gave me a doubtful expression and opened his mouth to say something. Before he could get a word out, I gently pressed two fingers to his lips. I stilled, a little shocked at my readiness to reach out and touch such a vulnerable, personal place on Squeak. I would never do such a thing to anyone else. I didn't want to touch anyone, nearly ever. But apparently that didn't apply to Squeak. I rarely touched Esther or my parents, the other people I was most comfortable with, and I wouldn't dream of touching their face. Not even to brush something horrific, say glitter, off their cheek or chin.

All I could do was stare at my finger touching his soft, warm, rich-with-nerve-receptors, and highly sensitive lips. I dropped my hand and held it with my other, resting them in my lap.

He closed his mouth and turned watchful but stayed silent. I looked straight into his eyes, trying to keep my expression soft so that his limbic system didn't take it to be a threat. In the animal kingdom, holding someone's gaze can be seen as aggressive. I had to be sure I wasn't too intense.

As I held his gaze, I was, for the first time, aware of the uniqueness of his hazel eyes. It was an eye color I'd always thought of as nondescript. I met his eyes, ever so briefly, several times a day, every day, but now, when I was really looking into them, they were far more interesting than I'd realized. Green, brown, and gold seemed to shift as I looked at them. More green than brown, with specks of gold. I'd noticed the green of his eyes seeming to take dominance over the other colors from time to time, but not like this. Several of the articles I'd read about the effects of intentional eye contact said that it could create a sense of closeness and affection, but I wasn't prepared for how strong the pull toward him would be.

I nearly forgot myself while examining them, until I saw the subtle wrinkling around one of Squeak's eyes and not the other. One corner of his mouth twitched, and I could see him fighting the smile.

Smiling, especially among friends, is contagious. And whenever Squeak looked at me like that, I couldn't stop myself from smiling. I tried to hold it back. But when his laughter erupted, so did mine.

"Stop it." I shoved his shoulder.

He took a deep breath and made a show of being serious. That lasted about two seconds and then he lost it. As usual, so did I.

I tried to get the giggles under control. I needed to do this while pretending I was staring into Theo's eyes. I wanted to be sure I wouldn't be too awkward with him so the moment would work as I intended it to. Squeak was the only one who could help.

In an attempt to get back on task, I pressed my palms against his cheeks and held his head still so I could hold his eyes with mine. I had already touched his lips today and it had been strangely nice. Touching him like this wasn't nearly as intimidating and felt as if it were a natural gesture between us. When had that changed for me?

My hands were cold against his warm face. He lifted an equally warm hand and laid it against mine, holding my hand in place.

He blinked. I blinked, and his expression changed from silly to serious. It was—intimate, much more than I'd expected. I couldn't move. I didn't want to move. And the last thing I could do was pretend it was Theo. It was Squeak and only Squeak.

His face relaxed, and his gaze softened. He leaned toward me just a fraction. I realized I'd moved a little closer to him.

My hand under his was warmer now. Too warm. I pulled it back and dropped my other from his face, but he reached for me before I was able to completely pull away. Holding my hands together between both of his, he brought them to his lips and blew gently, warming them. Then he gave them one last quick rub and released them.

He looked down, breaking eye contact. "Your hands were really cold," he said quietly.

The minute he let go of them, they felt even colder than they had before I touched his face. "Yeah, they were."

He was still looking down and away from me. I was feeling awkward, holding back the urge to either start babbling or rush into the house without saying good-bye. But there was a third alternative: pretend like nothing had happened.

"So!" I clapped my hands once and stood up, ready to be the researcher and not some girl still staring at a boy's warm, soft lips. "Tell me how that affected you. It should have given you an oxytocin release and sent some dopamine oozing into your nucleus accumbens. Making you feel, if not attracted to me, then closer, maybe giving you a deeper feeling of trust. I mean, in our case, because you're like my brother, it probably didn't really change your feelings for me, or maybe more like what you feel for me."

It seemed the sibling space that Squeak occupied in my brain was becoming confused. Of course I was fond of Squeak. There was no question about that. But all this time focusing on male physical traits and the effectiveness of those traits on female physiology had caused me to overanalyze my own responses. That must be what it was. My familial affection for Squeak was being misinterpreted by my hyperaware brain as attraction. Temporarily crossed wires.

Squeak said, “It didn’t change how I feel about you. I knew it wouldn’t.” His voice had a strange edge to it.

My body felt heavy. I wasn’t sure how this reaction in response to physical contact with a male would be of use in terms of mating behavior or survival.

“Oh. Of course not. Why would it? We’re old friends, immune to such attractiveness cues.” I heard the timid high pitch of my voice as I said the words. I hadn’t meant to say it like that. I mean, I knew it wouldn’t—this was Squeak.

“If you say so. You’re the expert.”

“Right. But did you have any kind of a response? Feel anything different?”

“Did you?” he asked.

“Yes—I mean, any eye gaze held between people, people who are close, good friends I mean. There’s an involuntary response from the brain. Oxytocin and dopamine happen.” The experiment was not going as I had planned. My response toward Squeak was unsettling and unexpected. It was also inconvenient, considering it interfered with the experiment. Time to get back on track. “So then, this is good. I can try this out on Theo—”

“Stick tosser.” Squeak pursed his lips.

“On Mon-Monday,” I finished, stumbling over the word.

Squeak leaned back, resting his head against the porch post, and closed his eyes. "You do that."

He seemed distant now. Tired almost. Physical and personal interactions can be very draining. I knew the feeling all too well. Changing gears would be good for us both.

"Come on, Esther is coming over in ten minutes so I can help her with her lab report." I started for the front door, but Squeak didn't follow.

His phone buzzed. He took a deep breath and exhaled as he sat up and slapped his hands on his knees. "Can't hang out, I'm afraid. I have to get going or I'm going to be late."

"Late? For what?" I struggled not to yell at him. Sometimes I felt frustrated with Squeak, but my reaction to his leaving surprised me in terms of its intensity. Something was seriously off with me today.

He stood, and once again I couldn't imagine how I'd been so unaware of his . . . growth spurt. The appearance of strong male traits. I couldn't even say I knew when it had happened. Last summer? Christmas?

"Bee, I had around an hour free, so I came over when you texted me." He glanced at his phone again. "I have to go," he said.

"Is this about Pom-Pom?" I asked.

"Her name is Taylor, and yes, she needs a little extra help today. So it's about her. She has to get through this class and manage to keep her GPA up enough to get into Caldwell College. She's got a provisional acceptance, but now she has to make it a full acceptance," he explained, frustration starting to color his voice and face.

I wasn't accustomed to trying to convince Squeak to do something. I didn't know how to effectively argue with him, much less be persuasive. I wasn't sure I could be persuasive in general. That took the ability to intuit things about people. Maybe if I got Esther to talk to him.

"Iris . . ." He shook his head.

Now I was worried. He never called me Iris unless he was mad at me, or when he was being very serious. It never boded well. Serious was more unsettling than mad. It made me self-conscious. I'd take mad any day.

He sighed heavily and then met my eyes. "I'm sorry. I have to opt for cash over intellectual stimulation."

He shrugged and then jammed his hands into his pockets. Unwilling to budge, that much was clear. Such a posture sometimes shows lack of interest or reluctance. It can also indicate deceit or hiding. What wasn't he telling me? Was he trying to hide something from me?

"You know that makes you sound like a stripper, right?" I said.

"Nice! Bee makes a funny—but I really gotta go."

"Fine. Go. I have work to do." Without looking back, I walked into the house and slammed the door closed behind me.

I raced upstairs and grabbed my phone, opening up my thread with Esther. **PESTER WHERE ARE YOU!**

## Prom Theory Notes

### Esther's Observations

*Iris is grumpy after testing things out on Squeak. Can't say how Squeak reacted to being lured by lollipops and then being forced into a staring contest. I'm not sure this will work on Theo. He doesn't look at anyone for more than a few seconds. He needs to rest his eyes so he can stare at himself in the mirror. I'm having doubts about Theo as a good subject. Are you sure you want to stare into his eyes? Let me know how that works out for you.*

## My Observations

The test on Squeak had positive results. It did create an intimate atmosphere, but that in turn made both participants uncomfortable, since both would rather not think of each other in any physical sense.

## Plan

Find opportunities to hold TG's gaze for more than nine seconds. Make note of TG's physical reactions, especially if he seems unaware of them (e.g., moving closer, physical contact, or breathing rate).

# CHAPTER THIRTEEN

## Monday
## Days to Prom: 12

I was up before my mother, which wasn't unusual. But it was unusual that Squeak was tapping on the kitchen door. I went over to the sliding doors to let him in. He dangled his car keys from his index finger.

I momentarily froze, drawn to his eyes. His interesting eyes. Some of the feelings that had indicated a burst of oxytocin to my system began to threaten. I broke eye contact with him, and looking at the ground, I stepped to the door and opened it wide enough for him to come in. He stood in the doorway, looking particularly groomed and bordering on fashionably dressed. Out of the ordinary for him, especially for so early in the morning.

"Do you have to give a presentation or something today?"

"No, why?" he asked, looking confused.

"You're wearing a new shirt and it looks like you ironed your khakis." I pointed at his midsection. "I didn't even know you owned a belt." I considered it for a moment. "It is a very nice belt."

A large smile crossed his face and he nodded. "Nice of you to notice. But so what?"

"Well, you must have had a reason. You never iron anything. Also, when have you ever been ready this early in the morning?"

"You make me sound like a loser—never iron, late for stuff. Both not true."

"Oh, so no occasion?" I didn't believe him. He was obviously trying to impress someone. I felt a bit sick to my stomach. There could be only one person he was trying to impress by looking so groomed and, as Esther would be sure to point out, hot. There was no other word for it, really.

"Oh, there's an occasion," he said as he took a step forward so we were nose to nose. "Have you had any time to think about Saturday's experiment? What do you think about how it affected us? Scientifically, that is."

I stepped aside to let him into the house. He wanted to talk about Saturday? Why? Did he suspect it had affected me more than I indicated? Was he going to make fun of me? Or did he want to tell me something else? Either way, nothing good could come of it, for me or the experiment. Best to ignore that particular topic.

"What occasion?"

Instead of tugging my ponytail as usual, he brushed a strand of hair that had escaped from my hair band and tucked it behind my ear. My neck tingled. Normally, anyone reaching out to touch me unexpectedly would have me moving away. But this was unsettling in a way I'd never experienced, and not at all unpleasant. It was much too early in the morning for anyone to be touching me to begin with, and I hadn't had breakfast. That must be it—my blood sugar was low and I wasn't fully awake yet.

"I have gas money and changed the oil yesterday. Let's go split a bear claw and a mocha," he said as he headed for my light denim jacket hanging on a hook in the hallway. He picked it up and returned, holding it out front-facing, as if he meant to help me put it on. He was being so odd that I was confused enough to let him do just that.

I supposed it was a thoughtful gesture. As strange and somewhat antiquated in terms of polite social behavior as it was, it felt kind of nice. After I'd turned with my back to him and slid my arms into the sleeves, he turned me around and adjusted my collar.

"Well, yeah, um, okay." I shook my head in an effort to clear my thoughts or lack thereof. Feeling more grounded, I said, "I have no desire to tempt type two diabetes. But since you're offering, I wouldn't mind a muffin and tea."

My mother shuffled into the kitchen. Eyes half-closed, hair impressively mussed, she ignored us and made her way to her coffeepot. It was the expensive type that began brewing at a set time. She used the aroma as a backup to her alarm. It never failed to draw her downstairs. She poured a cup, and then, sipping her coffee, she padded barefoot toward us.

Her eyes lit when she saw Squeak. "Seth! Good morning." She yawned. "Why are you up so early and dressed so nicely? Are you interviewing at nearby colleges today?"

Squeak groaned. "You too? No, I don't have college interviews today or anything else. Can't a guy look good once in a while?"

"Sorry, dear, I didn't mean you don't always look nice. Of course you do. Coffee?"

"No, thanks. Actually, I just came over to see if Iris wanted a ride and to grab something on the way in."

"So sweet!" She nudged me and grinned at Seth. He blushed. "Have fun. I'm going to grab another few minutes of sleep, since I'm not needed here." Mug in hand, she headed upstairs.

The Crusty Cruller was a popular coffee shop for students, since it wasn't far from the school. It was often too crowded for my comfort level, but since we were early, there was only a short line. Squeak told me to grab the corner closest to the storefront window, where the seriously worn but most comfortable armchairs were located.

I sank into the chair cushions and glanced at the local art that hung throughout the seating area, spotting one of my mother's neon birch forests. It wasn't my favorite painting she'd done, since the colors were a bit too bold and bright. But her hand and style were so present and distinctive, it made the shop's eclectic collection of mismatched furniture and secondhand knickknacks less jarring to me.

"That's one of your mom's, right?" Squeak said as he set our drinks on the table along with the bag containing my blueberry muffin and his bear claw. He followed my gaze and quieted for a moment, taking in the painting. "I've always really liked that one."

"Not my favorite, but it is very good. It's nice to see her paintings away from her studio. It—oh, I don't know." I leaned forward to reach for my drink.

"Makes the place feel familiar? Comforting, maybe?" He picked up my cup before I could and handed it to me.

I shrugged and took it. "Um, thank you." His attention to me this morning was making me feel shy. My world seemed to be shifting right beneath my feet. He wasn't making it any easier to accept that times like these were becoming less frequent and soon would be gone altogether. "Yes. I suppose that's it, isn't it?"

Squeak was often good at interpreting my reactions to places, people, and things when I couldn't quite do so. Senior year without him wouldn't be the easiest to navigate. Before I could start obsessing on that additional inevitability, the espresso machine hissed uncharacteristically loud, and the girl behind the counter shrieked in surprise, thankfully changing the course of my thoughts.

Picking up his coffee, Squeak stared down at the white plastic lid and picked at the protective cardboard sleeve, along the seam that cut through the purple doughnut logo. "Hey listen, I felt bad for cutting out on you on Saturday. I wanted to make it up to you. You know, for not really being around much." He took a sip and then lifted his eyes, meeting mine over the rim of the cup. His pupils widened, so much so that the small black discs made the now-thin green-gold band of his iris sharp and bright in contrast. The feelings brought about by the eye gaze test returned, and I felt my face warm—I looked away.

"I mean, if this works and he asks you . . . do you think you'll say yes?"

That was a quick turn in the conversation. What was he getting at? Was what happened Saturday making him think I might be onto something? Squeak was gracious in most things, but he didn't relish being proven wrong. That must be what was prompting this. Trying not to look smug, I fixed my attention on taking the lid off my tea and lifting the tea bag from the cup. As I wrapped it in a napkin, I said, "Why would I? Prom is so loud and crowded. I don't like even thinking about it—not really."

"Bee, look at me for a minute and listen. Don't you think that you might be changing your own neurochemistry by all this pretending to be interested in him? I mean, what if your 'prom theory' affects you more than it affects him?" He was still holding his coffee cup with one hand, so he made the air quotations with just one two-fingered quotation gesture.

"It won't. By being aware of the effect it has on me and knowing why it is affecting me, I won't be fooled into thinking it's genuine.

Which, if you remember, is one of the reasons I'm pursuing this. To prove the point that we can have control if we are aware of our brain's and body's instinctual reactions," I said.

"Okay, point taken." Squeak raised his eyebrows, and his forehead wrinkled accordingly. "But isn't thinking so much about prom making you curious about going?" He wasn't just asking me hypothetically, he was waiting for, and expecting, an answer. I didn't say anything.

"I mean, if you want to go, you shouldn't be embarrassed to admit it. I think all girls secretly want to go. I mean, if you really want to go to prom after all . . ."

"Why would I?"

"It doesn't make sense to spend so much time and effort on something you're not interested in. Theo, I mean. Not to mention something that might not work. You can't still be doing this to prove me wrong."

"It's important I see this through. I've told you why. I'm focused on the effectiveness of the methods on the brain and endocrine system, and how that then is interpreted by the frontal lobe in order to give meaning to the chemically induced sensations. No experiment is wasted time, despite the outcome. Besides, it will work." I patted his arm and smiled. Done. No more talk about actually going to prom. The fact that I had considered it was just my own false reasoning brought on by the instinctual but nevertheless mild and occasional attraction I'd been having to an athletic and physically attractive male. Or even the possibility I could dance with Squeak. Both were equally ridiculous ideas.

I'd most likely been subconsciously programmed by all the teen-focused media I'd been exposed to that presented proms and weddings as things all females should have as life goals. When really both were inventions by the fashion and entertainment industries to force women to buy expensive dresses and other pricey accessory activities. It was sinister when you really thought about it. I mean, what great minds were focused on getting dressed up for something so insignificant as a dance? I bet Marie Curie never went to prom, or even wanted to, for that matter.

"Well, okay, but I still think you should ditch this experiment."

The earth's rotation and the time passing as we sat across from each other increased the sunlight filtering through the leaves of the maple trees lining the streets of our small town's business district. The angle was just right so as to spotlight Squeak where he sat by the window. The light created shadows on his face, drawing attention to his cheekbones and angled jaw. His hair's dark red undertones showed, and the deep green of his oxford button-down shirt highlighted his eyes. He radiated masculinity and kindness.

That was the difference between Theo and Squeak—the open ease I felt when I was with him. Squeak. Why was I experiencing extremely uncharacteristic and illogical attraction to him, of all people? Was I experiencing a hormonal and biochemical imbalance due to the increased daylight brought on by the changing season? The more he talked about prom, the harder it was to expel the image of him dressed in a well-tailored suit, leading me onto the floor to dance.

I looked out the window and silently began going through the periodic tables to get rid of the completely ridiculous and wholly impossible image of Squeak.

"Earth to Bee," he said. I turned away from the window.

"Hmm?" I briefly examined my muffin before taking a big bite.

Maybe if I couldn't answer him, he would change the subject.

"Forget it. What is your plan for today?" he asked.

Swallowing, I looked up. More in control now, I felt like I could chance a look at Squeak again without imagining us dancing. That would be a disaster. If it ever happened—and I couldn't see there ever being a reason for us to dance together—I would likely step on his feet or take him down with me when I tripped. "For what?

"You know." He hefted an imaginary pole. I assumed he was gesturing to indicate Theo pole-vaulting. "Are you going to do that eye contact test today?" His voice had fallen, and his tone was quiet.

"I was hoping to. Depends on if I can catch his attention long enough." Back onto the topic of the experiment, I began to think about having a chance to get a positive outcome from someone other than a friend. Better proof I was on the right track. My mood brightened considerably.

He took a sip of his coffee, turning his head away from me. "Are you *sure* this hasn't gotten you thinking about going to prom?"

The conversation was becoming circular in its logic. Perhaps Squeak should have gotten a larger coffee. Caffeine helps with mental focus, but his tolerance was probably higher than it had been, since he was drinking more of it. Pom-Pom seemed to frequent coffee shops and used them as study locations.

"Squeak, have you been listening to me? You know this isn't really about prom. It's more about testing theories I've been reading about for the past year. How are we—and by 'we,' I mean Esther, you, and I—supposed to function in society if we have faulty information to guide our understanding of people?"

"I know that's your primary goal in life, but, practically speaking, in real-world consequences—what if it fails? What will you do about prom then?"

"Nothing, I—"

"Well, well, well. Is this Squeak—unthinkably early?" Esther appeared beside us, holding an extra-large drink topped with an enormous peak of whipped cream. "And Iris, not racing to school and looking relaxed. What happened?" Esther stopped talking as her eyes narrowed and she cocked her head to one side. It was a questioning gesture, but I could never really ascertain what its real meaning was in any given instance. However, she was considering us in a way that made me suspicious of her intent.

"Stop looking at me like that. The only thing that's happened is Squeak had gas money. I suppose I should thank Pom-Pom for that," I said.

"Yes, you should," Squeak said to me. "As well as for your early-morning tea and muffin," he added. I decided not to acknowledge that tidbit of unnecessary detailed information. Honestly, Pom-Pom didn't have anything to do with it. It was Squeak's decision to treat me, not hers.

Esther's eyes lit. She set her drink down on the small table and scampered—there was no better description—to the closest chair, then dragged it noisily between Squeak's and mine. She dramatically dropped into it. "I'm liking this coffeehouse meeting. How come we don't do this more often? Oh, we could be just like *Friends*! I got dibs on Phoebe or Chandler. It's a toss-up. Iris is definitely the Ross of the group. So that would make Squeak Rachel."

Both Squeak and I looked at her, equally insulted.

"Okay, so that's a no. Well then, it must be official. Up early. Out to breakfast." She was ticking off some list of qualifications on her fingers. "That must mean . . ."

Was she still teasing me? Squeak? Both of us?

She pointed at Squeak. "Nice to know you finally decided to cowboy up and asked—"

"Bee if she needed a ride to school. Yes, I did." He fixed her with an intent look, not blinking.

Esther's cheeks reddened. "Well, yeah, of course. I mean, what else would you ask, right?" She tucked her chin and looked down, slurping her coffee before wiping the cream off her face with a paper napkin from the stack on the table.

Something had just happened, and I wasn't sure what it was. "Why would he need to 'cowboy up' (or alternate) to give me a ride to school? He does that once in a while."

"So, we should get going soon so you have time to get your locker in order, huh?" Squeak asked, somewhat loudly.

I glanced at the clock on the wall above the counter. "We were really early this morning, weren't we? But yes, I would like to get to school while I still have time to get all my materials ready for the day."

Esther sighed and stood up, holding her cup. "Let's go."

## Prom Theory Notes

### My Observations

*During the course of these experiments, this researcher has been experiencing unexpected reactions to exposure not only to Theo but also to a friend. Most likely this is due to the time away from Squeak, his suddenly unusual behavior, and spring's neurological* and hormonal effects on all animals (the increase in daylight and so forth). However, since this researcher is not the subject of the experiment, and considers these dual attractions an anomaly, she concludes they are not significant to the outcome or in general.

## Esther's Observations

Wait. What?????????

## Researcher's Note to Above Comment

Disregard. I am somewhat sleep deprived. I've been getting up earlier than normal this past week. It's important to note that without adequate sleep, a person's levels of leptin fall, whereas the level of ghrelin rises. Ghrelin is an appetite stimulant. As an additional result of the lack of sleep, a person's body releases higher levels of insulin, throwing blood sugar levels off. This, in turn, affects perceptions, mood, and other cognitive abilities. So my above observations carry no weight and have no basis in logic or reliable emotions.

# CHAPTER FOURTEEN

**Mere-Exposure Effect and the Amygdala:**

*Repeated Exposure (to a Person) Increases Interest and Motivation to Seek More Contact and/or Information*

*Well tested and reliable, the effect is strongest when the unfamiliar stimuli are presented for short periods between ten and twenty times.*

Sneaking out of the morning's junior assembly was easy enough. All I had to do was sit in the far-left corner of the back row. Theo would be walking past the auditorium on his way to class, and I knew I could place myself in his path if I got out before dismissal and ahead of the stampede. If I "just happened" to be walking in his direction, I could walk with him and might even be able to get two solid minutes with him.

During a burst of applause for the class president's announcement of the record profit from our last fund-raising sale, I slipped out. With my hand on the side door of the auditorium, I eased it closed. Just when the door's lock met the strike plate, retracted, and clicked, someone tapped me on the shoulder. I stiffened, not moving, not turning around.

Caught.

"Don't you want to see how it ends?"

*Squeak*. I turned around.

His wide grin and bright eyes caught me off guard as much as his ambush had. I considered him warily. "What's up with you?"

"The guidance office just called me in for a meeting. Seems I've been offered several local scholarships. All I have to do is accept. Want to celebrate? Whatever you want from the vending machines, on me," he said. His hand shot out and grasped my hair, giving it a small tug.

I'd been scanning the hallway, staring over his shoulder, generally focused on looking for Theo, when my right brain deciphered what Squeak was talking about.

"So soon? I mean, do you have to do that today? Doesn't that mean you have to choose a college or something?" Other things, important things, needed my full attention. Just the idea of deciding what far-off college he was going to attend . . .

This was not on today's carefully planned schedule. Losing my best friend in three months—no, let's talk about something else. I wasn't ready for that conversation, and he had dropped it on me from out of nowhere.

I stepped back, getting ready to head toward the main auditorium doors so I could see the hallway in both directions. Then, to put a little distance between Squeak, his college discussions, and me, I took an additional step back. "I'm busy right now. Maybe we can talk about this after I've finished my experiments."

He followed, standing on my left side and blocking my view of the hallway. "Bee, come on. I have to make my decision soon. I can't wait until you've had your way with some brainless jock. This is an important decision that's going to change the rest of my life, not just my prom plans. I want you to be part of it. I've been helping you with this research project when you really needed me to for the past week. Now I need you."

"Why do you want my opinion? Besides, what can I—wait, how does this change your prom plans? You really have prom plans? I thought you said that you probably wouldn't go."

Just then the bell rang. Both doors to the auditorium swung open, and the entire junior class of 375 students rushed out, en masse. Squeak and I were crowded and pushed against the back-wall corner, pinned behind the open door. Thrown backward, I hit the back of my head against the brick and concrete wall. "Ow," I said as the air momentarily left my lungs.

Squeak flung open his arms and slapped his hands against the wall as he was pushed against me. His hands were on either side of my shoulders and I was trapped. I felt panic threatening to take over. However, as soon as I realized Squeak wasn't cornering me, but keeping me out of and away from the rushing crowd, the threat of an anxiety attack subsided.

"Are you okay?" He managed to move one of his hands to the back of my head. I winced. The point of impact was definitely going to swell, and I'd have to go through the day with a bump on the back of my head.

Possible mates who were obviously clumsy were a bad bet. They were more likely to trip and drop a baby or get trampled by livestock, or the junior class. So much for fulfilling their Darwinian imperative. The spot was tender, but Squeak's hand provided a cushion between my head and the unforgiving surface of the wall.

"Stay put. We'll get crushed if we try to get through that crowd," said Squeak, his breath hot against my ear.

"I am not going anywhere until the tide of humanity subsides," I promised.

He laughed. He was so close I could feel the air rush from him, his chest falling and then rising again as he took a deep breath. I'd never been this physically close, from head to toe, to Squeak. As far as I could remember, he'd never smelled this good. It was almost distracting enough to override the dull ache that had now settled in my head.

Pine and spice. It had to be his deodorant. No one smelled this good. Or at least I didn't think so. Hadn't really smelled too many people. I knew I was leaning in so I could get the full effect of his scent, but there was no helping it. In order to elicit a reaction like this, especially in me, it had to have something to do with pheromones, his pheromones. Would this cause my body to secrete some scent in response?

I wanted to be able to reach the crook of his neck to get the full effect. I needed to know if whatever he was wearing was mixing with his body heat as a catalyst to release his natural scent. Whether it was Old Spice or male pheromones, it was having a strange effect on me. But I couldn't have my head hover over his shoulder without standing on my tiptoes and pressing even closer to him, or lifting my head off the wall and Squeak's hand.

If I'd run into him in a darkened alley and been unable to see his face or hear him speak, I wasn't sure I'd have recognized him. His body had morphed from a lanky kid to this muscled, lean frame. I tried to stop the thrill that had started at the very base of my belly and was rushing through me at the thought of running into him in a dark alley. This had to stop.

It was *Squeak*, for pity's sake. *He's like your brother, remember?*

The reality check broke the hold Squeak's pheromones and full-body contact had on me.

I opened my eyes and blinked a couple of times. Most of the crowd had cleared out. Was the end of the assembly that bad that they couldn't get far away fast enough? I was just glad things had quieted down as quickly as they had.

I met Squeak's eyes. He was still looking concerned. His brow was slightly furrowed and his gaze soft. He really did care about me. But he was leaving.

Enough. I had other projects to focus on. Esther needed my help with getting Darren to ask her to prom. I needed to focus on her now, in her time of need. She would be here, with me, even after Squeak was gone.

Right, I was looking for Theo. If I didn't start paying attention to what was going on around me, I'd lose my chance to catch up with him before the last bell. I stepped a tiny bit away from the wall, toward Squeak, and he also stepped back, dropping his hand.

Then my own hand, the traitorous appendage, reached up and felt the hard curve of his bicep. Maybe I had alien hand syndrome. There was no other explanation for it. I rarely, if ever, sought to touch someone. Recently, it felt like I was becoming more accustomed than I had been to Squeak's friendly physical gestures of pulling my ponytail and warming my consistently cold hands.

I traced the line marking the muscle beneath the rolled-up sleeve of his flannel shirt. He'd always worn flannel shirts. Usually, he picked them up in thrift shops. He said he liked the hunt and the unexpected score, like a Doctor Who bow tie or a trench coat for a couple of dollars. Esther was wrong; he was much more of a geek than I was. It would seem that secondhand flannel shirts were not at all scratchy. In fact, likely due to their age and numerous washings, they were very soft.

My hand was examining his arm while I was busy looking at the strained fabric of his shoulder seam—

"Bee?" he whispered in my ear.

"Yes?" I glanced up and peered over his shoulder. The hall was clear.

I quit my exploratory examination of his arm when I saw how he was looking at me. He held my eyes for a moment, and then his gaze drifted to where my hand rested on his shoulder.

"Oh!" I said as I pulled my hand away. Squeak stood close, but he was no longer pressed against me. He must have taken a step backward when the crowd cleared. His expression still held concern, but it was making my stomach flip. He didn't move or drop his other arm from where he had his hand pressed against the wall, half caging me.

"Sorry, I . . ." Suddenly my head was filled with thoughts of the garment industry, and wiki mode threatened. I bit the inside of my cheek to stop myself.

"Listen, Bee. I want—" he started.

Just then Theo strolled past, and it was the perfect time to escape. I slipped under Squeak's arm. "I've got to catch up with Theo before I lose my chance." I had to get away before he started to talk about his college choice again. I couldn't deal, as I was still feeling muddled from our literal run-in. It probably didn't have anything to do with Squeak and everything to do with what I suspected was my mild concussion.

"Right. Later," I heard him mumble before I was out of earshot.

I was blushing and felt like I had a low-grade fever. Part of it was being embarrassed for treating Squeak like he was nothing more than a fine physical specimen. He probably thought I planned to get him on the dissecting table with the way I'd focused on his tendons and clearly defined muscle mass. I was flushed and felt like the lightweight snug sweater I'd worn that day to draw attention to my meager but certainly adequate physical attributes was one layer too many.

It was a good time to ask Theo a question. Why waste the eye-catching color of my chest and cheeks, and my more-than-likely wide eyes?

"Theo," I called out to him. I took a few quick steps to close the distance between us. He stopped and turned around. A couple more steps and I had caught up with him.

"Hey, Lily." He looked down at the pendant I had been wearing since Esther loaned it to me. "It's Lily, right?" he asked.

"No, it's Iris. I'm Iris. Like the necklace."

"Looks like a lily." He shrugged a shoulder, and one side of his mouth turned down in a dismissive gesture. Best to move on and attempt to regain his attention.

"Anyway, I'm glad I saw you. I wanted to ask you something." I hesitated before reaching out to touch his bare arm, exposed due to his short-sleeved linen shirt. I fought not to pull my hand away too quickly.

"My friend Esther wanted me to help her at the water table and to bring cookies to the meet, but I can't find her and she must have her phone off. When is the meet, again?" The words came in a rush. I took a breath before I gave him a shy smile. Then I held his eyes with mine until it was uncomfortable, which didn't take long, and looked away for a second.

He was looking over my shoulder, and I leaned in to appear interested in what he was about to say. Plus, getting closer would make it easier for him to pick up on my natural scent.

"Wednesday," he said, while looking past me. He lifted his chin, indicating something behind me. "Is he that asshole physics tutor?"

I glanced over my shoulder. Squeak was still watching me, standing where we'd been just a moment before. He was taller than Theo, not by much, but enough so that it was noticeable when the two were standing in the same hallway. He was leaning against the wall with one knee bent, foot pressed against the wall, arms crossed over his chest. When I fully turned around to look at him, he pushed himself away from the wall and glared at Theo. Squeak was always lighthearted, easy to get along with. But the way he was looking at Theo right now turned whatever low-grade fever I had into a chill. He shoved his hands into his front pockets and turned his back to us before walking away.

"I *think* he tutors physics," I said to Theo. I watched Squeak walk down the hall, his back stiff. I suppressed the urge to run after him and stop him, tell him I'd share a packet of trail mix with him from the vending machine, and that I was proud of him for getting those scholarships. But I wasn't sure that was the right thing to do. He wouldn't want to stop me from proving my theory, would he? I had to remember that these experiments were important not only for Esther, but for him, too. He had to understand that biology ruled us, and if we didn't understand that, we'd never be in control of our lives.

It was only when he was out of sight that I was able to turn back to Theo.

"Tutoring Taylor, right?" he asked.

"I think so," I said.

His eyes were still focused on the hallway where Squeak had been.

Suddenly his focus shifted to me and he smiled. No wrinkling at his eyes, but still, his attention had turned my way. Maybe the opportunity hadn't been ruined by the tension that had sprung up between him and Squeak, probably over Princess Pom-Pom.

"You said you're working the meet on Wednesday?" he asked, and I nodded. "Great, see you there." He winked and strode off with a noticeable swagger. I tried to consider his buttocks. His gluteal muscles were obviously strong. But nevertheless, it was hard to find anything attractive about someone who'd just called my oldest friend an asshole. Squeak was anything but.

Maybe I wasn't the only one to have noticed Squeak's recently acquired physical strength and superior height. Maybe Pom-Pom had noticed before I had, and Theo considered him a threat. Any sort of territorial threat or competition over a female could result in a real altercation between the two.

Not having laboratory conditions for these experiments was problematic. Too many uncontrolled elements and conditions were making this much more complicated than I had anticipated. I needed to stay focused and keep my methods specific and my hypothesis for each experiment clear. Most of all, I needed to be aware of my responses to the stimuli I initiated and introduced, and not let my own involuntary physical and hormonal responses affect the outcome of the experiments.

I could do that. Right?

# Prom Theory Notes

## Esther's Observations

Iris loves to volunteer me for things. Thanks, girlfriend. How many cookies do I have to bake for the team? The only reason I'm agreeing to do this is to sweeten Darren up.

## My Observations

Esther is kind and a gifted baker.

This researcher made use of knowing TG's schedule of classes and was able to create an opportunity to establish a connection. Eye gaze seemed to increase his interest, but his physical responses were, perhaps, so subtle as not to be noticeable. Although, due to an uncomfortable and distracting conversation with Squeak, it made it difficult for this researcher to be objective and closely observant of TG. Also, Squeak's increasingly adversarial relationship with TG may complicate things going forward and turn TG's focus more toward Pom-Pom.

## Personal Note

Elementary students should be taught more about the various types of flora, especially how to recognize commonly known flowering bulbs. It's a rather noticeably weak area of knowledge in the soon-to-be-adult-and-in-control-of-important-things generation.

# CHAPTER FIFTEEN

## Tuesday
## Days to Prom: 11

"Esther!" I grasped her arm just as she was reaching the door that led to the cafeteria. It was sixth period and we both had lunch.

"Hey! I'm starving!" But she didn't put up a fight as I pulled her the few steps to the girls' bathroom.

"You can wait. We have work to do," I said as I let go of her arm and pushed the door open with both hands.

"You're bossy, you know that?" Esther asked. She followed me in and gave the still-open door a little push.

The hydraulic door hinge hissed loudly as it slid closed. I took a deep breath to slow my heart rate. I needed to appear normal and nonchalant for this exercise to be productive. I didn't want to tip Squeak off, or the results wouldn't be useful. I needed Squeak's untainted reactions to help me determine which stimulus to include in the experiment on the real subject—Theo.

I slipped out of the straps of my backpack and set it on the floor. "No, I didn't know that."

"Well, you are, which is especially annoying when I have low blood sugar. This better be worth it." She wrinkled her brow, and her eyes narrowed as she stared at me. She could be doubting me or suspicious. Or both. I wasn't worried. Once I told her what we were going to do, her mood would undoubtedly improve.

I bent down beside my backpack and unzipped it to pull out a large hardcover book I'd found in my mother's studio the previous night. I held the book out to her.

"What the hell is that?" Esther stared wide-eyed at the cover.

"*A Pictorial Dictionary of Body Language: How to Recognize Lies, Love, and More Emotions Than You Can Name*. Isn't it perfect?"

Esther took the book and, with a smirk, sat down on a small bench next to the row of sinks. She flipped through a few pages before saying, "A little strange, but I see the appeal. Where did you get this?"

"My mom had it with her art books. She said she uses it for a drawing reference."

"So what are we going to do with it?" Esther asked, still turning pages, pausing only a moment to look at the series of photographs of people squinting, laughing, scowling, and so on. At one page she paused and then laughed, short and high, in surprise. "Now I know what you want to do with this. You want to learn how to flirt."

"Give me that." I snatched the book away from her. "I know how to flirt. I've read at least six books on the subject in the last week. However, some of this body language is far subtler than you would expect. Like this . . ." I knelt down next to her and flipped through some pages. I found the one I was looking for and pointed to a paragraph with an explanatory photo below it. "'The first signals a woman will give a man she is interested in are submissive cues.'"

Esther frowned. "I don't think I like the sound of that."

"No, it's nothing about letting him tell you what to do. It's just that some simple body cues are interpreted as weakness and vulnerability in a possible mate by the male primitive brain, the amygdala. It's a subconscious response that drives the urge to protect, therefore insuring safety for possible offspring."

"And that's sexy?" Esther asked.

"Apparently so. So, okay, if I'm tossing my hair around and touching myself—"

"Whoa!" Esther put her hand in front of her eyes.

"Would you stop thinking like a hormone-riddled teenager?" I said. She drew her hand away from her eyes, and I could see she was very amused.

She laughed. "What if I *am* a horny teenager?"

I closed the book. "Your words, not mine. But if you are, then maybe I shouldn't be sharing this information with you. It's probably safer for everyone if I do this without your assistance."

"You would keep this potentially powerful information to yourself? Iris Oxtabee, that's not very sporting of you."

"So you're not serious?" I asked.

"Only a little," she said.

"Hmm, well okay. I'll have to trust you, I suppose. I could use your help."

Esther carefully took the book from me again. I let her. "Okay then, let's see these submissive cues you're talking about, and then you can explain the bit about touching yourself in public," she said.

I ignored her attempt at masturbatory humor. We were wasting time. "They include lowering your body to appear smaller, playful, exposing your neck and wrists, glances, giggling and laughing, touching your neck, head tilting, downcast eyes, turning your toes in—that's called pigeon toes, or tibial torsion."

"Didn't you already do the eye gaze experiment with Squeak?"

she asked.

"Yes. It went pretty well, but now I need to see if casual touch will change the way he responds to me." I considered Squeak's and my encounter outside the auditorium yesterday. It seemed that his manner hadn't changed during the intimate circumstances. They had changed mine—but that was erroneous and had nothing to do with prom theory.

"Does Squeak know about this?" Esther crossed her arms and frowned.

"No. If he did, it wouldn't work at all. I have to do this with him as a blind subject. I think I can pull it off and it should work. I just have to be sure I'm not giving off body language that says, 'I want to run away as fast as I can.'"

"Yeah, that probably would make Theo leave. I don't think he sticks around unless someone is fawning all over him. You could just pretend it's Squeak when you're testing your subtle touching. That might help," Esther suggested.

"I just need some practice. I'm only going to get one shot. If I creep Theo out, I'll never get another chance. That's why we're in here right now."

"Why, exactly?"

"Because I'm going to rehearse some of these things. That way, I'm comfortable doing them. Then I'm going to try them out on Squeak during lunch," I said.

Esther seemed to consider something as she looked up at the ceiling. She clicked her tongue and then dropped her gaze to the book. She was still looking at it when she said, "Are you sure you want to do this?"

"Yes. Why wouldn't I?"

"It's just, well, it's kind of mean, leading someone on like that, even Squeak." She looked at me. Her expression was soft. Her voice was gentle. Like she was carefully explaining something. As if I didn't fully understand what I was about to do.

"That's the point, it's only Squeak. He won't mind. Besides, I'm not leading him on. I'm just going to practice some of this flirting and see if he responds or just thinks I'm acting strange. If he picks up on it, then I'll know I need to work on my moves." I smiled and brightened my expression and demeanor in an effort to lighten her unexpectedly serious take on the plan.

Esther drew a deep breath and then let out a loud sigh. "Still, Squeak likes to know what's going on, and he's having a hard enough time with you doing this project. He wants to help you, but . . . I just think you could actually hurt him."

Hurt Squeak? How? Why would he care if I was fake flirting with him? It was in the name of science. I didn't have anyone else I was comfortable enough with to practice on. I just had to hope that my seemingly out-of-whack endocrine system wouldn't respond to Squeak as it had when he unintentionally made full-body contact with me outside the auditorium. I needed to stay objective. Reminding myself that I had long thought of him as a brother should do the trick of eradicating the attraction I might be experiencing in response to his recently matured male traits. He obviously still saw me as a little sister. He'd said the eye gaze experience didn't change the way he felt about me.

For some inexplicable reason, I suddenly felt sad.

"He'll be fine. This is me, remember. It's not like I'm going to break his heart or anything."

"Don't count on it," Esther said softly. When I started to ask her what she meant, she cut me off. "What about the whole not-ethical-experimenting-on-humans thing?"

"Squeak has agreed to be a guinea pig. So he expects some of this. I'm just slipping in a small experiment," I justified.

"Okay, but just remember if this goes south, I'm the one who thought better of it." She stood and retrieved a lipstick from her bag. Leaning over the sink to get closer to the mirror, she traced her lips with the pink gloss before turning around to face me.

She held out the lipstick. "Your makeup has been looking great, but it does wear off. You need to reapply. We talked about this."

I took it and moved to the sink next to her. "The only way this could go south would be that I make a fool out of myself in front of Squeak and he teases me for the rest of my life."

"Nah, he'll probably only tease you for the rest of the year," Esther said. She watched as I carefully applied the lipstick. When I first started wearing some for the sake of the experiment, I thought it made me look strange—not clownish exactly, but close. Now that I was becoming accustomed to my face having certain attributes enhanced, I thought it looked quite nice.

I turned to smile at her before saying, "I don't think he'll give up that easily." I handed the lipstick back to her.

"Oh, he never does. But he'll be away at college, and I doubt very much he's coming home to visit his father on weekends," she said.

"Can we not talk about that?" I spoke a little louder than I meant to. So loud, in fact, that Esther caught my eye in the mirror and raised one eyebrow.

This was not the conversation I wanted to be having.

"Pigeon toes, huh?" Esther said as she slipped the lipstick back into her bag. "Who knew?"

After practicing a few moves and getting suggestions from Esther on how to appear less stiff, we were only about ten minutes late for lunch. Esther had gone into the cafeteria before me to keep Squeak from suspecting anything, with me following a few moments after. I spotted them as soon as I walked in. Easy enough. Squeak always sat in the same place. We didn't always sit with him, as he tended to be surrounded by his science bros, and usually things escalated into arguments about topics that, honestly, neither Esther nor I cared about. Too much about probability and not enough about actual testable theories for me, or animals for Esther.

Esther must have told him to save me a seat, since his messenger bag was on the stool next to him. I began walking straight to them before I realized I would get more scrutiny if I sat down without at least a drink and an apple. It was worth the few minutes it would take me to get through the line.

While I stood in line, I attempted a coy head tilt and tried to soften my posture. Earlier Esther had pointed out I should take a deep breath and relax my shoulders. I did so and held my tray with a loose grip, so as to make my inner wrists more visible. Exposing my neck and wrists supposedly made me appear vulnerable.

I lifted my right shoulder slightly and lowered my head so that I could peer over my shoulder and catch Squeak's eye. It was supposed to be a shy yet come-hither look that would trigger a protective response in a male. I turned my head and looked backward but instead caught the eye of Josh Patel from National Honor Society. We sat next to each other at the meetings, for alphabetical purposes. He stared at me for a couple of seconds before color crept up his face. He grabbed a tray and raced to the line for the salad bar.

Either I'd just successfully flirted with him, or I'd scared him. Either way, it was success on some level. Feeling a little more confident, I managed to work my way through the line, all the while trying to lower my voice, stay relaxed, make eye contact, and giggle when appropriate. With mixed results and no clear evidence that I was going about it in an effective manner, I took a few deep breaths and meandered, while rolling my hips, over to the table where Esther, Darren, and Squeak sat.

My hands were shaking. What was wrong with me lately? This was Squeak. Good old like-a-brother Squeak. No need to be nervous. I walked up to the stool and quietly said, "Squeak?"

Esther must have said something funny, because they were all laughing. Squeak didn't hear me.

I spoke a little louder but tried to keep my voice low. Esther was sitting on the other side of Squeak and across from Darren. She looked up, saw me, then elbowed Squeak. "Yo, move your bag so Iris can sit."

Squeak glanced up at me as he reached for his bag. "Why didn't you say something?"

He slid his bag beneath his stool.

I smiled softly and, still looking at him, placed my tray onto the table before taking off my backpack and setting it under the table. I slid onto the seat hip-first. "I did. You didn't hear me." Tilting my head and reaching around, I moved my ponytail to the other shoulder, exposing my neck. I straightened my head a little and looked down. It was difficult not to ask him if it was working, or even launch into a discussion of the book from which I'd gotten the information. This was, perhaps, the hardest thing I had ever tried to do.

"You okay?" Squeak asked, leaning back a little bit and examining me.

"Yes, why?"

He shrugged. "You seem a little off."

I shook my head just the tiniest bit. I didn't want to send a negative signal. I turned toward him and pointed my toes inward. Esther stood halfway up and peered over Squeak to look at my feet.

"Now what are *you* doing?" Squeak asked Esther.

She smiled widely and laughed. "Nothing."

Squeak swung around so he was facing me. I kept my head tilted downward and looked up at him. Wide doe eyes were good. I opened my eyes a little wider. This caused Squeak to pull back and screw up his face in a way that said he was either worried or confused or both. I didn't know his forehead could have such deep burrows. Something about how I was approaching this was incorrect. What was I doing?

"All right, something is seriously wrong with you. Esther, did you slip her a sedative or something?"

"Nah, she's like this sometimes." She took a big bite of her apple, chewed, and then said, "I think she's flirting with you." She waggled her eyebrows at Squeak. Darren laughed and set to work on his second pudding.

I sat up straight and glared at her. Some partner she turned out to be.

"Okay, Iris, you're off the hook. Esther is the one all hopped up on something," Squeak said.

Darren had swallowed the entire snack-size pudding in a matter of seconds. Esther offered him hers. He quickly took it. The smiles and looks between them were full of genuine affection. Real smiles, lifted cheeks, and bright eyes that kept Darren from attacking his pudding the moment he got it. His third pudding.

"There is a good deal of sugar and preservatives in those. That isn't very nutritious. It can't be the best food for a training athlete." I said.

"Huh?" Darren looked at me with a blank expression. Squeak laughed. He leaned next to me and bumped my shoulder with his before straightening. "She's definitely feeling better."

I was certainly feeling something. Even as far back as the late nineteenth century and William James, the theorist and early proponent of positive psychology, researchers and psychologists have held the theory that creating the physical expression of an emotion or feeling, even if you aren't feeling as such at the moment, soon creates that feeling. Were my attempts at appearing submissive to a strong and protective male setting off any response in his brain? Was I instead fooling my brain, with my repeated attempts to exhibit mate-seeking behavior, into thinking I was attracted to Squeak? That was not my intention.

I realized I'd leaned into him and was now resting my thigh against his, our hips touching. With just a small movement I could easily tuck into his arm and rest my head on his shoulder. The strange thing was I wanted to do just that.

Squeak relaxed against me and turned to catch my gaze. He seemed to be searching my eyes for something. Darren coughed.

We straightened, pulling apart. Esther was looking at us oddly, and Darren was grinning, as he usually was, but this time there was something mischievous about it.

"Fynne, sure *you're* not on something?"

How long had we been leaning against each other, staring and saying nothing?

"Yeah, I'm all hopped up on preservatives and red dye number four—you?" Squeak answered as he looked down and intently studied the Tater Tots and strawberry gelatin still on his tray.

"Sugar's my power food of choice. Hey, Esther, I got the car today. Want to hit the Shake Place?"

"You are awesome! Let's go—"

She started off while Darren laughed. "I meant after school," he said.

But she was already moving. Her foot collided with my backpack, and it moved out from under the table and past my seat. I must not have zipped it closed, because the body language book slid out of the top far enough for the title to show. I reached down and grabbed it, trying to block the cover from view. But I knew it was too late.

I chanced a look at Squeak. He was looking at the book, and his expression was slightly . . . hurt. He hadn't reached for my ponytail once since I sat down, and I wished that he would do so now. Anything to give a sign that what had just happened, what I'd done, hadn't changed anything between us. I looked away and concentrated on my salad. "I'm sorry," I mumbled.

"So am I," he said. Without another word or glance in my direction, he grabbed his things and walked out of the cafeteria.

### Outcomes

*Undetermined. Study was corrupted by subject discovering purpose of test situation. To put it otherwise, the subject discovered it was a test situation.*

## Esther's Observations

I hate to say told you so, but told you so. It's probably a good idea not to test things out on Squeak. You're the one who knows what all this can do to some poor unsuspecting boy's brain.

## Personal Note

My assistant makes a good point. I will cease treating Squeak as a test subject. It doesn't result in useable outcomes or information. Conclusion: Good friends aren't good candidates for test subjects.

# CHAPTER SIXTEEN

## Tuesday After School
## Days to Prom: 11

Esther was happily licking one of the beaters she'd popped free from the electric mixer. She was humming.

"Are you humming? Why are you humming?" I asked.

She stopped and wiped cookie dough from the inside of the beater blade with her finger. She paused before putting it in her mouth, then said, "I was. Making cookies make me happy, and I hum when I'm happy."

It was becoming increasingly clear since I started testing the prom theory that I, more often than not, failed to notice important things about the people closest to me.

"You do? Have you ever been happy around me?" I asked.

"I was humming. You're here." She shrugged and smiled at me.

"No, I meant before now."

"Since I am generally a happy person, then yes, I sometimes hum when you're around." She walked to the kitchen sink and dropped the beaters into the warm, soapy water. She'd filled it when we started cleaning up.

"You really don't notice?" Her face showed the signs of genuine sadness, but I couldn't understand why. Was she sad because I wasn't a very good friend? Or was she sad *for* me?

I swallowed nervously. "Did I hurt your feelings? I never meant to be such a lousy friend, but I guess—"

"You guess you never thought about it." Esther came around the island and sat on the stool next to me. "I know. There are so many wheels turning all the time in your head—I know it's hard for you to worry or notice if someone has a cold, or a huge, ginormous boot on her foot."

I didn't know what to say. I had an urge to say, "Thank you," but it didn't seem like an appropriate response to having been told I was inattentive and oblivious. Esther saved me from myself, as she often did.

"Did you know," Esther started, picking up a snickerdoodle cookie from the cooling rack, "they're discovering that old wives' tales, folk medicine, and other stuff like that actually work? I know some things too." She winked. "So, these cookies I just slaved over—"

"Hummed over," I interrupted, relieved at the quick change of topic.

Esther grinned. "These very hummy cookies are ready and willing to prove that the way to a man's heart is through his stomach."

"I'm the one trying to win his heart, as you say, but I didn't make them. You did," I said.

"You helped, and you measured. You're really good at the measuring part," Esther said. She popped the small cookie into her mouth, rolled her eyes, and groaned. "So good," she said around chewed-up cookie.

"Baking is chemistry. It's important to measure accurately," I said, reaching for a larger one on the rack.

"Exactly! So you made these just as much as I did," Esther exclaimed. She posed, tilting up the rack with one hand, and made a sweeping gesture toward the cookies with the other.

I took a bite and thoroughly chewed and swallowed before I said, "I've tried to make cookies by myself. They never taste as good as yours or my mom's."

"That's because perfect measuring is important, but the ingredients we toss in when you're not looking are even more important." She started stacking the cooled cookies onto a plate.

"That makes no sense."

"It's true."

"Like what?" I asked. I hated not knowing things like that. "You can't just tell me you put things that aren't in the recipe into cookies—into anything, for that matter—without fully explaining yourself."

"Baker's secret. Sworn to silence. It's those little extra-special bits you need to keep in mind when you're plotting your love potions." Esther reached into the cabinet drawer and pulled out a box of plastic wrap. She pulled a long strip from the roll and, with an expert tug, neatly sliced it along the serrated edge. That told me more about Esther's secret powers than anything else. Had that been me, I'd have cut myself and bled all over the torn, wadded piece of plastic wrap.

"Again, with the magic potions," I mumbled, and then said, "No such thing."

"You need to remember that no matter how perfect the lab experiments you're cooking up, there are going to be a few ingredients tossed in that you can't measure. Sometimes it's good, and sometimes it's not so good, because there are things you can't always predict."

"We've had this discussion before. I still disagree."

"Cookies are a good example of my point. If he thinks you made them, all the better, right?" Esther asked.

They were really good. Good cookies impress everyone. I could do worse than establishing a connection between myself and the pleasure of the dopamine rush he'd get when he tasted the cookie.

"Right," I agreed, and reached for another cookie.

"Hey, we need to save these for the track meet tomorrow." Esther took the remaining plate of cookies and dumped them into a Ziploc bag.

"Esther?"

"Yeah?" She started to put the packed cookies into a tote bag. Her head was turned away from me.

What else didn't I know about Esther? Probably a lot. What did she know about me, for that matter? And Squeak, he hadn't spoken to me at all after lunch. He was obviously avoiding me. It seemed there was a lot I didn't know about him, either. Like how he would react to discovering that my flirting, even in the name of science, wasn't genuine. It wasn't, was it?

Shouldn't friends tell one another things that other people don't know about them? Shouldn't friends take their friends' feelings into account no matter what? Had she ever noticed my occasional toe taps, hops, and rocking back on my feet? . . .

I wet a kitchen towel under the faucet and squeezed the excess water out. "Sometimes I . . ." I began wiping down the island top.

Esther stopped and turned toward me. "Sometimes you what?"

I glanced at her. She was tilting her head slightly to the side, and one corner of her lips subtly quirked. I'd started this conversation and I had to finish it, or she'd pester me for days to find out what I almost told her. I concentrated on scrubbing a small area of dried cookie dough.

"Have you ever noticed, um, sometimes I shuffle my feet?"

"I've seen you walk, yes."

"No. I don't mean that. Like . . . I mean . . ." I could feel my face heating up, and I was gripping the kitchen towel with both hands now while I wiped it around the countertop. "Sometimes, when I read something, or someone says something, about a topic that suddenly interests me, I get excited—"

"And you start tapping your toes or swinging your legs if we're sitting, or stand on one foot—"

"So you notice?" My face must have fallen a bit, or my voice indicated that I was embarrassed or maybe even a little ashamed. I think I felt ashamed.

"I notice it, and so does Squeak, but we just figured you had a lot of energy on those days." She paused before adding, "Nobody else notices."

"Really?" I asked.

"Really," she assured me. "Did you just want to know if I noticed you doing those things?"

"No, well, yes—I guess I wanted you to know why," I said.

Esther didn't say anything. She looked like she was thinking about something else. I just wasn't sure what it was.

"It's extra energy, I guess. My toes tingle, and sometimes it feels like they're going to go off like sparklers. I used to really hop around when I was little. I hopped up and down and flapped my hands. But people didn't react well, especially adults. Preschool teachers didn't have much patience with my disruptive behavior. So anyway, I don't do that anymore. Or I try not to, anyway."

Esther was pressing her lips together, and her face reddened. She swallowed and looked away. Was she going to cry?

"What? What did I say?"

"Oh, Iris!" She reached for me and caught me in a tight hug before I knew what she intended. "You've never told me anything like that before."

I struggled a little, trying to loosen her arms so I could breathe. I really wanted to pull away. "I might not ever again if you don't let go of me."

Esther sniffled and laughed, then released me and stepped back.

"I'm sorry, Esther, I didn't mean to upset you even more, but you know I'm not a hugger."

"I know." She wiped her eyes and gave me a huge smile.

She looked like she was about to grab me again. I held up my hands. "Don't."

"Come on, bestie, let's get this put away so we can do something seriously exciting. I want to know what extra-special ingredient I can sneak into your next experiment."

"Take me home and I'll fill you in—and don't plan on adding extra-special anything, except a few cookies." Esther grabbed her keys, and I quickly wrapped a stack of cookies in a paper towel. It was quick energy, but the brain needed glucose and fat to function optimally.

Esther sat on my bed, leaning back into my oversize brain-shaped pillow. She had given it to me for my last birthday. It was very comfortable.

"You ready?" I asked as I pulled out my notebook and slid off the elastic binding. I turned to the page I had marked with the ribbon.

"Hit me," she said.

"Thursday I'll test the dilated pupils effect."

"Go on," Esther said.

"Recently it's been shown that women's pupils dilate the widest when looking at a potential mate during ovulation." I tried not to sound too excited, but it was really fascinating. It said so much about the evolution and hardwiring of our brains.

"Why did I ask?" Esther asked.

"No, wait, listen. This is such a great example of our evolutionary biology giving our subconscious mind clues about other people's physical conditions. Those clues enable us to constantly be aware of who is a receptive and fertile mate, even when we don't know that's what we're looking for. It's all about fulfilling our Darwinian imperative."

"It always is with you, isn't it?" Esther dug a quarter out of her pocket and held it up. "Tails, you don't tell me anything else about ovulation—not a sexy topic, by the way. Heads, you explain yourself but in two sentences or less."

"But—" I started to protest.

Esther flipped the coin and caught it in the palm of her hand. She looked at it and swore. "Okay, fine, but remember, two sentences or less." She narrowed her eyes and pointed at me in warning.

I took a deep breath and tried to think it through so I could sum it up the best way possible. "Men are instinctually attracted to females whose pupils are widely dilated. Researchers have linked this involuntary response in both sexes to arousal and interest."

"Got it. Your pupils go all Disney-princess big when you're looking at someone hot, even though you don't know it's happening." Esther nodded in understanding.

"Yes! Therefore the person I look at with my big Disney-princess eyes feels attractive and thus is attracted to me. Then that person's pupils will likely dilate in response. It's like a good-feeling feedback loop." I grinned at Esther. If cookies made her happy, this made me equally so. Maybe I'd start humming.

Esther, scooting to the edge of the bed and leaning toward me, said, "So how are you going to pull this off? Since I'm going to assume you're not ovulating. My God, you've got me talking about it now." She held up her hand to stop me from answering. "No. See, you don't have to fill me in on your calendar. Let's say for this conversation you're not. So how are you going to cast this big-pupil love spell?"

Ignoring the love spell comment, I said, "During the middle ages Italian women used eye drops made from belladonna to dilate their pupils in order to make them look more seductive. But it contained a toxin that could poison them over time."

"You're not going to use that, because it's a very bad idea," Esther said.

"Don't worry. I'm not going to use belladonna. There are a couple of safer ways. For one, your pupils dilate in a dark room to allow more light into the eye so you can see better."

"So you want me to help lure him into a dark corner of the school's basement, where you will be waiting with your big black eyes," Esther said. Her excitement was obvious.

"No, of course not. Besides, that sounds like a scene from a horror movie," I said. I didn't like horror movies. It wasn't so much the fear of the unknown or the blood and gore—it was the foolishness of the characters being attacked. I watched them only because Esther seemed to enjoy them so much.

"I love horror movies. Let's do it. Maybe Squeak will give in and help film it or something. This could be fun," she said, laughing.

I narrowed my eyes at her.

"Fine. It was just a suggestion. What else?" Esther asked.

"Well, amphetamines can dilate your eyes, as well as some other street drugs," I said.

"And you want me to score you some speed?" Now Esther looked at me suspiciously.

"Of course not, you don't know any dealers." I paused. If I hadn't known she hummed when she was happy, maybe there were a few other things I didn't know about her. I shook my head. No, Esther didn't have time to hang out . . . well, wherever drug dealers hung out. "Plus, it's hardly safe."

Esther laughed lightly. I must have had a funny look on my face, which happened sometimes when I got caught up in thought and forgot there was another person in the conversation.

"So go on . . . you were telling me how you were going to dilate your eyes so that Theo would find you irresistible. We've tossed out the illegal and potentially poisonous blinding methods. What's left?"

I tapped my fingertips on my notebook. I wasn't sure how Esther would feel about the approach I'd chosen. "Well, my mother has some eye drops left over from when one of her eyes was inflamed and the muscles that control the iris had frozen. The drops dilated her eyes, which reduced the pain and allowed the inflammation to go down more quickly."

After a moment Esther said, "It's generally a bad idea to use someone's prescription medication. But I guess it's the safest way to do it. Will the drops mess up your eyes? You don't need to relax the muscles—what if it takes a really long time to wear off? I mean, whenever they dilate my eyes at the eye doctor's, I hate it. I can't even watch TV. Then I have to wander around in those big, ugly sunglasses they hand out."

I went to the top drawer of my dresser and pulled out the very tiny bottle of atropine ophthalmic eye drops. "I've thought about this. It's prescription, but it isn't a controlled substance, like amphetamines. I've researched it a little, and the side effects can be a little strange but extremely rare. Just to be safe, I think we should test it first."

"Okay. But what are the rare side effects? I should know what I'm watching for before I call nine-one-one," Esther said.

"They are so rare that doctors probably tell their patients to read the box if they are curious. But if you must know, the side effects can include lethargy and sleepwalking, hallucinations, loss of neuromuscular coordination, and agitation." I paused while double-checking the label for dosage. "It says two drops twice a day. So one drop is probably enough."

"How long does it take to wear off?" Esther asked.

"That's what we need to find out."

## Prom Theory Notes

### Esther's Observations

*One drop of the eye drops should be enough to give Iris the Belle eyes she's looking for. (See what I did there? Oops, I did it again.) It only took around ten minutes to wear off. This might be very interesting. I plan on watching carefully and taking notes, if I can take my eyes off the action long enough to jot things down.*

*I'll help you Thursday morning. Best time will probably be after homeroom.*

## My Observations

*One drop per eye caused partial dilation for a reasonable time, enough to effectively appear aroused and interested to TG. It should be relatively easy to judge the effectiveness in this further eye gaze experiment. If TG's eyes dilate in response, it will be a clear indication of attraction.*

# CHAPTER SEVENTEEN

## Wednesday
## Days to Prom: 10

**Step Three: Role of Adrenaline in Creating Perceived Excitement of New "Love"**

*There are a few hormones, such as norepinephrine, that are linked to adrenaline. They all work in concert to increase heart rate, alertness, attention, and sense of excitement. Experiencing these physiological responses to a situation or stressor in the presence of another person can increase your attraction to that person. They are perceived as the cause of the excitement, whether or not they are.*

"Thanks for coming with me," I said as I handed Esther the soft pretzel I'd just bought for her at the snack stand. We'd arrived at the track meet early to drop off the cookies and hadn't eaten before we left. I needed to get food into Esther before she started to faint or gnaw on me.

Esther's tongue peeked out between her lips as she took the pretzel. "Hungry?" I asked.

"Yeah, how did you know?" Esther asked before she took an enormous bite and chewed happily.

"I think the fact you were obviously salivating was a pretty good clue." I sat beside her and started to carefully smear mustard on my pretzel from one of the little packets I'd grabbed at the condiment table.

Esther swallowed and wiped her lips with her napkin. "That," she said, gesturing to my pretzel, "I don't get."

"What? You mean the mustard?" I began nibbling at my pretzel. I was a lot hungrier than I'd thought. It tasted good. On any other day I'd say it was a nice piece of warm sawdust. Which was why I normally found the mustard a requirement in order to successfully swallow it.

Esther suddenly stood up, her pretzel falling from her lap. It slipped between the metal bleachers and landed on the dirt below us. "Darren! GO—GOGOGO!" She started waving her hand at me while never taking her eyes off the track. "Look at him!"

Before I could take my attention away from my pretzel and look up, the race was run and Esther dropped back down into her seat.

"Did he win? Where is he?" I was scanning the field, but there were so many multicolored team tank tops, I couldn't pick him out.

"No. Came in third," she said. She stood up again and began searching around her seat.

I took a bite of my pretzel, tapped her on the leg, and then pointed to the ground below us. She bent down and looked through the space between the risers. "Well, that's not cool." She pouted and sat back down, landing hard.

I chewed and swallowed the last of mine. I disliked it when she pouted. It indicated she was sad or disappointed. Since I was physically the closest one to her, I felt I was somehow responsible, which in turn suggested that I needed to do something to rectify the situation.

"Come on, Theo isn't vaulting any poles for a while. I'll get you another pretzel." I stood up and brushed the salt from my hands.

"Oh thanks!" she said.

"It's what friends do," I said. I was trying to do more of such things. After making our way to the end of the row, we jogged down the steps to the track and made a sharp left toward the snack stand.

"Speaking of friends, did you apologize to Squeak yet? I saw him right before I met up with you, and he seemed strangely okay with everything. So I figured you guys made up or something."

"He avoided me all day yesterday after lunch and canceled on coming over for dinner. I called him late last night and tried to apologize, but he wouldn't let me. He's kind of acting like it never happened," I said, still unsettled by his change in attitude. I had been nervous about calling him. We never really had a reason to talk on the phone, since we lived next door to each other. Also, I didn't like talking on the phone and avoided it as much as possible. There was something about a bodiless voice that confused and disturbed me. However, it seemed the best way to apologize, since there was a chance he didn't want to see me. A text seemed too impersonal, and I was trying to be more aware of my sometimes distant behavior with Esther and Squeak.

"That's kind of weird, but you know Squeak, he doesn't like conflict, so he avoids it when he can. It's probably easier to pretend it didn't happen than to have a heart-to-heart with you. Maybe he thinks it will freak you out or something. He's busy, but I know he still wants to spend time with you while he can," Esther said, her tone warm and reassuring.

"Maybe." I was quiet for a minute, searching for an idea of how to change the subject. "So, has Darren asked you to prom yet?" I asked.

"No, not yet. But . . ." One corner of her mouth lifted to a half grin.

"But?" I prompted.

"But he asked me out for tomorrow night." Esther's words rushed out of her mouth and basically formed one word. She hopped up and down a couple of times and then spun around.

"Esther! That's great. Do you think he'll ask you then?" I knew she really liked him, and I wanted Esther to know that I appreciated her and that I was thinking about her. I was trying to be a good friend, even if I was starting a little late in the game.

"Yes. But I don't want to expect it, you know? I want to make him feel like I'm totally surprised." Esther was still hopping around as we got in line.

"Think you can act surprised?" I asked while I was digging in my pockets for my money. I hated handbags. I never had much to carry around: School ID, maybe some money, and a house key. And if I remembered, my phone. Pockets worked exceedingly well, especially when I wasn't carrying a backpack full of books. Which I tried not to do unless necessary. I was wary of potential neck and shoulder strain.

However, when things got busy or stressful, I would forget what I put in which pocket. So maybe a purse could be better. At least I'd never put it through the wash, unlike my phone.

"I think all I have to do is squeal, throw myself at him, and say, 'Yes, yes, yes.' He'll be so overwhelmed by my response he won't even worry about whether I knew he was going to ask me or not," she said.

Still digging, my fingers curled around something that felt like it might be money. "Aha!" I pulled out three fives, crumpled together. Esther gave me a thumbs-up.

"Do you know what kind of dress you want?" I asked.

"Not sure. I can't decide whether I want to go with the big dress. You know, the southern belle look." She had a dreamy look in her eyes.

"You'll look like a cake topper," I said.

"I have told you that you're no fun, right?"

"Twice today. That makes number three." I grinned at her. I could get used to spending time at track meets. This was fun. I hadn't gone wiki since at least before lunch, and I was feeling pretty relaxed, all things considered. It would have been the perfect day if Squeak had been able to come. Unfortunately, he had a previous commitment to tutor *her*. I pushed the thought away.

"You've been looking at your mom's prom pictures again. That was the eighties. They all had big hair and big dresses. My mom said she wore a hoop. Every time I think about it, which isn't often, I picture my mother sitting at the table and the front of her hoopskirt popping up in front of her face. Her underwear exposed for all to see."

Esther laughed. "I doubt that happened."

"How can you be so sure? This is my mom we're talking about."

"Exactly. I doubt she would have bothered with the underwear," Esther said.

"You have a point there. So consider it a cautionary tale. Don't wear a big, obnoxious dress with a hoopskirt. At least not without making sure you have donned proper undergarments."

We were next in line, and I scanned the menu again, not that there were many choices. Coke, Diet Coke, water. Nachos, soft pretzel, hot dog. It was looking like water for me. I couldn't choke down another pretzel, no matter how good the last one tasted.

"What do you want?" I asked.

"Diet Coke and another pretzel. I guess the big dress would take up too much room. Darren wouldn't be able to sit close enough to hold my hand. Besides, everyone wears cocktail dresses," Esther said.

I stepped up to the counter. "A Diet Coke, a water, and a pretzel, please." I handed over a five. Esther reached up to grab the drinks and I took the pretzel.

"What kind of cocktail dress?" I asked as we started back to the bleachers. Pole vaulting was coming up in about ten minutes, and I wanted to be high up enough to have a good view. I'd seen him do training drills but missed the few times he'd actually vaulted at the practices, because I was working the water table.

It wasn't so much that I wanted to see Theo perform, but I did want to see the vaulting itself. The physics of it was simple enough, I supposed. What was the first instance of pole vaulting? Most track events seemed to have come from actual life or survival skills. The javelin throw, even the shot put, came from hunting and warfare. I'd have to do some more research.

"You haven't thought about this at all, have you?" Esther asked.

"What?" I'd lost track of our conversation while scanning to see if Theo was approaching the pole-vaulting area.

Esther huffed a little in annoyance. "A prom dress."

"Oh. No, I haven't thought about a prom dress because there is no reason to. I'm not going. Even if I were, Theo isn't a sure thing. I'm closer than I was, but there are a few more things I need to test on him, especially if I'm going to try and seal the deal," I said.

"Fair enough. But maybe you could still go. I'd like you to be there."

"I guess I could tag along with you and Darren," I suggested. I'd spotted Theo warming up and was focusing on what he was doing. Which muscles were most important? It seemed he was stretching his back out the most.

"Um, no. We'll deal with that later, when we know what the Theo sitch is. Okay, cocktail dresses—the slinkier the better. All the it girls wear the classic little black dress. Last year most of the cheerleaders tried to outdo each other by being classy. Little strands of pearls, gloves. It was like a parade of some old movie star clones, what's her name? . . ." Esther trailed off.

"Audrey Hepburn," I finished for her.

"Yeah. Audrey Hepburn. Anyway, they looked good, but with all of them at one table it must have looked kind of creepy. I don't think that was the effect they were going for. I bet there is going to be backlash. Like, classy is out, and sexy is in." Esther waggled her eyebrows.

We started climbing the bleachers. "Keep going up. I want to sit near the top."

Esther nodded in agreement and started taking the steps two at a time. She was in a hurry to get started on her pretzel. She hadn't eaten much of the other one before losing it.

I pondered the prom dress topic as we climbed. I wasn't even sure I knew what a sexy prom dress looked like, much less what one would look like on me. Not that I was going, of course. Esther would be there—a niggling nervous doubt was starting to plant itself in my mind. Maybe I did want to go to prom. Did I? Would I enjoy it if I were with Esther and Darren? I hadn't attended many typical high school social events, with the exception of pep rallies or other events held during school hours. Those times had been stressful enough to scare me off from anything else Esther had tried to get me to attend over the years.

My coping "tool kit" had become quite extensive. There were a lot of things I'd thought I could never do, like having fun at a track meet, that I was managing just fine. Esther always had a way of making things fun.

If Squeak went with Pom-Pom—I supposed I had to face the fact that Squeak would be making new friends and spending time with other people when he went to college. He'd have girlfriends. It was bound to happen. The reality of the rest of our lives couldn't be avoided forever, no matter how hollow it made my chest feel to even consider it. Maybe it was time to stick my foot out into the world a little further—test the waters, as it were. It had to happen at some point, right?

"So, what defines a sexy prom dress?" I asked as we neared the top.

Esther moved into the second-highest bleacher and sat, patting the corrugated metal beside her. I sat, and she gave me my bottle of water as I handed over her pretzel.

"Okay, a sexy dress is low cut in the front or back or both. It can be short-short, or long but with side slits going up both sides, preferably ending somewhere around your hip bone."

Honestly, the girl had a dreamy look in her eyes.

"No," I said.

"What do you mean, 'no'?" Esther looked at me, confused.

"I mean I don't think you should wear something that should be a camisole under a dress as a dress to prom."

"Iris, you are a genius!" she said.

"Don't even think about it," I said.

"You're no fun." She leaned back against the bench behind us.

"That makes four times today," I said.

* * *

Theo's pole vaulting was awe inspiring. It was like dance. It took a level of coordination I was pretty sure, up to that point, I hadn't imagined was possible.

Watching Theo catapult himself into the air, all the while twisting his body midflight and curving his back, gliding over the bar, was thrilling. By the time he landed and popped nimbly to his feet, I'd risen from my seat, shouting and applauding. My reaction was instinctual, its intensity brought on by the crowd's reaction, I was certain. Theo as a person wasn't all that impressive; he certainly didn't spend much time developing his intellect. So I was surprised by how much I felt my heart racing and the excitement I was experiencing.

It seemed to be the perfect time to test his mirror neurons, since my attitude toward him, in that moment, was one of heightened admiration. I tapped Esther's arm. "I'm going to go and congratulate him."

Esther gave me a thumbs-up. "Good idea!"

I went down the bleachers and met him as he walked back to where the track team was gathered.

"Theo," I called out to him.

At first he looked up and didn't spot me, or he did and he didn't know who I was right away, but I didn't care. I walked quickly to him. "Theo, wow, I had no idea. That was perfect, it was . . . beautiful." It was shocking to me how genuinely he had impressed me. Perhaps I should attend more track events. I obviously enjoyed them.

He laughed and then said, "That's what all the girls say."

I didn't care that he might be sincere, that all the girls, in fact, said that. My heart rate was elevated, my cheeks were flushed, my hair was messy in a wind-tossed way. The way he looked at me gave me goose bumps. How strange. Why would his attention trigger my pilomotor reflex? That particular reflex had always fascinated me. We no longer had thick enough body hair that the contraction of the tiny muscles that caused our hair to stand up straight made much sense. It didn't make us warmer or even make us look bigger as a warning to potential attackers as it did for most other mammals. It was, in a sense, a wasted effort of the sympathetic nervous system. I wasn't cold and didn't feel threatened, so the goose bumps must mean I was excited. There was no doubt the event had been exciting, and most importantly, I had his attention. And I was reluctant to admit it, but for the first time he had mine.

Somewhere beneath the buzz of adrenaline and the oxytocin/endorphin rush, I also remembered there had been studies in just this—the bond that often forms between people during exciting or traumatic events. I needed to be around him during another exciting moment, and I was sure it would cement his growing interest. I knew it was working on me. Because to be honest, up to this point I hadn't liked him as a person very much.

But at the moment, I was attracted to him, perhaps for the first time. And if I was attracted to him, while that was something I hadn't planned on or intended, it would increase the likelihood that he, in turn, would mirror my responses to him, thus increasing his interest and attraction to me. How could we have a moment like this again?

A sophomore track team member, who seemed to be Theo's personal assistant or his fanboy, jogged up to us and tossed Theo a cookie from the stack he held in one hand. Theo took a bite, and his eyebrows lifted in surprise and appreciation.

I saw my opportunity. "Glad you like them." I could still feel myself glowing, so I had no doubt I managed to sound flattered and confident.

He pointed at me with the remainder of his cookie. "You?"

"Yes. I made them." Not a lie. I was there. I helped. So what if Esther's magic something or other made them taste so amazing? She had encouraged me to take credit.

I was obviously also benefiting from his experiencing the heady mix of sunshine aiding the release of serotonin, the adrenaline from his success, and the endorphins from his intense exercise. He took a step closer and brushed some hair from my face with the lingering touch of his fingers. I started to jerk away from him but caught the reflex in time, so it wasn't so obvious I was reacting negatively to his unexpected touch.

"Hey, Lily, you going to the spring carnival on Sunday?" he asked.

"Maybe," I managed to say. All thoughts had left me and I had no idea how to react, though I knew this was a crucial moment to the experiment. I couldn't do anything wrong. It could completely undo all the work I had done to this point.

I didn't know why I thought of Squeak in that moment, but I did. If I pretended he was Squeak, I might be able to speak. I remembered how it felt to flirt with Squeak and held on to that. I touched my iris pendant but didn't correct him, in case it ruined this chemically induced rush.

It was nice not to have to try so hard to remember how to flirt. In the right moment it was instinctual, just like it had been with Squeak in the cafeteria. There was something scientifically significant about my reaction and how I was dealing with the situation, but I didn't want to examine it then and there. Maybe later, while I was writing out my observations. Maybe. Best to leave Squeak out of my notes. Esther would overreact and be convinced all my confusion about him meant something other than what it did.

What did it mean?

"Cool, maybe I'll see you there." Theo nodded and winked as he pointed his index finger at me, then turned and jogged back to the water table.

It just meant that I was controlling my reactions to the opposite sex logically and applying said reactions in the manner that I had preplanned since I started this.

Esther came up behind me and grabbed my arm. "Well, he must be in a good mood. Maybe your science magic *is* changing his brain. All right, spill it, all the gory details. What was that about?"

"I might see him at the carnival Sunday," I said simply.

"Might? What is that supposed to mean? Either he asked you to the carnival or he didn't," Esther insisted, annoyed she wasn't getting the story she had hoped for.

"No, I'll see him there. It's the perfect place to further test excitation transfer." I grinned. Everything that should be working was, and it looked like there was a steady path to success ahead of me. Squeak would change his tune about this, I knew he would. I wouldn't have thought it possible, but the idea of Squeak acknowledging my successful efforts lifted my mood even more.

"That transfer thing. Sounds dirty. Maybe even messy. I think I want to know more."

"Come with me to the school's spring carnival on Sunday afternoon, and I will tell you all you want to know about it. It's exciting, and sometimes a little messy, but only when there are bombs going off or natural disasters," I said.

Esther looked a little disappointed. "Oh. No bombs?"

"No bombs. Come on. I need to catch the bus or I'll be walking home," I said.

"Come home with me! My mom texted and she has snacks," Esther said.

## Prom Theory Notes

### Esther's Observations

*The track meet was awesome. Darren was awesome. And okay, Theo was impressive. I'm keeping awesome for Darren. But, dude, who's turning whose head here? Be careful. You catching feelings is not the goal. Don't do it. But otherwise, he's looking at you, he thinks he knows your name, and he's asking about your plans—though he isn't making any with you. . . .*

### My Observations

*This researcher is aware of her increasing subjectivity and susceptibility to the unconscious reactions to an attractive male that are further enhanced by excitation transfer. The day at the track meet increased this researcher's adrenaline and dopamine to a degree that was unavoidably affecting.*

*However, this only further highlights the importance of this study. This researcher is fully aware, and her logical brain is able to process what and why she is experiencing the attraction to the opposite sex and TG. This researcher knows it is not a legitimate attraction—just a response to the availability of an attractive male. TG, in particular, is a shiny thing, but not one this researcher* would like to permanently acquire. By seeing this through to its successful conclusion, this researcher will allow her friends to carefully monitor their own reactions to others (as this researcher is doing successfully), enabling them to make better choices and not be swayed by their lizard brain.

## Plan

Due to the success of an exciting event enhancing TG's attraction to this researcher, preparations will be made to increase the chances of sharing a fast-action ride, preferably a frightening, spinning ride, if available, with TG. Not sure what preparations could be made in advance. This researcher may have to wait until arriving at the carnival to assess her options.

However, first things first. Tomorrow is slated for testing the eye gaze theory.

# CHAPTER EIGHTEEN

## Thursday
## Days to Prom: 9

### Eye Gaze and Attraction—Part Two

*Dilated pupils: When a person is looking at a someone to whom they are attracted, several involuntary reactions take place. Eye gaze becomes slightly off focus in order to be able to see the entire person. Pupils dilate and appear shiny. This is often referred to as doe eyes and can often be a sign of sexual attraction, or as Esther so aptly pointed out, a Disney character.*

Standing by my locker and waiting for Esther, I played with the small dropper bottle I had slipped into my pocket that morning.

I told Esther I would wait for her. But she was running late, and I couldn't. I needed to make sure my pupils had time to fully dilate before I ran into Theo. Besides, she might try to talk me out of it, even if she did help me with the trial run. Or if I stalled too long, I might lose my nerve. I couldn't wait until after homeroom.

I pulled the bottle out of my pocket. *Do, don't think.* Leaning forward so my head was in my locker enough to hide me from view, I opened the bottle. I took a deep breath and tilted my head back, carefully squeezing one drop in each eye. That had worked well during the trial run.

But a couple of extra drops would probably work faster and last a little longer. Not knowing how soon I would find Theo, I quickly squeezed two more in both eyes.

"Good golly, it's the Bee in my bonnet," Esther sang in no particular tune. She paused at her locker and swatted at my ponytail. "Hey, I thought you were going to keep your display of luscious locks of lust this week. Are you back to your ponytail for good?"

"Don't you start with that. It's bad enough I never broke Squeak of the habit," I said, quickly slipping the atropine drops into the back corner of my locker. I closed the door and spun the combination lock.

"So?" Esther asked.

"So what?" Now what was she talking about? I was still trying to decide if "luscious locks of lust" would be an appropriate description of earlier experimental attempts to include in my notes.

She reached out and flipped my ponytail over my shoulder. I turned my head and looked down at my hair. "Oh." I sort of waved my hand around, trying to indicate, *Whatever*. It was one of those gestures I'd seen Esther use, usually to end a conversation she didn't want to have. It always worked for her.

"Oh, come on, fess up. It was because Taylor pulled her hair back. Since when are you the jealous type?"

I must have done the dismissive hand wave incorrectly. "Jealous of Princess Pom-Pom? Don't be ridiculous." I flipped my ponytail back over my shoulder. "Besides, I accomplished what I wanted. Theo noticed me, and I'm quite certain his medial preoptic area noticed my 'luscious locks of lust' and stimulated his reward systems, especially the nucleus accumbens. This, in turn, dulled his prefrontal cortex, thus making him focus on me and search for stimulating clues."

"Whatever." Esther waved her right hand while using her left to press against her temple. I'd never noticed the temple bit before, but perhaps that was more a sign of a headache than a response to my reply. Although that, too, might effectively change the course of an awkward conversation.

"Do you need an ibuprofen? I'm sure the nurse has some," I said.

"Huh?" Esther rubbed her forehead a little before dropping her hand. "No. I'm fine. You, however—you know, all you'd have to do is to give your tight T-shirt a little tug, and you'd actually be showing cleavage."

"Everything I told you about cleavage and breasts is basically accurate. The exact reason for the evolution of large breasts—well, it's only speculation. But breasts do not have to be large in order to be effective in breastfeeding . . . ," I explained. Trying to maintain polite eye contact with Esther was starting to make my head hurt. The drops were taking effect.

With a quick turn of my combination, I pulled my locker door back open and tucked my head behind it. I began rearranging my books and straightening my file folders. I didn't want Esther to know I'd put in more drops than I should have. She would definitely overreact. My headache should subside as my eyes adjusted, and then I could just explain to her that I'd been too impatient to wait. She'd understand. I hoped.

Esther wasn't saying anything, but my urge to try to act normal kept me blathering on. "Because of that, the male brain doesn't seek signs of potential high milk production. But femininity is very important. However, being confident and kind can be just as important. Males don't want to go out with a female who is insecure and constantly asking for reassurance that she's pretty or whatever." It was getting almost impossible to focus on the contents of my locker. The light was dim, but it still made me feel like my eyes were, well, much too open. I couldn't help squinting and moving my head in an attempt to keep things in focus.

"Those don't sound as scientific as the reasons you gave me before," Esther said, turning her focus to trying to open her locker.

"Well, they are and they aren't—they're tips from a dating book." I knew I couldn't hide behind my locker door forever. Sighing, I closed the locker and turned to meet Esther's eyes.

She looked up, stilled for a moment, and then gasped. Loudly. My eyes must have been close to fully dilated. The sunlight streaming into the hallway from the enormous windows near the stairwell made me wince.

"You were supposed to wait for me! Why didn't you wait for me? We were going to do this after homeroom!" I could hear the panic in Esther's voice.

I wanted the result of the drops to make my eyes appear attractive and to signal my interest, not look like I was in a freak show. "Shush. Relax, it will be okay. Theo usually comes up this hall early on Thursdays. I'll catch him, talk for a couple of minutes, and then head to the nurse. I'll say I have a headache." I pressed the heel of my palm into my temple, as Esther had earlier. "Which isn't a lie. I'll lie down until it starts to wear off."

It was getting increasingly difficult to look at things and people, and my head was starting to pound. My eyes were trying to focus and constrict to control the amount of light shining on my retinas but couldn't. I hadn't considered that people are usually aroused in dimly lit settings. Candlelit dinners. Moonlit walks. The bright sunlight pouring in from the large windows at each end of the hallway was the exact opposite of romantic lighting.

Esther frowned and crossed her arms. I had to look away from her. She was not doing anything for my intensifying headache.

"Why didn't you wait for me? This is nuts!"

"I remembered he'd be around this morning, and you were late. I just figured I'd get a head start on the day," I said. It was a poor excuse.

"I'm taking you to the nurse's office." Esther was gritting her teeth. She only did that when she was seriously serious or very upset. In this case, it was likely both.

"No, really, I'm fine. I'll track Theo down, and then I'll go to the nurse. I promise." I blinked, as I thought I saw a huge rabbit hop past us and down the hall. I stared after it for what must have been a little too long, because Esther slapped her hand onto my forehead like she was checking for a fever. Which, it turns out, she was.

"Are you sure? What about those nasty side effects? Maybe they aren't so rare as you think. You look like you saw a ghost." Esther began fussing, and I knew I was about to be taken to the nurse's office against my will unless I took control of the situation. It was obvious Esther hadn't seen the rabbit, so I must have been hallucinating. Best not to mention it. I pulled her hand off my forehead.

"I skipped breakfast today and I'm feeling a little woozy. Should have known better. The drops will wear off. My eyes hurt because they're probably overdilated, if that's a thing," I said.

So maybe I didn't skip breakfast. But I was feeling a little woozy, that much was true. I'd never been very good at lying. Yet somehow I was doing a fine job of it this morning.

"Okay. Wait, I should have a granola bar in here somewhere. . . ."

Esther began digging through the black hole that was her backpack.

This could only end badly, and I needed to find Theo. I stepped away from the lockers and tried to spot him—he should be walking by any minute. And there he was. I mean, I couldn't be positive it was him, but how many other blond guys with enormous shoulders did we have in this school?

"Hey, there's Theo. I've got to catch up with him before this wears off."

She grabbed my arm. "Iris, really, you don't look good. I don't think this is going to work the way you think it is. Let me take you to the nurse's office," Esther pleaded.

"No, really. I'll be right back. I just need to talk to him for a couple of minutes. I don't want to waste this cleavage; I don't let it out much, you know." I tugged the hem of my shirt and tried to give Esther a reassuring smile. The way she was frowning told me it wasn't working, but it was hard to be sure of her expression, as my attention was really on the increasing number of squirrels and hedgehogs racing past us. Who knew that hedgehogs could run as fast as squirrels?

"Iris, please, this is not going to make anyone fall in love with you, much less get Theo Grant to ask you to prom," Esther said.

"Shh. If somebody hears you, they'll tell him and he'll avoid me. And besides, love isn't the goal here," I hissed as quietly as I could and still be heard. There was a dust cloud drifting up the hallway in the wake of the small stampede. I coughed. "Now, if you don't let me go, he'll only know me as the girl who knows her way around the library and hands out water at track." I was getting desperate and Esther knew it. She didn't let go until two guys stumbled into us, a girl chasing them.

"Give me my shoe, asshole!" Laughter erupted as the shoe sailed past my head. Someone snatched it out of the air and rushed back past me to the girl. He was tossing it from one hand to the other above the girl's head while she protested. They both blocked Esther from reaching me. I started toward where I'd just seen Theo as more unrecognizable things rushed by me. I put my head down and walked as fast as I could.

Then something was suddenly behind me, and it was huge. I fought the instinct to run.

I failed. Turning the corner and running down the hallway that led to the guidance offices, I stumbled and tripped, slamming into a tall blond guy with broad shoulders. Did I get lucky and run into Theo?

Somehow he stayed standing, and I landed flat on my butt, my books scattering around me. He picked up one of the novels I'd been carrying and held it out to me. He leaned in closer and I saw that it wasn't Theo. This particular experiment was not off to a great start.

He was saying something, but I couldn't hear him. The blur of words spilled out of his mouth as two strong arms lifted me to my feet. I grabbed at the arm holding me and tried to steady myself. A flannel-covered bicep. Squeak. Good old Squeak. Sir Squeak, white knight. Always there to save me.

"I won't always be," said Squeak. I must have said that out loud. I would never, ever live that down. He'd be bringing it up when I was on my deathbed.

I closed my eyes. They were still dilated and my head hurt. A lot.

Squeak opened a door, pushed me into an empty classroom, and sat me on the floor.

"Where are we?" I asked.

"The bio lab. Don't worry, it's empty this morning," he said.

I knew I was hallucinating. His voice went from sounding like it was coming from the end of a tunnel to being accompanied by wind chimes. I hated wind chimes. The sound of them made me itch.

I opened my eyes and tried to focus on Squeak. The atropine drops seemed to be slowly wearing off, but I was still confused.

"This shouldn't be happening. I tested it." It was hard to concentrate. The bright room made it impossible to look at Squeak. There were windows everywhere. Why would he bring me in here when there were plenty of dismal, windowless classrooms? "Why are you doing this to me?" A sharp spike of pain shot through the back of my head. I closed my eyes again and pressed the heels of my hands against them. The pain dulled a bit.

"I'm not doing anything to you. Bee, you don't look good. Did you take something? What were you trying to do?" The concern in his voice should have soothed me—it didn't.

I opened my eyes and saw that Squeak was squatting in front of me. I didn't need his interference with my plans. What did he care? It's not like he'd said more than a few words to me since Tuesday. If he hadn't interfered, I'd have charmed Theo by now and been headed for the nurse's office for some analgesics. "I was trying to dilate my eyes with drops. I mean, I did dilate my eyes. Not that it's any of your business." Being angry with him felt good. Maybe a fight would speed up my metabolism and the drug would wear off faster.

"What? Where the hell did you get drops to dilate your eyes? You need to go to the emergency room." Leaning forward, he grabbed his backpack. He took out his phone from the top pocket.

"No, don't tell anyone!" I dived at him. He caught me.

"We have to get you some help, in case you're having serious side effects!" he said as he pulled us both to standing. My knees buckled. He grasped me around the waist with one arm, holding me up.

"Let go. I'm fine." But the weight of his arm holding me was nice, comforting even. He was warm and I relaxed, almost instinctively. Just leaning into him felt so much better than having to struggle to focus and stand upright. Then, in an instant, my body was burning up and I was panting, trying to breathe.

Pushing him away, I used every ounce of strength I had in order to stay standing. My feet were beginning to feel more stable beneath me, and my body cooled now that I was away from the source of heat.

He was watching me, holding out his arms, prepared to catch me again. But I could stand on my own, and there were no small, furry animals in sight. It was almost over. He took a step toward me.

"Don't touch me. I'm fine." In my currently weakened state, I was less in control of myself than I was comfortable with. Being physically close to him just made me more confused. No matter how good it felt, it was putting me on edge.

"Bee, you're not okay. You're not making any sense. Let me get some help, please." Squeak spoke in low tones. "Tell me exactly what's going on, or I'll carry you out of here and deliver you to the hospital myself." He leaned in and made the threat real. "I drove today."

I folded my arms across my chest. "Fine. I was dilating my eyes with atropine drops so they'd look bigger and more attractive."

"Damn it. What are they and where did you get them? Actually, it doesn't matter. You could have seriously hurt yourself. Maybe you already have. What the hell, Bee? You know how to look stuff up. Didn't you even think about checking the side effects?"

I scowled so hard my eyes almost closed. How could he think I'd done this without careful research? "I did check them."

He jammed his hands into his hair. "That's a prescription drug, right? I'm pretty sure it's not yours. And you put it in your eyes so you would look pretty?" He threw his arms up in the air and began pacing between the door and the lab table we'd been standing beside.

He sounded frustrated and angry with me. That wasn't fair. If he had been talking to me instead of avoiding me, I would have kept him in the loop. His reaction to this situation was, in turn, making me angry. I stumbled toward him, with the intention of poking him in the chest or on the shoulder to emphasize my dissatisfaction with *his* recent behavior toward me.

If I'd thought the atropine drops were wearing off, I was wrong. The minute I reached for him, he instinctually caught me, his hands holding me at my waist. Squeak looked at me, my enlarged pupils—and everything stopped. And then time rolled forward in slow motion. His breath was hot and slow against my cheek. My chest ached and I couldn't catch my breath or move. I reached up and gripped his shoulders.

"Damn it, I hate when anything happens to you. You know that, right?" He took a hand from my waist and drifted it up my arm to rest on my shoulder. His eyes were half-closed, but I could still see his pupils. They were dilated. Had I somehow gotten the atropine drops in his eyes? When would I have done that?

While everything around me slowed, Squeak became larger than life. I searched his eyes. "You do?"

His light complexion, his strong jaw, his hazel eyes. I knew his face so well, every asymmetrical feature, every spot of melanin . . . his slightly crooked nose, his bottom chipped tooth. But did I really know him—what he felt or thought? Why didn't I? Could I? I should, given all our time together. Right then I wanted to, more than anything.

We stared at each other, and it felt like it did when we were on my porch. But more so. I felt all the annoyance at him drain from me. My eyelids were drifting closed, and I couldn't stop from lifting my chin, trying to reach up to him. His lips looked like they'd be warm and soft. I slid my hands up from his shoulders so I could touch his neck. He sighed. He leaned forward a little and brushed his cheek against mine.

The bell rang, and I jumped and dropped my hands.

I'd almost kissed Squeak. Or did he almost kiss me?

It was my enlarged pupils. He was responding to them as though I were showing signs of being attracted to him. This was not what should be happening at all. His mirror neurons had been responding to my big, black, come-hither pupils. That's all it was.

I was exhausted from my physiology trying to compensate and cope with the side effects as well as my uncharacteristic rapid mood swings. After making my way to the lab table, I pulled out a stool and sat down. When I looked up, I saw Squeak's warm expression was gone. He clenched his jaw, and his lips pressed into a thin, down-turned line. He could be worried or angry. Probably both. The sudden jolt of the bell had likely reminded him of why we were hiding in here in the first place. It certainly wasn't to make out. I made a move to stand up, but the room started to spin again. I dropped back down onto the stool.

"Jesus, I should have stopped this before it got started," Squeak said. He started pacing, shaking his head slowly, his hands jammed into his pockets.

My head still hurt, and I slapped a hand across my forehead and squeezed. Squeak made a small sound of concern but didn't rush to my side, like he normally would have. The ache moved from my head to my chest.

"Why? Why would you want to stop it? Why would you choose tutoring some *pom-pom* over spending time with me? Where have you been?" And why was I yelling at him? Was my mind misinterpreting my confused senses as anger when it was really something else? A small voice of reason, superior insight, and knowledge whispered in the fog of my thoughts. I shook my head, hoping things would fall into their proper places. It just made me dizzier.

"I have been here, with you as much as possible, waiting to talk to you. Trying to talk to you about school, about my future, hell, about us! Do you even care? And what was that—flirting with me at lunch? Do you care about my feelings at all? Did you even think about how it might hurt me, or affect our friendship? Do you care about me at all? Have you even noticed how I feel about this ridiculous stunt? And for what? To prove me wrong? What the hell? You shut me down every time. So tell me, where the hell have *you* been? You checked out as soon as school started this year."

"I've been right here, like always," I insisted, but now I had a nagging feeling I really had done something horribly wrong. The voice, the properly informed one in the back of my head tried to explain something that I couldn't quite make out.

"Have you ever listened to anything I've ever told you? Ever?" Anger and hurt were growing in his voice. When had he stopped squeaking? When had he become someone else?

"I don't even know you anymore," I said. And as soon as I said it, I realized it had come out all wrong.

"I'm starting to wonder if you ever did," he said.

A cold sensation ran down my spine and I felt shaky. It didn't seem like it was the effect of the atropine drops. I hadn't read that side effect in any of the online sources. I felt out of control and losing my footing with every word he said.

"You don't get it at all," I mumbled, looking away from him.

"I don't get it? All you understand is your little projects. You think you know how people work because you know a little bit about the brain, about monkeys—"

"Primates," I interrupted.

His jaw muscles twitched. He held up his hand to stop me. "You don't understand people at all. Do you know why I haven't chosen a college yet?"

I thought about it—my head was starting to clear—but I still couldn't find an answer.

"I thought you'd want me to stay close to home, maybe go to Caldwell, but I can't get you to talk about it. Did you know a couple of impressive colleges gave me *very* generous academic scholarships?

"I *have* to work. I'll need extra cash if I stay here. Caldwell is crazy competitive, and by the time I could afford to get my application in, all the major scholarships had been handed out. It kills me not being able to be with you. Can't you see that? I know your social skills aren't the best, but I thought I was different, that you knew me, recognized how I was feeling. But obviously you can't. Or you don't care."

He paused, looked down, and took a deep breath. His shoulders slumped. When he looked back up, his expression had shifted from anger to sadness. "I'm tired of you falling all over someone you just randomly picked out of a crowd. A person is more than their damned limbic system, their hormones, and their heart rate. I don't care about prenatal testosterone or how it determines the length of my index finger in proportion to my middle finger—"

"Yours indicates a very impressive—"

"Would you stop? I know I'm a man. A lot girls have made it very clear they were interested in me. What you're doing is going to fail miserably. And when it does, don't come back to me and say I didn't warn you."

He paused, waiting for me to respond. I didn't know what to say. I'd never seen him like this before. I had no understanding of how to respond. So I didn't.

"You think you know so much. But I'm starting to doubt you will ever understand what a real friend is or how to be one. In fact, you really suck at it." He spun and walked toward the door.

"No—Squeak, please," I said as I moved, reaching for him. My voice cracked, but I managed to get the words out.

He stopped but kept his back to me. "Iris, just stop. I . . . I just don't want to do this anymore. I can't be your filter for the world. I've got to start thinking about myself and where I'm going, because I'll be out of here soon. It's just easier this way." He took a deep breath and sighed. "I'm done."

He went out into the hallway, the hydraulic hinge hissing as the door slowly slid shut behind him.

I reached for the lab table and lowered myself onto the stool, gripping the edge of the table with one hand. I'd been so warm when he touched me. It wasn't a side effect from the atropine drops, it was Squeak. Who'd left. Who'd said he wasn't my friend anymore. I was cold and shaky. My chest ached.

I'd been scared of things changing. It was too late to face the changes and be a part of any kind of decisions. They had already happened.

I knew a lot about a lot of things, but I didn't know anything that could fix this. What fix was there for a broken friendship—and a broken heart?

The door cracked open and Esther leaned into the room. "Iris?"

"Yeah?"

She exhaled and her shoulders slumped in relief. "I couldn't find you, and then I saw Squeak rush out of here. From the look of him, I figured it was better if I didn't ask." She came into the room and over to me. I let her wrap her hand around mine. She looked at my eyes and squeezed my fingers. "Your eyes look better. You ready to go to the nurse for some ibuprofen?"

I nodded and she led me out of the room.

# CHAPTER NINETEEN

The rest of the school day was exhausting and complicated. When Esther took me to the nurse's office, I was able to get by with the excuse that I'd gotten something in my eyes in the chem lab. The nurse didn't check my schedule, so I didn't get caught in the lie. She made me use eyewash and rest, and then she called my mom. I was sent home, and my mother fussed over me nonstop until I convinced her I was fine and to go back upstairs and paint.

Squeak was done with me. He'd said that, but had he really meant it? He'd been so angry.

Getting angry is part of fight-or-flight. It triggers the body to pump adrenaline and norepinephrine, urges us to take charge and get things back in balance. Fix the injustice perpetrated against us. Fight against the wrongs we've suffered. And the good old amygdala, dealing with emotions as it does, goes crazy. It jumps up and rushes forward, and a quarter of second later, or less, your mouth opens up and "I'm done" comes out. Our filter, our rational brain, isn't quick enough to catch it. It's been said.

What's even worse is our brains like to reverse interpret. Squeak says it, and his usually kind and thoughtful brain is like, *You said it, you must mean it*. So then he believes he means it. So that happened. But did he really? Did he really mean it?

I'd texted him twice, apologizing. He'd left them unread. I'd have to give him time for his residual anger and its effects on his brain and body to fade. It was too soon to try. I hoped he wouldn't need too long. Having never fought with him before, I didn't know what his recovery time was from extreme emotion. Physiologically speaking, his stress-induced cortisol levels had to be extremely high. As soon as I'd gotten home, I'd looked up how long it takes for the effects to subside. It often takes several hours for levels to fall after an incident of extreme anger. Despite this reassurance, I suspected it was going to take a lot longer than that for things to return to normal. If they ever would.

I'd been uneasy and frightened to face how little time was left before he went off into the big, wide, overwhelming world. Now it seemed I'd lost every day from now on.

Bells chimed in bouncy rhythm down the stairs from the attic as I heard my mother heading for my room.

Was it six already? She was going to ask even more questions than when she'd brought me home. It was almost dinner, and we had made plans last week, before everything fell apart, for him to come over tonight. She'd be looking for Squeak. I'd spent the last few hours alone and trying to fix what I could, since I couldn't fix things with Squeak. I'd tidied my room and organized everything I owned, from paper clips to underwear. Made everything all right. Or something.

I was just about finished taking all of my books out of the bookcase when the jingling stopped. Silence in my house spelled doom. When my mother stopped moving, it was only because she was planning some sort of strategic motherly attack.

I had the hardcover of *The Trouble with Testosterone*, by Robert Sapolsky, the neuroendocrinologist, in one hand and a battered paperback titled *Make Him Worship You in Five Easy Steps*, which I'd picked up at the Hillcrest Public Library freebie bin, in the other when she tapped softly on my door before opening it a crack.

"Hi, Mom," I said, dropping the paperback behind my back, cover down.

"Oh, sorry, honey, I didn't know you were cleaning. I hate to interrupt such a momentous event." She leaned against the doorframe, rested one hand on the knob, and looked at the books on the floor and the neat piles of clothes on my bed, sorted by color and carefully folded. "Did something else happen today? What's wrong?"

"Nothing. I couldn't find something I needed and had some extra time," I said without meeting her eyes. I kept my head down, pretending to scrutinize the cover of *Mind Wide Open: Your Brain and the Neuroscience of Everyday Life*, by Steven Johnson.

"Okay. I'll leave you to it. I just wanted to see if Seth was tutoring late tonight," she said as she opened the door a little farther. She took a couple of steps into my room. But only a couple. My mother believed in a child's right to privacy. She never asked for my passwords or read my text messages to check to see if I was sexting. Actually, I think she didn't bother because she knew my texts consisted of making study plans or checking on homework assignments. She'd be bored stiff and probably a little disappointed in my lack of teenage rebellion. If my secret teenage life were juicier, she might be more interested.

"I don't know," I said, shrugging.

"Oh?" Her voice lifted a bit higher than usual, sounding genuinely surprised. She looked around my room again, probably searching for other clues to explain my sudden change in attitude and behavior. The reminder that life as I knew it had ended with one thoughtless argument was something I didn't want or need. I began shelving my books as rapidly as I could while maintaining subject-then-author sorting.

"Oh well," she continued, "I was going to hold dinner. He's usually here by six, hovering around the kitchen and waiting for me to ask him to stay. Did his father's work schedule change again?"

"Mom, I don't know. I'm not his keeper," I snapped.

"No, you're not, but he appointed himself yours a long time ago," she said quietly but with a little smile.

"Well, not anymore. He resigned." I tried to sound casual. I couldn't let her go on thinking he would be by anytime soon. My mom was Squeak's biggest fan. She was likely going to be more upset than I was that we'd had a fight.

"What?" She probably thought she'd heard me wrong.

I slammed a book down on the pile beside me. "I said, not anymore."

That shut her up. She crossed her arms and leaned back against the doorway, examining me, her eyes narrowed with suspicion. "What did you do?"

"Why does it have to be my fault? Why can't Squeak be in the wrong?" I said, insulted, and generally unhappy the conversation was lasting this long. I could think of a hundred things I'd rather be talking about. Well, not really. I didn't want to talk at all right now.

"Seth has been eating here a couple of nights a week for the past six years. And the two of you pretty much know whenever the other one sneezes," she said.

"Like I said, not anymore," I said, trying to get across that the conversation was over.

"So, what happened?"

"Nothing. More like he did nothing. I got mad at him. He got mad at me. The end. He's got better things to do. Princess Pom-Pom probably has him cornered somewhere dark and cozy," I said, before standing up to throw myself dramatically onto my bed. I managed to avoid landing on my sorted clothes. I stared at the ceiling.

"Princess Pom-Pom, huh? You mean the girl he's been tutoring." It wasn't a question. I turned my head to the side and looked at her. She nodded, her blue eyes peering out from behind a curtain of messy curls spattered with bits of paint. She'd been working in oranges lately. "Well, that explains it."

"Explains what?" I sat up again. I was irritated at having my orderly, self-soothing process interrupted. At any moment I was going to either run from the house or scream at my mother.

"Why you two are fighting—you're jealous because he's interested in someone. I knew something like this was going to happen sooner or later. I just hoped . . . well . . . you're teenagers and he's leaving for college soon. Probably best it happens now. Still, though . . . ," she said with a little nod and a sad shrug.

"Why would I care if he was interested in someone? I don't care who he's attracted to. Why should I?" Good question. Why did I care? That was something I'd been asking myself a lot lately. Because the truth of it was he didn't feel like a sibling anymore. Not that it mattered. It was too late to think about those implications now. Especially since he'd sped up his leaving by leaving me.

Maybe I didn't know what was going on with him. He'd been right about that. Had he stopped telling me things and I hadn't noticed? Was it because I'd stopped listening? How many times had I refused to talk about his college choice or anything about what came next? Thinking about it, I realized he had tried to talk about it, almost every day, since the start of the school year.

It was my fault. I was the one who had done something wrong. Like always. I was doomed to be alone. At least I hadn't messed up with Esther. Yet.

My mother straightened away from the doorjamb, uncrossed her arms, and waved a hand, beckoning me to follow her. "Come on, let's eat. Go tell your dad dinner is ready. He's out back reading in the hammock. You might need to wake him up. He's still jet-lagged from his trip."

"Okay," I said.

She turned, and the jingling receded as she went down the steps.

## Prom Theory Notes

### Esther's Observations

*Don't you ever, ever, ever do anything like that ever again. Don't ask for my permission, consider me a functional fool who makes bad decisions.*

### My Observations

*It is imperative that researchers never put themselves or the test subjects in seriously dangerous situations. This researcher has learned her lesson. Also, in terms of the study, an experiment doesn't have results if it is not fully executed. Unfortunately, this researcher ended up testing instead the side effects of a prescribed drug without a doctor's approval or guidance.*

### Personal Note

*An experiment is particularly a failure if the researcher (me) loses her best friend.*

# CHAPTER TWENTY

## Friday
## Days to Prom: 8

I tried, not very convincingly, to act too sick to go to school. My mother had none of it. "Buck up, soldier. Nothing gets better until you face it," she said as she pulled me out of bed.

She was wrong. I made it to school, and of course, the first person I saw was Squeak. I did what my mother had told me to do. I faced him, even stopping to give him the warmest hello I knew how to. He walked past me, never turning his head. Never acknowledging me. As if I didn't exist. The ache in my chest swelled. Dazed and attempting to will myself numb, I made my way down the hall.

Esther stood at our lockers, obviously searching for someone. I had no doubt that someone was me. She grabbed my arm the moment I was close enough. "Oh. My. Freakin'. God. What *exactly* happened with you and Squeak yesterday? I mean, I knew you had a fight but—"

"Doesn't matter," I said. I went to work opening my locker. On my second failed attempt, Esther gave a snort.

"Right. Doesn't matter. And that's why the ever-capable Iris can't open her locker," she said.

I yanked my locker open on the third try. "Just leave it, okay? It's not a big deal."

"For not being a big deal, he is royally pissed. And he's never pissed at you, at least not like this. Ugh, he called you Iris. He never calls you

Iris, like, ever. The way he said it too—I'm surprised he didn't use your middle name. It sounded like he was on the verge of disowning you or something."

It was my turn to snort. "He's not on the *verge* of anything."

"Okay, this is actually starting to scare me. Spill it. I want every word and a dramatic reenactment. What happened yesterday in the lab?" She stared, and stared some more, waiting for me to answer her.

I could have sworn she was actually biting her tongue. It must have been taking great physical and mental effort on her part to stay silent. She wasn't someone who would wait very long for anything or anyone. I knew if I didn't say something soon, she'd bolt and head straight for Squeak. I couldn't put him through that kind of interrogation.

"I—I was confused. I'm not sure I remember it all. I said something very wrong. Something I should have never thought, much less said. I know that much." I turned away from her, yanking a couple of books out of my locker. I dropped them into my bag and slung the strap over my shoulder. With one hand on my locker door, I closed it and then leaned forward, resting my forehead against the cool metal.

Esther was mercifully quiet. When she placed a tentative hand on my shoulder, I knew she wasn't going to push me for more information. She knew the last thing I wanted when I was upset was anyone touching me, but the momentary light pressure of her hand was reassuring. Knowing she wanted to comfort me—I knew I wasn't entirely alone. I lifted my head and she dropped her hand.

I didn't want to talk about Squeak, but I needed to know what he'd said about me. If he had indicated in any way that he was willing to forgive me.

I hesitated a little before asking, "Did he sound at all like he would accept an apology?"

She shook her head and then looked at my sympathetically. "You know, maybe you should drop the experiments, for a day or two, and go try to talk to Squeak. Smooth things out."

"I don't know if I can. I've never seen him this angry, about anything. The effects of anger on the brain are significant. The rush of glucose through the bloodstream and muscles, further enhanced by stress, causes the neurotransmitter catecholamine to flow through the entire body and increases the anger. I would think that the brain and body chemistry would take some time to normalize after that. I couldn't find any research that indicated how long that could take. A couple of hours can't be right." I was talking so fast I barely took a breath.

Esther placed her hands on my shoulders. "Breathe. He just needs some time to cool down. It'll be okay. He'll miss you before too long," Esther said. She gave me a small smile and squeezed my shoulders before letting go.

"Maybe. I don't know. It feels like he'll never talk to me again." I shrugged. I didn't really want to think about how long it might take for Squeak to cool down. I had nothing to go on, no past behavior on which to base a calculation of time needed. He'd never been mad at me. Not that I knew of, anyway. That thought made my head hurt more than it had yesterday.

"I need to stay focused on something or—I don't know. The only thing I've got to take my mind off of Squeak is the experiment."

"Well, he's probably too mad at you to be jealous. So what's the point? Okay then. What now?" Esther asked.

I pushed up my breasts with both hands. "Onward," I said.

"Pulling yourself up by your bra straps, are you? Nice, but I think you need to do a little more than display your monkey butt to keep yourself going right now," she said. For the first time that morning, she gave me a real smile.

As if I could get my mind off the disaster that was, most likely, my last day with Squeak. But having tried to get my mother and father off the subject of Squeak last night for the whole of dinner, distraction was definitely called for. The sooner I proved this theory, the sooner I could try to make things right with Squeak.

His leaving felt real for the first time. Or maybe I let myself actually acknowledge that it was happening. I was so overwhelmed by everything that had changed and was changing that trying to sort it out made dealing with two people and problems at the same time an impossibility. One person, one problem, at a time. It was what I did best. Which is another way of saying, I could interact with and understand only one person at a time. Theo and his base, primal reactions currently made more sense to me than the increasingly murky boundaries of my friendship with Squeak. Simplest things first. And while interacting with Theo was far from intellectually stimulating, it wasn't very complicated. Plus, I could show Squeak that he didn't really have feelings for Pom-Pom. It might work as a stepping-stone to start reestablishing our friendship.

"I think a retake of yesterday is called for. Only without illicit substances. I need to make sure he'll be looking for me at the carnival, and enticing eyes should help trigger that response." I pulled my very dark sunglasses out of my bag and then hesitated, realizing that pretending Theo was Squeak wouldn't help me hold his gaze. It would make me both sad and uncomfortable. I needed to get this done, if only to follow through with my plans. I slipped the sunglasses on. Esther laughed softly and gave me a little pinch as I walked past her and stepped into the traffic of the hallway.

Theo practically tripped me. Just like yesterday, my books went flying. As least this time it was Theo. That little fact seemed to signal today would be more successful than yesterday.

"Oh shit, sorry." He scrambled to pick up my books.

"No worries," I said.

When he started to stand and hand them back to me, he got a particularly good view of my cleavage, thanks to my red V neck T-shirt. He paused. But being the savvy alpha male he was, it was an almost imperceptible stutter in his movements. I'd caught the glance, and unable to stop myself from smiling, I gave away that I'd seen him take note.

"Oh, hey, Lily. Didn't realize it was you I crashed into. What's with the sunglasses?" He tilted his chin upward to indicate them.

I slipped them off. My pupils should be significantly larger. The hallway was filled with the morning sunlight. I knew they would contract almost immediately. The few seconds I had big, interested eyes might be enough, and worth the try. "These? Nothing really. I was running late. I forgot to take them off. Just grabbed my books."

His eyes drifted downward. I had the urge to say, "Hello, I'm up here." But I didn't, and after the crappy day I'd had yesterday, I actually felt more flattered than insulted. I hated to admit it, but it was something to keep me from thinking about Squeak. Maybe it could help me forget he was done with me. I needed some success.

I coughed, a little. I couldn't help it. He jerked his eyes up to look at me. I knew I should be acting a little shy and sweet. But come on. . . .

"Iris. My name is Iris." I pointed to the necklace. "IRIS."

"Right, yeah."

"So, hey. Are you still going to the carnival?" I asked.

"Sure."

"Great! See you there." I gave him what I hoped was a dazzling smile. It couldn't hurt to flash my straight white teeth. In fact, I was starting to feel like maybe I was good mating material. Though I had no intention of taking it that far. Right now I was shooting for good prom date material. Plain and simple.

I into my first class and glimpsed Squeak sitting in the back of the room. I hadn't thought about the fact that we normally sat together in the front row. Looked like going forward I'd be sitting alone. I suddenly felt an ache all over and found myself tucking my shoulders forward in an instinctual, unconscious reaction to protect myself. It was as if I'd taken a hard and sudden blow to the chest. Only it was, more accurately, one to the heart.

## Prom Theory Notes

### Esther's Observations

*Iris drops her books when she runs into tall, blond, and handsome, no matter who it is. That's my hypothesis for the day. I'm out.*

### My Observations

*First, it is important to make note of some research that has taken place over the last few years in pain management. As this researcher can attest, emotional reactions to negative life events often manifest as physical symptoms (e.g., tensed muscles resulting in a buildup of lactic acid, painful muscle spasms,* and chest pains). In the case of what is commonly referred to as heartbreak, common idioms also accurately reflect and describe the very pain this researcher feels in the areas of her chest and heart. Because it is physical, muscular pain, it has been found that common pain relievers such as ibuprofen and acetaminophen do reduce the pain of heartbreak. It does, in my experience, help a little bit.

It was difficult to determine whether TG's invitation to go to the carnival had been prompted by the signals my briefly dilated eyes were sending to his ventral tegmental area (where the seeds of romantic love reside) or by the reaction of his hypothalamus (seat of sexual attraction) to my very visible and padded-bra-enhanced breasts.

While it could have been one or the other or a combination of both, the results certainly suggest the validity of the hypothesis.

Note: The spring carnival is the focus going forward.

# CHAPTER TWENTY-ONE

## Sunday
## Days to Prom: 6

### Step Four: Moving from Increased Attraction to Romantic Arousal

*Misattribution of arousal occurs when people mistakenly identify the physiological responses to fear as romantic arousal.*

*Responses to fear include rapid heartbeat, elevated blood pressure, and elevated temperature. Accompanying adrenaline response can enhance feelings of arousal and excitement, which can be associated with the person who is involved in the experience.*

After a short walk from my house, I met Esther where she was waiting for me at the entrance of the spring carnival. Not our usual pattern of behavior. I was normally the first one to arrive when meeting Esther somewhere. Today, however, I had reluctantly left for the carnival ten minutes late.

The prospect of jangling, chaotic music from the rides, and screams from their riders, without the soothing presence of Squeak had done nothing to motivate me to face the day. However, it was an opportunity to advance the likelihood of a positive outcome for the entire project. Esther, at least, was there for support. I could never have faced an event that was in every sense too much alone. I hoped Esther's ability to make things fun was up to the challenge.

We walked down the small path lined with ticket booths, food vendors, and games designed to take advantage of the brain's response to intermittent rewards. Even though it was only the second day, the smell of old grease hung in the air, and litter was scattered along the paths to and from the rides. We were standing in front of the milk jug toss, which was right next to the ubiquitous fish pond.

"I guarantee everybody wins," barked a young man wearing a faded band T-shirt and holding a fistful of long plastic fishing poles. Things were now officially in full swing and getting more crowded by the moment as evening approached.

Esther spun around, obviously trying to take everything in at once. I was getting disoriented simply by looking at her. She stopped spinning, grabbed my arm, and began dragging me to a booth near the end of this section of games. "Look at the teddy bears. Hey, Darren will be coming later. Maybe he'll win one for me."

"So much for feminism," I said.

"Oh, lighten up, Lily."

I shot her a glare.

"It's a carnival. Tell you what, I'll win you a teddy bear and we can be BFFs forever!"

"That's redundant. 'BFF' is 'best friends forever.' You just said 'best friends forever forever,' and forget it. No need to get scammed out of your life savings for a chance to win me a stuffed bear made in a sweatshop with child labor," I said.

Esther took another look at the stuffed bears, this time with concern. My nervousness over the need to act charming and interested in Theo while surrounded by *everything* at once was making me irritable.

Esther looked back to me and caught me gritting my teeth and tugging on the hem of my shirt. “Ouch, you’re in a mood. Come on, it’s a carnival! The games are meant in good fun. And besides, why in the world would anyone play enough to lose their life savings? This isn’t Las Vegas. There’s no million-dollar jackpot,” she said.

“Still, everyone is susceptible. In behavioral terms, it’s known as partial reinforcement. We know there is a prize, and when we win, we get a rush of good old dopamine flooding our reward system. We like this. We want more of this. But when we don’t know if or when the win will come, to get the reward, the rush, we keep trying again and again in case we win the next time. And so we throw the Ping-Pong ball into the black-rimmed cup in the center of all the other cups that have no prize at all—or what prize they do have is majorly crappy—and we get just enough of a taste of success and reward that we try again, shooting for the big prize we rationally know we won’t get, because the game is fixed so we don’t win.”

“Iris, you are supposed to be having fun. Leave the wiki behind for the day,” she said as she lightly punched my shoulder.

“You’re right.” I exhaled loudly. “Just a little nervous, I guess,” I said, bringing my attention fully back to why we were there. I needed to get Theo on a ride, something thrilling with me seated beside him.

“You know what? If you need a boost, I’m here to help you. Riding something will boost your adrenaline whether or not it has any effect on Theo. So let’s do this. We’re going to grasp this sunny day by the thorns.” Esther gave a little “whoo” and reached out to give me a fist bump. Before I could recognize the gesture and bump her back, her phone buzzed with a text. She glanced at it and smiled, the corners of her eyes scrunched up in apparent pleasure. She looked at me and started to say something, perhaps what the text had been, but her attention shifted to somewhere past my shoulder.

"Oh, oh, oh, Iris, look—over there. Theo is hanging out at the Tilt-A-Whirl. Here's your chance." Esther started pulling me across the field behind the school district's administration building.

We stopped behind a small ticket booth, just out of sight of the crowd lining up at the ride.

"I'll get some ride tickets." Esther scooted around to the front and came back a minute later with a fistful of tickets.

"How many rides are you planning to go on?" I asked.

"Darren just texted me. He's going to meet me here, and we'll go on a ride while you and Theo get cozy spinning around at high speeds."

I wished I felt as excited as Esther looked. But I had to come up with a plan, and soon, or Theo would be on the ride without me. Then I'd have to wait for him to get on another ride, and who knew how long that would take? I studied the scene at the Tilt-A-Whirl. Theo and some of his teammates were hanging around but not getting in line. It looked like they were planning to, though, talking and occasionally erupting in seemingly good-natured shouts.

"So, tell me how this excitement mind meld or whatever works. Maybe I can use it on Darren," Esther said.

"I don't think you have to. He's already responding in kind to your mate-seeking behavior. He's very 'into you,' as they say," I said, not taking my eyes off Theo.

"Oh, he is not. I mean, I know he likes me, but there is nothing wrong with keeping things fresh and making him deeply devoted to me." Esther grinned.

"Keeping things fresh? You're not even officially dating," I said.

She poked my side. I turned my head and frowned at her. She shot me a hopeful smile.

"Fine. And it is not excitement mind meld, or whatever you said. It's called excitation transfer. All it means is that in some cases people equate the excitement of one event or experience with another. Basically, you are both in an excited state, and it not only makes things more fun and gives you a shared moment to reminisce fondly about, but it also ramps up attraction. Since the situation is already thrilling and causing adrenaline to leak into the brain, being in close proximity allows for the psychological transfer of the reaction to one's response to another person."

Esther looked at me.

To simplify, I said, "It just makes things sexier."

Esther's eyes lit up. Her anticipation of the arrival of Darren and the carnival rides had increased exponentially, and Darren didn't stand a chance. As if to prove my point, my excitement was beginning to rise in response to Esther's. I considered the guy who was running the ride.

"Esther, I think I have a plan," I said.

"Do what you do best. I just spotted Darren. I'll meet you back here in half an hour." Esther tried again for a fist pump. This time I recognized her intention immediately and returned the gesture. Then she was off, jogging across the field.

"Excuse me," I said over the noise of the generator powering the ride. He didn't even twitch, much less look up from his comic book. I spoke again, loud enough to make my throat hurt.

This time he heard me. He looked up, and I waved him over to the barrier where I was standing. He slowly wandered over and gave me a smile. His front teeth overlapped, and he wore a Pink Floyd *Dark Side of the Moon* T-shirt, a clunky watch, and a leather band around his wrist that read STUD.

He leaned on the metal bars of the temporary gate. "Hey there, blondie, how can I be of service?" He waggled his eyebrows in such an exaggerated movement that they peeked up above his sunglasses, which were perched crookedly on his nose. He was probably only twentysomething but might be as old as thirty. He looked forty.

It was demeaning, but useful in this situation. I leaned on the gate too. "I really need your help."

"How could I turn those sweet blue eyes down?" He grinned again. He seemed like a nice guy at heart, a solid beta, so I rallied on.

"See that tall blond guy over there?" I asked as I pointed to Theo.

The ride operator's expression dropped a little. "Yeah, the pretty-boy jock?" The hopeful tone in his voice was gone.

"Yeah, that's him. I just need to get him alone for a few minutes." I raised my voice about half an octave. "I really need a date for prom, and his girlfriend just dumped him, so I know he needs a date—"

"Say no more, sweetheart. I understand." His voice registered moderate disappointment, along with an almost proud I've-done-this-before tone. "You stay right here." I thought I saw him wink, but it was hard to tell behind his sunglasses.

He strolled over to where the people were waiting for the ride to open. It occurred to me then that no one had lined up because the operator had been on break. Coincidence was working in my favor.

He had everyone line up, with the track guys right up front. He returned to where I was standing. "Come with me," he said, and motioned toward the line. He quietly slipped me in right behind

Theo. This time there was no mistaking his wink. He followed it with a thumbs-up. I smiled, laughed, and gave him a thumbs-up in return. This was getting interesting. So much so that the dissonance of the many rides and their tunes faded into the background. It was also getting my mind off Squeak—a little bit, anyway.

He went to the rope, but instead of just dropping it, he let only three or four people in at a time and then told them which car to sit in. In just a few minutes Theo and two of his friends were in the front of the line. My accomplice lowered the rope and let the two in but held his hand up to stop Theo.

"Hey," Theo protested. His friends were making comments and telling him to let Theo pass. "I can only put two people in the last two cars."

Theo looked at the guys and shrugged. "Guess I'm not riding today. My tough luck."

The darker-haired of the two boys who had climbed into one of the cars shouted, "You set this up just to get out of it."

"Yeah," said the other one, "aren't you the lucky one. We'll get you later."

Theo was laughing and started to make his way under the rope and out of line. The ride operator stopped him again.

"Sorry, dude. If you're in the line, you're on the ride," he said.

"But I don't have anyone to ride with. You put the last of my bros on the train."

"No problem, you can ride with blondie here," he said.

Theo looked back and was momentarily surprised when he saw me. But, true to form, he recovered and acted like he knew I'd been behind him the whole time. "So, library girl, you ready to man up and ride the Tilt-A-Whirl?" He grinned.

*Man up, my ass,* as Esther would say. I had enough experience of being on rides that I knew I had the stomach for it. I had managed to find a way to get on the ride with him, so the hardest part was over. This experiment was on track for success. I might not have to do anything else to prompt him to ask me to prom. And then I could get back to fixing things with Squeak.

I smiled sweetly and said, "I think I'm ready, at least I hope I am." I added the last bit so as to trigger his protective instincts, which would cue his brain to release more testosterone. The increased hormone in his system should further his attraction to me because it would put him on high alert for anything female. And there I was. A female. In close proximity. All the elements I had hoped for were lining up. Cue the adrenaline, norepinephrine, and eye contact.

Predictably, I noticed, he stood up straight, increasing his height. He slightly puffed out his chest, not unlike the male red-chested grouse trying to attract a mate. All he needed to do was bellow and fill up his large red chest with air until it looked like a balloon ready to pop. My smile was genuine—at his expense, of course—but he took it as a smile of appreciation just for him.

He grabbed my hand and began pulling me to the remaining car. I had to suppress a squeak of surprise and keep myself from pulling away. Then he dropped my hand and grasped me at my waist. This time I wasn't able to stop from giving a small shriek and batting at his hands as he lifted me into the Tilt-A-Whirl. He didn't seem to notice. The initial shock and discomfort passed quickly, and my attention was drawn to his hands. They weren't particularly large, which was somewhat surprising given his overall stature. But they were strong. To be expected in a pole-vaulter.

Although, the physics involved in vaulting certainly had more to do with the momentum than any particular type of strength. I was sure Squeak could explain it in terms of physics—if he were still talking to me, that was. The satisfaction I'd felt when I realized Theo would be my partner on the ride faded, and my heart felt heavy in my chest. I was scanning the crowd for Squeak's dark, unruly hair before I realized what I was doing. I immediately forced myself to think of something else.

"The Tilt-A-Whirl is known as the Waltzer in Europe," I blurted out while looking straight ahead and pressing myself against the back of the seat.

"Huh?" Theo glanced at me as he hopped into his seat beside me.

"It's also one of the best-known flat rides." There would be no stopping me until I got out all the bits of trivia. As awkward as it was making things, I'd be much more on edge if I forced myself to stop. I turned to look at him in order to appear as normal as I could, despite my less-than-normal coping behavior.

"It's considered a flat ride because it's on a platform, and the car never rises off the ground. There are always seven cars, and they're attached at a central pivot point on a rotating platform. Centrifugal and gravitational forces cause the spinning of the car as the platform rises and falls. It's really quite amazing." I finally managed to halt the wiki flood. I took a deep breath and felt some relief after the small surge of distress at the thought of Squeak.

Theo leaned back and looked at me. His friends continued to shout at him and toss insults from the next car over in order to posture and make subtle challenges to his dominance. I felt my face heat up. I knew that in the social hierarchy of high school, I was the chatty, dreadfully boring "smart girl" that a "jock" normally wouldn't be caught dead with. I had to redirect him, and fast, by turning his attention from me and my awkwardness back to himself and reinforcing his high-ranking status. "Rides like this make me a little nervous. I'm glad you're riding with me."

"Hey, don't sweat it." Instead of paying attention to me, he leaned forward and called out to his friends. "Yo! Just because I'm not sitting with you doesn't mean the bet's off. I'll be chasing you down for my twenty bucks."

"Right, keep telling yourself that. Glad you won't be in here when you lose." They jostled each other, both of them laughing.

"Yeah, you're so gonna owe us twenty bucks," the dark-haired one said.

"Let's up the ante, then. If it's one of you guys, you owe me forty," Theo shouted.

"In your dreams, asshole," one of them yelled.

Theo gave them the finger and flung himself back into the car, arms crossed.

I wasn't clear on what their exchange had been about. What I saw was roughly the equivalent of chimps throwing feces at one another. "Why would you owe them twenty dollars or why would they owe you forty? Are you betting on something?" I asked. A competition of some sort with a significant prize for the winner would somewhat explain their somewhat exaggerated behavior.

He dismissed my question the instant I asked it. "Aw, it's nothing. Just asshole trash talk."

Was he blushing? If he was, it had nothing to do with me, except that maybe I'd seen the poo flinging and it looked like he'd been the recipient of most of the poo.

I must have been staring at him long enough to make him uncomfortable.

"Don't worry about it," he said gruffly. But then he sat up straight, his alpha attitude back in place. He gripped the safety bar in front of us. "Come on, let's see how fast we can get this spinning."

He grabbed the bar in a way that would never facilitate anything like a spin, especially not against the rotational force of the ride itself. For an athlete whose success relied almost solely on the ability to harness certain aspects of gravitational physics, Theo clearly knew nothing about them. *Not like Squeak,* said the little voice in my head. Ugh. Not only was Squeak not talking to me, now he was interfering with my thoughts and making it impossible to stay focused on Theo and my research. What did I care that he wasn't talking to me? It didn't matter. It didn't. Or that's what I told myself.

The ride started and I reached forward to grab the bar. Quite honestly, I loved carnival rides—the faster the better, and upside down was the best. Besides, the more extreme the ride, the better the adrenaline rush, and the better the bonding moment for us. I felt much better. That was the voice I needed to hear inside my head.

I looked into Theo's eyes with an intensity that surprised even me. "Let's do this."

Theo's grin was downright conspiratorial.

The ride got up to speed quickly, and the rolling movement beneath us brought the car to the top of the first crest. Pulling as hard as I could and leaning to one side to take advantage of the direction of the tilt, I fell against Theo. His cool arm in the spring air felt solid and very masculine.

Then Theo slid into me, pinning me against the side of the car. I was already out of breath. My heart was beating fast and hard in my chest. I could feel that the same was true for Theo. If I could catch his eye, it might raise the likelihood that he would associate me with his automatic responses to the thrill of the ride.

We crested, slid right, left, and then right and right again. I had him temporarily pinned. I lifted my head from his shoulder and turned so I could see his face and eyes, which I expected to include flushed cheeks and wide pupils, two clear signs that what I meant to have happen was indeed happening.

But his cheeks weren't flushed. He was pale and perspiring. Sweat glistened across his forehead. He hung his head and sagged forward just as our car crested. It seemed to hesitate for a moment as Theo swallowed and then said, "I don't feel so good." We began swinging with a downward arc in the opposite direction. As he slid against me and we both shifted to the left, he lifted his head, and I saw that his face was a pale gray. He started to speak. "This sucks—"

But that was all he was able to get out before he vomited.

In my lap.

The ride began to slow. I was in shock. Any release of adrenaline or oxytocin or vasopressin, not to mention anything that had been attractive about his natural scent or the subtle nuances of his pheromones, were completely obliterated by the stench of vomit.

As soon as the ride slowed enough to disembark, his friends got out of their car. When they caught sight of Theo, they burst out laughing and trotted over to pull Theo off the ride. He was still groaning and retching. But of course, he had nothing left to vomit; he'd spent the entire contents of his stomach, which apparently consisted of an extra-large strawberry slushy, onto me.

His friends, obviously no worse from the ride, were slapping him on the back and still laughing. "Twenty bucks, pal!"

Theo, breathing heavily, managed a "sorry" before he was dragged off into the park, hopefully in search of a restroom. And though he hadn't spoken while looking directly at me, his words . . . or word . . . was certainly meant for me. If it wasn't, it should have been.

The ride's operator appeared beside me and tried to help me down, while at the same time being sure to keep his distance. His arms were fully extended in front of him as he took my hands.

"Oh man, that sucks, blondie. If I were you, I wouldn't be thinking about making out with him tonight. You better get cleaned up. Ladies' room's that way. I'd walk you over, but I got a mess to clean up, and I don't make money unless I'm collecting tickets." He paused, looking at me with more of an apology in his eyes than Theo had been able to muster.

I let go of his hands and held up one of mine. "No, really. That's okay."

And it was Esther to the rescue. She was at my side so fast I hadn't seen her coming.

"Shit. Come on." She flashed the ride operator an apologetic look and mouthed, "Thank you." Poor guy had to shut down his ride and sanitize it. I bet that was the last time he tried to help a girl out.

"We need to get you to the ladies' room and cleaned up so you don't smell so bad. You think you can walk home? You can walk home, right? I don't mean alone, I'll go with you," Esther said. She stopped in her tracks. "Oh no, don't look."

I was still gasping a bit because I was trying not to breathe through my nose. I looked up, hoping to get my nostrils clear of the acidic stench, and there was Squeak. Of course. And there was Princess Pom-Pom.

Squeak with Princess Pom-Pom.

"Oh man, I told you not to look," Esther said with both sadness and regret in her voice.

"Are they on a date?" Of course they were.

"Iris, I wasn't going to tell you this—well, not right now, anyway—but he, um, asked her to prom."

He saw me and then, with a grimace, took Pom-Pom's hand, turned away from me, and eased her through the crowd.

"Esther, I think I'm going to be sick," I gasped, and felt a pull in my stomach.

"Again? How can you have any left?" Esther marveled.

"This isn't mine. It's Theo's." I choked as bile burned the back of my throat.

"Coming through, out of the way, puke happening here . . . ," Esther was shouting as she made a beeline for the restroom just inside the entrance to the sports equipment storage area, dragging me behind her.

Esther threw me into the extra-wide handicapped stall. I dropped to my knees, held the sides of the toilet bowl, and vomited everything I'd ever eaten and some I hadn't.

# Prom Theory Notes

## Esther's Observations

*Well, that happened. I won't describe it in your notebook if you won't.*

*Is there anything this assistant (me) can do to cheer up the researcher (you)?*

## My Observations

*Excitation transfer does not take place if one of the participants vomits in the lap of the other.*

*The smell and experience may well form a stronger association than earlier, more pleasant associations. Unfortunately, the memories of negative experiences tend to negate the positive ones and can create an association between the person and the negative event (i.e., the sight of this researcher causes TG to have an urge to vomit). Worst-case scenario, TG vomits when he sees this researcher.*

# CHAPTER TWENTY-TWO

## Monday
## Days to Prom: 5

Esther and I stood shoulder to shoulder at the sinks in the senior girls' bathroom. I stared at her. "When did this happen? How do you know about it? You weren't even there. You came home with me."

Esther leaned forward toward the mirror and expertly applied her lipstick. She pressed her lips together and turned her head from side to side, examining her work.

It appeared that she was in no hurry to answer any of my questions. My hands were starting to shake. I can be patient, when I have to be, such as when I'm in line for something. But even then I'm never entirely comfortable and always have some difficulty standing still.

However, when Esther started to tell me some gossip that she knew was of utmost interest to me, waiting was something I was physically and psychologically unable to manage.

"Esther, come on," I pleaded, standing behind her now. She met my eyes in the mirror.

"Chill. I'm getting to it." Esther fluffed her hair with both hands.

"If you don't tell me the big and shocking tale of Squeak at the carnival, right now—"

She turned around and rested her hands behind her, on either side of the sink, leaned back a little, and crossed her ankles. I relaxed the tiniest bit. She had taken the you-are-not-going-to-believe-this stance.

"Okay. So. Turns out, Theo was at the carnival with those guys because the entire track team was working the dunk tank to cross off their senior community service requirement. And before you start grilling me about who my informant is and lecturing about carefully considering the source from which I obtain my information, Darren told me the whole thing this morning. He was there and heard everything. Mostly everything, anyway," she said.

I nodded, indicating I found him to be an acceptable source. I didn't want to say anything to interrupt her. So even though the "mostly everything" comment was cause for some concern, I needed to hear everything that had happened before I started questioning the details.

"So after the tilt-a-hurl incident, Theo went home, cleaned up, and changed clothes. He must have gotten his attitude adjusted while he was there, because he came back acting like he'd never puked in public." She paused for questions. I nodded. I wasn't about to interrupt her to acknowledge the "tilt-a-hurl" comment. I wanted her to tell me in the fewest possible words.

I needed to know what Squeak had done to Theo. It was important. Nothing had ever felt more important. I wasn't sure if whatever had happened would give me any clues as to Squeak's receptivity to my apologies, or if it would somehow jeopardize my efforts to salvage the outcome of prom theory.

"And?" Even I could hear the annoyance and impatience in my voice. Esther closed one eye and pursed her lips. That meant she wasn't going to tell me anything unless I played nice. "Please?" I bit out as sweetly as I could manage.

"That's better. Okay, basically, what happened was Darren was standing with Theo and some track guys when they saw Squeak with Pom-Pom. Theo went right for them. Darren hung back a little, so he didn't catch every word, but Theo said something, then Squeak said something, and then Squeak said another thing about puke. Darren was just waiting to see who would swing first.

"Then Theo said something else, Squeak lunged for him, and Pom-Pom pulled him back," she said.

"But what was it about?" I couldn't imagine Squeak being angry enough to even consider getting into a fistfight with anyone for any reason.

Esther hopped up and leaned into me. "Well, apparently, it was about you."

"What? Why? No. It must have been about Pom-Pom." There was absolutely no way this had anything to do with me.

Esther shook her head. "No, Darren said he heard Squeak say 'stay away from.'"

I shook my head. "It had to be about Pom-Pom. Theo was obviously harassing Squeak because he was with his ex," I said. That made sense. Even though they were no longer dating, Theo, as an alpha, would still consider her his property. And Squeak was, as he had told me, done with me. I pressed my hand against my stomach as I felt the familiar nausea return. Luckily, Esther didn't notice.

"So you'd think, but when Theo came back, he asked the guys, 'Who the hell is Iris Oxtabee?'"

"What?" It felt as if wires had crossed in my head and shorted out. I couldn't fit what she was saying into any logical scenario.

"Theo knows you as Lily. He doesn't know who Iris is, and he's probably never heard your last name," Esther said.

"But why? What would make Squeak say that?" I said. I didn't understand. "Especially since doing so actually helped me. It enhances my value in Theo's eyes." Was Squeak trying to help me after all? Perhaps he was feeling a little remorseful about our fight and he was trying to make it up to me. It couldn't possibly be that he was trying to undermine my efforts. No matter how angry he was with me, he just wasn't the kind of person who would go out of his way to hurt someone.

Esther's face scrunched in confusion. "I guess so? Wait, how so? That doesn't make sense. No, not with the way Squeak really feels about—"

I cut her off. If she was talking about me, she was wrong. I knew how Squeak really felt about me, and it wasn't good. "Theo, alpha as he is, isn't going to let Squeak tell him to do or not do anything. Plus, Squeak is also apparently with Pom-Pom in some way, and that ups the competition between them. Theo will make sure he finds out who Iris Oxtabee is and *not* stay away from her," I said. I knew my smile was confusing Esther even more than my explanation about what really happened between Theo and Squeak.

Esther half frowned and then nodded. "Maybe. You might be right about that part of it. But I don't think Squeak was trying to help you win Theo. Darren said Squeak looked like he was ready to punch him."

"No, it has to be that he was helping me." It didn't mean that Squeak's and my friendship was back on track. I had hurt him, and that was going to take some time. But perhaps . . .

"Anyway, that's all I know. One thing is for sure, those two are hating on each other in a really big way," Esther said, and then moved to the side of the sink and gave me a little shove. I took a few steps closer to the sink and mirror.

“Let me fix your hair. Your ponytail is a mess,” Esther said as she undid the hair band. “Can you get the brush out of my bag?”

I nodded and pulled it out of her backpack. She took it and began to brush my hair back in long, smooth strokes. It felt good. Normally, I didn’t like it when people crowded me or picked at me. But this was soothing. I thought about chimpanzees and apes grooming one another to strengthen social bonds, and smiled. “Thanks, Esther,” I said.

“No problem, girlfriend.” She smiled at me in the mirror.

Four seniors came into the bathroom, talking loudly and laughing. One of them glared at us—for being in there?—but didn’t say anything. They wore matching Pom-Pom T-shirts and bows.

I had never noticed them much before, but now I saw them everywhere. I knew it was ridiculous, but I was beginning to feel stalked.

Esther must have decided, for some unknown reason, that now was the appropriate time to bring up the Tilt-A-Whirl fiasco. Which, no doubt, she’d been dying to talk about all morning.

“Well, the carnival plan was a complete bust. I’m like, can he even look at you now? That had to be a big blow to his glorious ego—”

I reached back and lightly swatted Esther’s hand. “Shush.” I pressed my lips together and met her eyes in the mirror. When I gestured to the occupied stalls behind us, Esther’s eyes widened.

“Sorry,” she whispered. She leaned in and said in a barely audible voice, “I didn’t say too much. It’ll be fine.”

I was still nervous that Esther might have given away our plans concerning Theo and prom. Although in truth, she hadn’t said anything that the whole school wouldn’t already know about. THEO GRANT PUKES ON GIRL was too disgustingly juicy of a story not to have spread far and wide.

I looked at her in the mirror and frowned. She shook her head and mouthed, "It's fine." I hoped so. Granted, if they'd been the ones puked on, I was sure they would say the carnival was a complete failure as well.

The chatter started up as soon the stalls began opening. Esther went back to brushing my hair. Neither of us said anything else. There were a lot of slamming, swinging stall doors as they made their way to the sinks.

*"Oh. My. God. She is the most conceited . . ." "Did you see him . . ." "When's practice . . ." "Who's driving . . ." "Crap, I'm late for class. . . ."*

We ignored them and were ignored. Loud hand dryers went on and off, conversation never stopping, and then they were gone. We were alone again.

Keeping to almost a whisper, Esther said, "Sorry! I was dying to talk to you about this. It has to be the worst possible result of an experiment in the history of science. God, can you imagine the rest of the track team ragging him? He's never going to live that down. Do you still think you have a chance at this?" The words spilled out of her mouth like they'd been sitting on the edge of her tongue, just waiting for the go-ahead.

"I don't know," I whispered back. "It was a complete disaster and may have undone all the progress we've made. I just have to think about how to go forward from here. Though if I'm right about how Theo is going to react to Squeak's threats—"

"Not sure about that. It can't make up for the fact that you made him vomit—"

"I am not the reason he vomited!" I pulled away from her. Wiki mode threatened, but she stopped me before I could launch into a full explanation of the inner ear and the part it plays in our balance and sympathetic nervous system.

She moved me back into position in front of the mirror and resumed work on my hair. "Okay, not your fault—what I meant to say was you were right. Darren and I got on the swings while you were on the Tilt-A-Whirl, and now he grabs my hand every time he passes me in the hall. I mean, it really does work."

"I know it does. There's a lot of circumstantial evidence, like the number of pregnancies conceived during a blackout. I think the only even slightly positive thing after a disaster is that wedding planners make a bundle," I said absently.

"I have to say, Miss Oxtabee, you are managing to stay pretty calm after such a huge hiccup in your research. Do you know, you have not slipped into wiki mode all day?" She twisted my hair into a tight ponytail. The hair band snapped against my scalp as she tightened it.

"Ow." I rubbed my head and turned to give her a look. "I almost did. I'm trying not to think too hard about the fiasco at the carnival. Or anything else," I said. Anything else being Squeak, of course. In comparison, thinking about Squeak felt much worse than remembering Theo vomiting in my lap.

Esther handed the brush to me and gave my shoulders a quick squeeze. "Well, I won't bring anything else up. Come on, girly-girl, cheer up. There have to be at least a dozen super-secret science tricks up your sleeve. If anyone can trick the base of Theo Grant's brain, it's you, Einstein."

"Einstein was a physicist. He didn't know anything about evolutionary biology or neurology," I said as I bent down to put her brush back into her backpack.

"That's my Iris. Come on, tell me how I can help you get asked to prom."

I slapped my hand to my forehead as I straightened up. Talking about prom and thinking about the carnival reminded me that Esther had said Darren was going to ask her. "Esther, I'm so sorry. I forgot to ask. Did Darren ask you to prom?" Once again I'd dropped the friend ball. Poor Esther. I made a silent promise to her that I would try harder. She was everything I could ever wish for in a friend. She deserved the same. And I didn't want to lose her, too.

"Not yesterday like I thought he would . . . but he did this morning." Esther's expression softened, and it was obvious she was smiling at the thought of Darren and the carnival. I could tell she was very happy. I was too—for her, anyway. But it boosted my spirits regardless. Hurray for mirror neurons making my brain experience some of the joy Esther was feeling.

"Come on, Pester, I just might have a job for you. Prom theory is a go." I started for the door and Esther followed. It wasn't until much later—and much too late—that I recalled that only three of the four cheerleaders had left the bathroom during our conversation.

## Prom Theory Notes

*Note: I have had to switch to writing these notes up on loose-leaf paper, as my notebook was in my back pocket. It has been irrevocably compromised due to contact with my vomit-soiled clothing. I will have to replace it and transfer the content posthaste.*

### Esther's Observations

*I got nothing.*

### My Observations

*The possibility exists that TG's negative experience may have* completely undone all the mate-seeking and seemingly romantic physical and cognitive responses intentionally triggered by and then later associated with this researcher.

Since it is theorized that such events stay in short-term memory rather than immediately moving to long-term memory, if this researcher can quickly create several situations that result in the physiological signs of sexual attraction, there may be a chance the positive responses to this researcher may override the negative.

## Possible Plan

Several experiments that this researcher has not, as yet, been able to test:

- Being trapped in a dangerous or extremely stressful situation
- Repeated close physical encounters, which should increase desire for future such encounters
- Wearing clothing that conveys vulnerability. This appeals to the basic animal responses in one of two ways: suggests a possible mate who needs protection; suggests a possible mate who can be easily captured. This researcher intends to suggest a vulnerability that produces the need to protect.

## Personal Note

Planning ahead will be difficult because of TG's reduced schedule due to end of year and upcoming graduation. Must be prepared to take advantage of opportunities as they are presented in order to implement tests. Also, I've decided that after Squeak did not say anything when he passed me in the hallway, I am unclear about his motives in confronting Theo. Therefore, I am excluding the incident from consideration of the success or failure of the end results of the experiments. It is likely irrelevant.

# CHAPTER TWENTY-THREE

## Monday After School
## Days to Prom: 5

I wrote up my notes and then thought about Squeak in great detail, something I'd managed not to do in depth mostly because it didn't add to the data I was gathering about the stimuli that would elicit an attracted response from Theo. It also didn't have a clear cause and effect that I could follow. I lacked a piece of information about Squeak's overall motivations. All I could do was pace around my room like some poor, crazed zoo bear. I had to get out of the house.

It was raining, so I took an umbrella and made for the front door. My dad was working in his home office, and my mom had requested "do not disturb" before heading into her attic studio. She had a show coming up in a month and was in serious production mode. I'd be back before either one realized I was gone.

But just in case—I turned around and went into the kitchen. On the memo board my mother had put on the refrigerator for just such an occasion, I wrote, "Went for a walk to Scurman's. BRB." I put the marker down and once again headed for the front door. This time I made it outside.

It was warm and the air smelled sweet with ozone. But the light rain was misleading—I'd checked the radar earlier and knew that it was going to turn into a downpour. I was getting out just in time. Knowing what the weather would do and when it would do it made me feel like I was prepared and couldn't be taken by surprise. It was comforting to be able to rely on sound data, if only about the weather.

Originally, that was why I had felt so good about the prom theory project when Esther accidentally came up with it. It was a chance to test what I knew about the human brain and condition. Seeing my expectations as to how things would progress or turn out as expected had worked, so far as it went. But now I had serious doubts about the successful outcome. It seemed like such a trial-and-error endeavor, which is what all scientific discoveries are, when you get right down to it. But still, I didn't have a good way to examine the results. I certainly didn't have a control for comparison, and I had barely been able to control the environment.

The rain began to fall a little harder as I turned onto Main Street. I hurried down the remaining two blocks to Scurman's Stationery.

Nothing like a new notebook to lift my mood. All the blank paper waiting to be filled with observations and new insights into all topics that I sought to understand better had therapeutic effects and calmed me like nothing else.

I shook out my umbrella and closed it, then left it in the bucket in the entryway of the store and headed for the stationery aisle.

Paper, pens, and office supplies, in all their various incarnations and mutations, were creature comforts and my number one guilty pleasure. To be honest, I had a sticky note problem. But until the American Psychological Association recognized it as an actual disorder and there was a support group for it, I wasn't about to think of it officially as a problem. I was rounding the corner of the aisle of my destination when I stopped short and my stomach twisted into a tight knot. It felt as if my heart had crawled up to my throat, making it hard to breathe.

*Relax, it's only Squeak.* I would just have to be mature about the whole thing and share the aisle with him like an adult.

I swallowed hard and blew a slow breath out between pursed lips before I walked down the aisle. I stopped to stand beside him.

"Fancy meeting you here," I said, trying to act nonchalant, just out for a stroll past the stationery display. I held still, desperately trying to ignore the urge to flee. I had never wanted to be near someone and be as far away as I could get from him at the same time.

Squeak's head jerked up and he dropped the package he'd been holding—two packets of notepads. One was shaped like comic strip speech balloons and the other one was burst symbols just begging to have "POW" and "BOOM" written in them. I almost snatched them up. I didn't have those. But I took control of the urge before I bent over and made a grab for them. It would've been rude. I'd come back later.

Squeak liked office supplies—who doesn't?—but he didn't often purchase sticky notes. He preferred fine-point mechanical pencils and, although he would never admit it, brightly colored gel pens. So why was he looking at novelty shaped sticky notes? Didn't they remind him of me, and if so, why would he want to be reminded of me when he had ended our friendship?

His not speaking was making me anxious, so much so that I had to say something to end the silence between us.

"I just came in to pick up some . . . sticky notes," I said, internally kicking myself. I'd have to loop back for my notebook. "See, here they are! I need . . ." I picked up the ones closest to me without looking at them. "These. I just need these."

"Those are yellow. You hate the yellow ones. Here . . ." He tossed me a neon pack. I was beginning to think something might actually be wrong with my diaphragm, because my breathlessness was becoming disconcerting.

I hadn't expected him to speak to me. I thought he would just ignore me like he'd been doing for the past few days. I caught the package and stared at it in my hands like I'd never seen anything like it before. Squeak brushed past me.

"I have to go. I need to stop in to McCaul's before they close. I'm already past the deadline to order my flowers. And don't worry, I'll try to stay out of your way from now on," he said over his shoulder.

I was following him out before I realized I was carrying the sticky notes out of the store without paying.

"Flowers? Why flowers? Wait. Squeak," I said just loud enough for him to hear but not so loud I attracted attention. I was on his heels and out the front door of the pharmacy.

He stopped and opened his umbrella as he walked out from under the awning and onto the rain-drenched sidewalk. The rain had become heavier but was by no means the downpour that was coming. We both should get home. I should let him leave.

"Why do you think I need flowers? Did you think I wouldn't get flowers for my prom date?"

"No, I just . . . ," I faltered.

"You just didn't think about it," he finished for me.

I hung my head, unable to look at him. I hadn't made eye contact with him for more than a moment or two since the argument. "No, I suppose I didn't," I admitted.

"Right. Thought so." He turned and started down the street.

"Squeak," I called out.

He stopped and his shoulders dropped. "What now, Iris?"

So, I was Iris. No longer Bee.

"Uh, nothing." I smiled weakly. My impulse was to ask why he was taking Pom-Pom, but I couldn't bring myself to. Whatever his reason, I knew it wouldn't relieve the heaviness in my chest.

But then he spoke again, not apologetically, but with a little twinge of settling for something, giving in to the inevitable. "You know I'm going with Taylor, right?"

I lifted my head and bit my lip so I didn't say anything. I nodded again, but this time I met his eyes. The raindrops slowly slid off the slick black fabric of his umbrella, falling in thin, lazy lines between us. We stood there staring at each other, ignoring the impossibly slow movement of the rain and the world around us.

He looked away first, turning quickly and walking with long strides through the downpour as the speed of the world and rain returned. I went back into the store and headed straight back to the sticky notes. I'd need a stack of them, including the ones Squeak had been holding, and at least two new notebooks. Retail therapy has been proven to be a real thing. I definitely needed more than the dopamine release of just one notebook. I added gel pens to my mental list. A bar of chocolate was probably called for as well. I needed all the help my endocrine system had to offer.

# CHAPTER TWENTY-FOUR

## Wednesday
## Days to Prom: 3

Esther and I sat quietly on the hill overlooking the athletic fields. The weather was mild, warm with perfectly clear skies and a nice breeze. It was such a nice day that the administration, in acknowledgment that sunlight and time outdoors relieved stress, improved serotonin levels, and thereby improved mood, had given the students the option of eating lunch outside on the cafeteria's patio.

"It doesn't seem like Theo is on a quest to figure out who Iris Oxtabee is. He hasn't even said hello to me today, or even looked in my direction. I stopped wearing red, so maybe he doesn't recognize me. Or he doesn't want to after—you know."

Esther sat up and crossed her legs. "Good move, the not-wearing-red part. You don't want him puking whenever he sees you in some sexy little red number. I know one thing, I'm never having a strawberry slushy ever again."

"I doubt seeing me in what I wore that day would have that effect on him, but it's not unheard of. Just to be safe, I'm not wearing the necklace, either. Thank your aunt for letting me borrow it," I said.

"Thank you for soaking it in bleach before giving it back." Esther was serious.

"I hope it didn't ruin it."

"No worries, it looks fine. If it turns a funny color or falls apart, my aunt will just say it's a sign from the universe that she did the right thing by dumping his sorry ass."

"I could go into a rant about magical thinking and signs from the universe, but I won't," I said.

Esther looked worried. "Why?"

"Honestly, I haven't felt up to it for a couple of days." I could feel Esther's eyes on me, but she didn't say anything.

There were interesting theories about why we sense being watched. Squeak would say it was a seventh sense perceived by the pineal gland. He'd be wrong. The pineal gland is an atrophied gland—camp buddies with the appendix.

I drew up my knees and wrapped my arms around my legs. "Have you talked to Squeak?" I asked. I tried to sound casual and as if I didn't care. I knew she wouldn't buy it for a second.

"Yeah," was all she said.

"How's he doing?"

"Seems okay."

"Just okay?" I asked. Hearing my own voice made me wince. I was pathetic. I actually sounded hopeful, like I didn't want him to be okay without me.

Esther bent forward and started pulling up grass. It was apparent that we had similar displacement behaviors. It was uncomfortable to talk about Squeak. It was easier if we didn't have to look each other in the eye. "He's still not talking about you at all. It seems like he's not willing to forgive and forget. Plus, now he's taking Taylor to prom."

I dropped my forehead onto my knees and mumbled, "I know." I tried to hide my face. Tears were sliding down my cheeks.

"Iris?" Esther's voice was thick with concern. Was she starting to cry too?

I turned my head to the side, still resting it on my knees, and tightened my arms around my legs. It felt like I was trying to hug myself, and maybe I was.

"Are you crying?" She leaned in and put her hand on my arm.

I nodded. There was no going back now. I hid my face. All my grief came to the surface.

Esther slid next to me and gave me a small pat on my back. She probably wanted to hug me but knew that would make things worse. "Give him some time. I think he just needs to think through some stuff. He's got a lot of decisions to make in the next month."

"But I should be helping him make those decisions," I managed to say in between gasps for air. "He asked me to and I blew him off. For what? A popular jock puking on me."

"Does sound pretty pathetic. It also sounds a little bit like something you read about people doing on purpose for excitement. How could that be a turn-on?"

I hiccuped a laugh despite my tears. "Believe me, there was nothing sexy about it."

"Oh, I know, I was there," Esther said with a sad smile. I concentrated on slowing my breathing. When I was ready, I lifted my head. Esther waited quietly while I wiped my face with my hands.

"I just wish you guys could figure things out. It's going to be okay. It has to be," she said.

"I'm not so sure about that. I've made a fool out of myself. Everything we've—I've done lately has been a complete failure."

"Yeah, but you know, maybe you should just ask somebody. I'd love to have you at prom with Darren and me." I could tell she was imagining it because her eyes had a faraway look.

"I'm not that desperate for a prom date—but saying that made me pity myself even more than I already do," I said. Esther and Darren would be at prom. Squeak and Pom-Pom would be at prom. Everyone was moving on without me. I didn't know how to catch up. Would Squeak even want our friendship again? Did Pom-Pom just fill the space in his life that I used to fill?

After thinking about it all morning, I couldn't see a clear way to salvage the experiment. The only things I had managed to accomplish these past weeks were failing to get asked to prom and instigating a fight with my best friend that had probably ruined our relationship forever. And now I was feeling left out because I wasn't going to the dance. I hadn't considered the possibility that I would want to go to be with Esther and—yes, Squeak.

Behind us, the end-of-period bell sounded.

"How bad do I look?" I asked Esther as I wiped my fingers under my eyes. A silly move that likely did nothing except make the area around my eyes redder and more swollen. At least I wasn't wearing mascara. I'd been putting it on religiously since I started the experiment. Larger eyes in women is a sign of high estrogen levels. Nothing says good breeding mate like high estrogen.

"Well, if we run into Theo, now maybe his mirror neurons will make him feel your pain and he'll want to comfort you," said Esther as we stood and began walking toward the open exterior cafeteria doors.

"I'd rather he didn't. I feel pathetic enough as it is," I said. Esther gave me an understanding look and bumped her shoulder into mine.

It felt like a reassuring gesture. As if she was indicating that she was there and I wasn't alone.

By the look of several couples rushing back, Esther and I weren't the only ones to have taken a stroll. Of course, they'd had a different motivation for getting out of sight than we had. We went into the cafeteria with everyone else. I just had the afternoon to get through, and hopefully I wouldn't see Squeak. I hoped I could avoid Theo as well. Seeing him would just be a reminder of my disastrous attempts to control the world around me.

I slipped out of class just as last period ended to beat the stampede. Without the distraction of my research and grand plans for Theo Grant, missing Squeak was becoming gut-wrenching and bone-deep. I couldn't imagine ever feeling happy again.

As I approached my locker, the crowd in the hallway thickened. Which in and of itself wasn't odd, but no one seemed to be rushing to leave. People were talking in low voices and standing with locker doors open, but not doing much else. I was distracted by the odd behavior around me and didn't notice the condition of my locker door or the floor in front of it.

I finished turning the combination to my lock, but before I opened it, I looked up to find the crowded hallway had gone nearly silent. All eyes were on me. Why? I was fairly certain I didn't have anything sticking to my back or on my face. As I opened my locker door, I heard Esther shout.

"Iris, wait!"

But it was too late. The door swung open and what could only be described as a glitter bomb spilled out onto me, the floor—everywhere. There were small paper hearts among the tiny, static-ridden metallic bits. I barely registered their presence or potential meaning.

I couldn't breathe, at least at first. Then I couldn't stop panting, frozen to the spot, blinded by the one thing that set off every alarm and panic button in my brain and body.

Esther was there, grabbing my shoulders and forcing me to turn around and away from the glittering trap. It was everywhere, absolutely everywhere. On my books. On my graphing calculator. It would be ruined. It was all ruined beyond salvaging.

"It never goes away. You can never get rid of it. Esther, it's biologically persistent, it never degrades, it never ever goes away!"

"Iris, relax. Look at me," Esther urged, giving my shoulders a tiny shake.

"You can't clean it up. You can't. My locker. I'll need a different locker."

"School will be over before you know it. You can use mine," Esther said.

"And my books—"

"Just a few more weeks and you never have to see them again. I'm sure I can get someone to swap with you. Iris, look at me."

I couldn't. All I could see were the four-thousandths-by-four-thousandths-inch pink, purple, and silver specks, glinting and reflecting the fluorescent hallway lights.

"Esther, I can't breathe."

"Close your eyes. Listen to me. Breathe. Remember shiny things are good, right? Humans are attracted to shiny things, right?"

"Right." I nodded. I was able to take a deep breath. "Theo did this, didn't he?"

"He did—did you notice your locker is also full of red paper hearts? You got a promposal from Theo. It's a promposal," Esther said.

"Are you sure?" I opened my eyes, trying to focus only on Esther. "Is this revenge for trying to manipulate him? He knows. He must know," I insisted.

"No, Darren said he's been planning this. I would have stopped the whole glitter bit, but I didn't know about any of this until, like, five minutes ago."

My breathing started to slow and some of the panic response began to subside. Esther took her hands off my shoulders.

"This—this is punishable by law, you know. Some woman glitter-bombed her boss's office, and she got eighteen months and a thousand-dollar fine." Although I was feeling more in control, my voice was rising in pitch. "I'm sure they needed the money to pay for the ineffectual cleaning crews they had to hire."

"Keep your voice down," Esther warned in a quiet, still-gentle voice. "It's all good. We'll work around this—remember the shiny things, the good shiny things."

That was right. It was evolutionary. There was a new theory that said we are attracted to shiny things because of our instinct to search for water. Made sense, right? Of course that was right. Because over time humans misattributed those feelings for water to other valuable shiny things. Right.

Wiki mode threatened, but I managed to hold it back. I felt calmer now. Esther could see it. She patted my shoulder. "He's here."

"Who?"

Esther, despite her patience with me up to this point, rolled her eyes and let out a sigh.

I turned to face the newly arrived Theo. He held a bouquet of lilies in one hand, and as I looked at him, a sly half grin spread across his face. The smile seemed a bit strange, but bits of glitter floated across my field of vision as though their cast light had burned patterns onto my retinas. The floaters and the shock of everything did not, however, keep me from noticing the students with phones held high—recording the entire scene.

I stood mute.

Esther came even closer, standing behind me, nearly resting her chin on my shoulder, and whispered, "Come to prom. We'll have fun. Squeak's going. Why shouldn't you? Smile and say yes."

Theo moved closer and handed me the lilies. As I reached out to take them, red glitter sparkled across the back of my hand.

"Yes?" I heard someone say. Me?

"Are you asking or accepting?" Theo asked as he leaned in, crowding me.

"What was the question?" Me again. I'd managed to say something, and this was what I said? Hardly clever banter from a prospective prom date of the most coveted male in the school.

Theo laughed, "Will you go to prom with me?"

I struggled to look away from my sparkling hands. I bit back everything that was struggling to get out—how glitter worked electrostatically and further adhered to things due to a principle of physics called van der Waals forces. Squeak had told me that during one of my previous confrontations with the stuff.

And what about the wildlife that defecated glitter-laced feces—polar bears! Where did they even find it? Glitter poop. The uncaught mice in the building—statistically speaking, there had to be mice in the school—they would be ingesting glitter for generations with inevitable results. I swallowed it all. Squeak was going to prom. Squeak was going to prom with Pom-Pom. So why not? Why not Theo?

"Yes."

I forced a smile.

"Right answer." He winked and walked away. "Catch you tomorrow," he said over his shoulder.

"Sure," I said. But he was too far away to hear me. Tomorrow? It occurred to me that I knew little about Theo, other than a few facts, most of them sociological, such as his being the alpha male due to his status on the track team. I knew nothing about him as a person, his likes and dislikes. What would I say to him? I wasn't good at thinking of personal questions to ask someone. It was probably why I wasn't very good at making friends. If he did "catch" me tomorrow, what on earth would he do with me? Or me with him?

The hallway was now filled with people who blocked my view of Theo as he headed for the stairwell to the front entrance and then, no doubt, out to the parking lot, where his black Mustang was parked. I stood there for a moment, realizing that *it* had happened, the confirmation of everything I'd theorized. Of course, no one got 100 percent positive results when testing a theory. But this was the outcome my research and hypothesis had indicated should happen.

Yet, despite what should have been a great sense of satisfaction and accomplishment with my success, from the moment Theo asked me to prom, I'd felt on edge, waiting for something to leap out at me. From a survival standpoint, natural selection should prefer those with a more acute reaction to the combination of senses that make you believe there is something or someone watching you—a lion, a bear, a man with a spear. Those who can sense it before it comes bursting from the undergrowth are better prepared to get out of the way or to counterattack. Those who don't are lunch.

Maybe it was just because suddenly people were looking at me, wondering who I was, and what the attraction was.

I already hated it. At least, as soon as Theo left, there was no reason for the crowd to hang around. The hall emptied, and even Esther had been pulled away by Darren.

The initial rush of success and attention had drained away and left just a nervous tension crawling up my spine in the quiet hall. It didn't seem or sound like anyone was around. But I could feel someone staring at me. Trying to look casual, like I wasn't looking for anything or anyone, I glanced around. It turned out I was, in fact, being s tared at.

Squeak was at the water fountain at the end of the hall.

He was standing stone-still and staring at me. He had an asymmetrical smile and narrowed eyes. All that was missing was an eye roll and I would be certain of his contempt for me at that moment.

He looked down at the ground, shaking his head. I could see the shift in his body. He visibly clenched his jaw and took a deep breath before meeting my eyes again.

Everything, every success I'd had in the last few days with testing the prom theory, was now, in one moment, reduced to scraps of torn-up loose-leaf paper, meaningless report cards, and discarded lollipop wrappers, which now were nothing more than litter at my feet.

I was cold, inside and out. I wished for a sweater to wrap tightly around myself. I wanted to have a casual attitude, to walk past him and say "hey" without meeting his eyes. Instead I just stood there, unable even to blink.

There are seven main universal facial expressions in humans: happiness, anger, fear, surprise, sadness, contempt, and disgust. Nose wrinkled and upper lip raised, he turned and walked toward the exit. I knew disgust when I saw it.

# CHAPTER TWENTY-FIVE

## Friday
## No School—Teacher In-Service
## Days to Prome: 1

"Can you finish cleaning these brushes for me? I'm going to see if your father needs anything. He looked a bit wrecked after his red-eye flight home. I can't believe he didn't go straight to bed when he got back this morning," my mother said as she wiped the paint off her hands with a rag that looked suspiciously like my father's favorite old B-52's T-shirt. There was still a corner that read OVE SHAC. Having my mother claim his old worn-out T-shirts as paint rags was the chance he took when he left on week-long business trips to the West Coast.

Roof windows made up much of the ceiling of my mother's attic studio. They were open, letting the two large, industrial-like fans bring the cool air in and push the fumes from the oil paint and turpentine out.

"Sure, Mom. That's what days off are for," I said.

"I suppose so." She sighed and wiped her hands on her smock this time, before pushing my hair away from my face and kissing me lightly on the forehead. "You sure?" she asked. She'd been looking at me with constant concern ever since she found out about the fight with Squeak. Even the news that I would be going to prom, and with a popular athlete, didn't seem to lessen her worry. She was happy I was going, but only cautiously so.

"I'm fine. I want to do this. It's very relaxing. Go."

She nodded, seemingly satisfied I was sincere. Small, sweet chimes followed her out of the attic and down the stairs.

I needed some solitude after yesterday's adrenaline and dopamine high of Theo's promposal, followed by the crash caused by Squeak's obvious antipathy toward my acceptance. Not entirely surprising given that I had insisted throughout the experimentation I didn't want to go to prom, and certainly not with Theo. Just recalling how Squeak had looked at me released cortisol and stimulated my anterior cingulate cortex all over again. In other words, my body physically ached whenever I thought of him.

I dipped a clean rag in a small capful of turpentine and started wiping the wooden length of a paintbrush, using my fingernails to scrape off the thin layers of oil paint that decorated the handle and metal casing at the base of the brush.

It was easy to lose myself in quiet, focused tasks like cleaning paintbrushes or pairing socks. They gave me the quiet time to think through things. Like the prom theory. It had been working nicely, with a few unexpected disasters and some unintended consequences due to variables I was unable to control. But since Theo had asked me to prom, they obviously hadn't ruined the overall positive outcome of the trials.

The outcome might have been successful in ways I had expected at the start of it all, but I hadn't foreseen the disaster of losing Squeak. It felt like I was being replaced by Pom-Pom—someone who was nowhere near Squeak's level. What would they talk about? Despite Esther's persuasive argument about why I should go to prom, I was starting to think that I had accepted only because I was upset he'd asked Pom-Pom. That was probably wrong of me, but Squeak was going to move away to go to college. There was no getting around that. He was leaving. My chest tightened. Maybe it was better this way. I'd have more time to become accustomed to not being with him every day. He would still physically be here, so in some ways, it might make the transition a little easier. I would see him. I just couldn't speak to him or listen to him tell me physics fun facts.

But how does someone suddenly stop being with a person? The longer you spend with someone, the more pathways your brain develops linked to the person. Suddenly your brain has to build new pathways, while finding new ways to function and make sense of the world. All of which is what your brain experiences when you go through withdrawal. It's difficult. It can be physically and emotionally debilitating. I had to accept that I was going through withdrawal from morning chats by my locker, tugs on my ponytail, and takeout Chinese and horrible-movie nights with him at Esther's house.

They were going to be gone. They were gone. I didn't know how to fill the time. Our schedules and routines had been intermingled for years, and the constancy of his presence had kept me from feeling disconnected to the world around me. Squeak's presence had pull and gravity. I had to learn how to hold on without him so that I would not float off, into space, alone.

I lined up the clean oil paintbrushes on a dry linen towel and scooped up the ones thick with acrylic paint. Then, filling a quart jar with hot, soapy water, I dropped them in, brush first, to soak.

I walked over to the open window where I could look down into Squeak's backyard. He was sitting on his porch, hunched over what looked like a part from the mostly disassembled push mower in front of him.

I watched as he wiped parts with what was likely a gas-soaked rag—both of us spending the day with flammable solvents. I wanted to stay there and watch him. He could be so efficient and focused. I liked that about him. His hands were quick, and he seemed to know what he was doing no matter the task. It was comforting. He tried the mower's pull cord a few times. The engine sputtered once, twice, and then died.

Squeak stood and, obviously frustrated, kicked the rags out of his way as he went to the back door of his house. He opened it, leaned in, and said something about going to get fresh gas and a few other things I couldn't make out. I continued to watch him as he walked over to their shed and pulled out a red gas container and walked to his car. He put it in the trunk and drove off.

I heard my father coming up the stairs. I was still looking out the window when he leaned down and spoke softly in my ear. "What's wrong?"

"I miss him," I said

"Of course you do," he said.

I turned around and pressed my face against my father's warm chest. He wrapped his arms gently around me and held me close. I struggled not to cry and failed.

"Friendships go through stages. This is the first real falling out you two have had. Give him some time. When he's ready to work past it, he'll let you know. And you know, even long friendships don't always last. People grow apart, go their separate ways. And soon you'll go to college, make new friends, and maybe even fall in love."

I knew he was saying this to comfort me, but it made me want to sob. Didn't he know I didn't know how to deal with the world without Squeak? That I needed him? I bit the inside of my cheek in an attempt to keep from giving in to the urge. My head hurt. Nothing made sense.

My mother leaned into the room from the doorway. "Hey, you two, how about some lunch?"

I laughed a little and hiccuped, surprised by her appearance. I hadn't heard her ankle bracelets chime as she came up the stairs.

My father rubbed my back. "Let's get something to eat. You'll feel better with some food in your belly." He dropped a light kiss on the top of my head before letting me go.

"Still down?" my mother asked, her eyes full of sympathy. But then she brightened as something occurred to her. "I know, we'll go prom dress shopping right after lunch, instead of tonight. Call Esther and I'll take you both. It will lift everyone's mood, mine included."

Theo had asked me. I was committed to going with him. And I had been excited, sort of. My parents had been upset about Squeak's and my falling-out, but they were taking it in stride. They were trying to be upbeat and happy about prom, and what was essentially my first date. Theo had been very sweet after the promposal, texting last night to see if I had a favorite flower or type of candy.

Despite all that, I felt as if it wasn't going to be much fun. Especially with someone who didn't understand me or my reactions to crowds and loud noise. But I'd gotten myself into this and I needed to give Theo the benefit of the doubt. I'd do my best to be as normal and calm as possible and not ruin this one night. I'd already done enough damage.

Dress shopping wouldn't be much fun either, but it would be a distraction. Anything to get my mind off Squeak. Not thinking about Squeak was becoming my motivation for doing most things.

My mother headed back downstairs, giddy with the thought of dress shopping. This time I could hear her bells.

# CHAPTER TWENTY-SIX

Abigail's Bridal and Formal Boutique was one of the few places in Hillcrest to shop for a gown or rent a tuxedo. Even though it was last minute, and Princess Pom-Pom most likely had her dress by now, all I could do was imagine running into her at the shop. Her dress, of course, would be stunning and irresistible. Any rationally thinking male would be completely lost. He'd be made into a veritable zombie—he'd have eyes and ears and drool only for her. Princess Pom-Pom would no doubt be promoted to prom queen.

I'd be lucky if I found something that didn't make me itch.

But, as luck would have it, I had a wise and intelligent mother who, despite her earth-goddess leanings, knew how to convince a busy, overwhelmed small-town boutique owner to give us the large room in the back normally reserved for those shopping for bridal gowns.

It was a small store, after all, so the room wasn't enormous, but we all fit into it with enough space to crawl in and out of completely impractical dresses, in completely unreasonable colors. Many sparkled so brightly that I was shocked they didn't come with seizure warnings. That was bad enough, but my anxiety increased tenfold with the variety of shapes and sizes of the dresses—some of them had enough fabric in the skirt alone to clothe a village. Others would get you arrested for indecent exposure.

"Esther, I can see your navel," I said, sitting on a small stool while my mother piled possible "Iris-friendly" gowns onto my lap. Esther was on her tenth gown. I was getting irritable in the extreme, but that was no excuse for snapping at her. I had tried on fifteen and still hadn't found anything I'd be physically or psychologically comfortable in for an entire evening.

"I know, isn't it awesome?" Esther radiated excitement. I was beginning to think she might have other plans for the evening besides dancing and making out in Darren's car. She was the only person I knew who could talk about condoms without getting embarrassed. She was bold but smart, so I was fairly certain she could take care of herself, especially with Darren. He was one of the sweetest males I knew. I should probably be more worried about *him*.

"No, dear," my mother said, "it's trashy."

"Hear, hear," I said.

"This is prom we are talking about, people." Esther left the "duh" unsaid but suggested it with her upturned hands and incredulous wide eyes.

"Iris, would you help your friend so we can wrap up this little adventure?" My mother lay down on the short bench as best she could and covered her eyes with a bent arm.

"May I remind you this was your brilliant idea to lift everyone's spirits?" I said.

"Each of you, just pick out a dress so we can go home." My mother sighed her mom sigh.

"Fine, but what do I know about prom dresses?" I had no clue what to tell Esther or which dress I should choose. I was starting to doubt that my agreeing to go to prom had been a good thing. I hadn't thought it out to its inevitable end—actually having to go. "I'm beginning to think whatever fits and sufficiently covers a majority of my body will do."

"Hear, hear," my mother said.

Esther had slipped back behind the dressing screen, and the rustling of satin and the occasional crinoline persisted for at least ten minutes. I stood and placed the gowns I'd been holding onto the stool. I went back to the rack that held the gowns we'd already considered. There was a deep-blue satin one, with the occasional sparkle embroidered in random spots on the dress. It reminded me of the night sky at twilight, just as the stars became visible. I'd been too grumpy to really consider it. The fabric flowed over my hand as I lifted the skirt.

"That one is very pretty," my mother said softly.

I turned halfway around. She was sitting up now and smiling at me, a wistful my-baby-is-growing-up smile. It made me feel loved.

I looked back at the dress. "You think so?" I asked. My uncertainty turned the question into a whisper.

"I do, and you should try it on again," she said.

Just then Esther walked out from behind the screen. Holding her arms out to her sides, she turned in a slow circle. This one was an eye-catching red. It was low cut in the front, but she wasn't going to fall out of it while dancing. And there was a high slit, but only on one side, and the dress was long.

I nodded in approval. "You have done an admirable job of finding something that is at once nearly respectable *and* suggestive. I wholeheartedly approve."

My mother stood up and applauded. "Sold," she said.

The red was quite bright, but it didn't give me a headache looking at it. It was just dark enough to bring out the red tones in her brown hair. Her dark brown eyes shone, and although I'd never given much thought to Esther's appeal in general, she was very attractive in ways that spoke of health and vitality. She was nearly as tall as I was, but with more-enhanced female attributes—slim waist but generous hips, and medium-size breasts. Her complexion was clear, and all the time she'd been spending outside at track meets had given her face a bronzed glow. In other words, she looked beautiful.

"I guess I'll go try this on now," I said reluctantly. I slipped behind the screen before anyone could say anything encouraging.

I took a deep breath. No more stalling. I was going to try this dress on, and if I could stand it rubbing against my legs for more than a minute, and if we could cut the tags out, it was what I was wearing.

I slid the dress on and zipped up the side. The top was square cut and not even remotely revealing. It was sleeveless, and I liked how it showed off my long arms. I had some actual definition in them. Attractive, lean muscle from carrying around piles of heavy textbooks my whole life. It was knee length too, so I wouldn't be tripping over it all night. And I felt like I was wearing a constellation, such were the arrangements of the small, embroidered silver bursts. Several had long tails and reminded me of meteorites and comets. I took a deep breath and walked out from behind the screen.

Esther gave a little gasp. "I love it. It's you, all you, and I am not just saying that to get out of here. Really."

"Mom?" I asked, looking for an honest opinion. She was covering her face with her hands. And then she wiped tears from her cheeks as she pulled them away.

"Sold," she said.

Back at my house, Esther was curled up in my beanbag chair and I was lying facedown on my bed. We weren't really saying much, just hanging out, thinking our own thoughts but not feeling alone.

It was Esther who decided to bring up the one topic I didn't want to talk about.

"Iris," Esther said.

"Hmm," I answered, with my face buried in a pillow.

"Remember what I said a couple weeks ago about you rethinking the whole going-with-Theo-to-prom thing?" Esther said.

"Yes, but it's a little late to be bringing that up now, don't you think?" I lifted my head off the pillow and folded my arms so I could rest my chin on them.

"Well, I never told you why I really thought you might not want to go with Theo."

"What do you mean? I thought it was because Pom-Pom thought he was a dick," I said.

"Maybe . . . I just . . . there are some things I think you really should know, and then I need to confess something," Esther said without looking at me.

"Like what?"

She didn't answer. She was picking at her cuticles, her number one nervous habit.

"Esther, like what?" I asked again, sitting up and looking squarely at her.

Whatever she had to say, I wasn't certain I wanted to hear it. But she'd brought it up like it was a big, heavy secret, and there was no way I'd be able to stop thinking about it until she told me. I had to know, regardless of what it was. She looked up from her now-torn cuticle.

"It's about Squeak."

I didn't respond, waiting for her. She finally gave in and started talking, all of it coming out in a rush.

"Iris, he's been in love with you since grade school," Esther said.

"That's not possible," I said. I didn't know why Esther was saying that about Squeak. How she would even know. Besides, he told me everything. I didn't always listen, but I would have remembered him saying something like—well, like that.

"Iris, think about it. No—wait, don't think about it. He's never gone out with anyone. He's never admitted to having a crush on anyone. Have you ever seen him pay attention to anyone, of any gender, like he pays attention to you?"

"Well, no, but—of course he paid attention to me. I'm like a little sister. He probably wanted to protect me from being bullied and whatnot." Why was Esther trying to argue this point? It was absurd on so many levels, wasn't it?

"Do brothers give their sisters little gifts for no reason? Hold their hands whenever they get a chance? Stare longingly at them from across a room?"

"He looks at me longingly? How would you even know?"

"It would be sickening if it wasn't so sweet. Talk about boyfriend goals. You had it better than anyone else and you didn't even know it. If I hadn't thought of you two as a unit, I would have been jealous," she said. Then she paused and a small grin crept across her face. "Also, it *is* Squeak, so you know." She shrugged, now biting back a full smile.

"What is that supposed to mean?" I felt a sudden urge to defend Squeak. Was she implying he was somehow lacking because he was Squeak? There was nothing lacking in Squeak. He was intelligent, kind, caring, attentive, and sensitive. He'd been my translator for the social behavior of those around me since we'd met. He'd always made a point of understanding what it meant to be someone with NVLD, and not expected me to be just a diagnosis but also a person. He was also very attractive. He smelled fantastic. And maybe I didn't want him to be in love with me because I wasn't sure I could love him the way he deserved to be loved. I wasn't sure I knew how to do that.

"No. He's known me too long. We've spent too much time together for anything other than platonic feelings to develop." I was on my feet now. "That can't be right. It just can't."

But it could be possible. Not all evolutionary survival strategies worked the way we interpreted them. I started to pace back and forth from my bookshelf to the window, alternately moving a book from one shelf to another and fussing with the drapes. I needed to do something with my hands, and I needed to move.

Everything I thought I knew was breaking down. Everything I'd been doing to understand people had just confused me further. One minute the cause and effect of people's actions lined up and made sense, and the next, nothing did. But if it was true, I'd hurt him far more than I had even guessed and probably in ways I was completely unaware of. And what was I feeling other than missing a friend? If felt like more than just that, didn't it?

"I—I didn't know." I wasn't just confused. I was lost.

"I know. It was probably silly, but I thought maybe you saying yes would make Squeak jealous enough to make up with you, if not by now, then maybe after prom. Seeing you with Theo might make him realize he doesn't want to lose you."

"He's the one that decided to end our friendship, completely, and forever. If he loves me so much, why would he do that? Why did he ask Pom-Pom out? What is that all about?" I didn't realize I was shouting until I stopped to take a breath.

Esther shushed me. We both glanced at my closed door. No approaching chimes. Esther's shoulders relaxed a little. The last thing I wanted was for my mother to hear this. Esther must have felt the same.

"You hurt him, Iris. You should've seen him right after you guys fought. You scared the hell out of him with that belladonna stunt," Esther said.

"Atropine drops, it has the active ingredient—"

Esther cut me off and waved both her hands at me. "Stop it. This is no time to hide behind your vast knowledge of Latin names."

I knew Latin names, but honestly, there were other things I didn't know much about. Why was I so clueless when it came to other people? I knew all about the mating behavior of the Argentinian brown-eared woolly opossum, but I couldn't even tell when someone liked me. If I had known, I would never have explored this prom theory by pursuing Theo. Why did he let me? Maybe because he loved me. Since I couldn't accept that he was right about love, maybe he wanted me to find out on my own. Maybe he hoped that by trying to attract someone, I'd realize the only one I really wanted was him.

And if that was true, then he had been right to hope. I didn't want to be with Theo at all, much less all night at prom. But I'd said yes. I had to go. I was so frustrated I felt like my ears were about to burst, and my feet buzzed, every nerve felt like it was on overload. I wanted to scream and stomp. Instead I kicked my dresser once, and it felt really good, so I kicked it again. Twice.

Esther jumped up from the beanbag chair. "Iris. Take it easy, girl.

You're going to hurt your dresser and break your foot. Prom doesn't stand a chance of being a special, magical night if you have your foot in a cast."

"At least then I wouldn't have to dance. Oh my God, Esther, what was I thinking? I can't dance. Everyone is going to be watching us. Including Squeak! I'm going to make a fool out of myself. It's going to be fifth grade all over again." I was nearly in a panic. What had I done? Why had I even done it? "What am I going to do?"

I dropped onto the floor. I shoved my face into my bent knees and wrapped my arms around my legs, hugging tight. Esther knelt beside me and gave me a one-armed hug.

"I just don't get it," I said, not picking up my head. I turned so my cheek rested on my knees, and lifted my eyes to meet Esther's. "He's not even cute, you know." I tried to smile. Tried to make it sound like a joke. Esther just narrowed her eyes and frowned at me.

"If by 'cute' you mean"—and here Esther did her best impression of me, which was frighteningly accurate—"'symmetrical features, a jaw you can slice meat with, and really long middle fingers,' then maybe not. But even you know that Squeak is a cutie. In his own way. He's tall—you said that's attractive, right?"

I nodded.

"He's all muscle, if you haven't noticed. Lugging around all that drywall and lumber on weekends made him something of a badass. He's got amazing eyes—I always thought so. I'd kill to have his eyelashes." Esther sighed.

"That's a bit of an exaggeration, don't you think? I really don't think you'd kill anyone for something so—"

She lightly smacked the top of my head. "You know what I mean.

And he doesn't squeak anymore. We're the only ones who call him that. It keeps him safe for everyday use. Seth is a serious package even if his nose is a little crooked. It makes him look even more badass."

"He's not a badass at all. It's not like he broke his nose in a fight," I said.

"I didn't say he was a badass. I said he looked like a badass, and besides, only you and I remember how that happened."

"Oh, I'm sure he remembers. That doesn't win me any points with him either." I hid my face against my knees again.

"I'm sure it's not keeping him up at night," Esther said.

"Thanks," I murmured into my knees.

"No problem, girlfriend. I got your back," she said.

I sat up and straightened my legs out in front of me. "Esther, I don't know what to do. I can't stand it. I feel like—this is not how it's supposed to be. He's supposed to be like a brother to me," I insisted.

"Well, maybe, but would you feel this way if your brother, if you had a brother, refused to talk to you?" she asked.

"I'd care, but it wouldn't feel like this," I admitted.

"How does it feel?" she asked.

"Like I'm not whole anymore. Something is missing and it hurts where it used to be."

"Ouch, you've got it bad." Esther sighed and rested her head on my shoulder.

"I ruined it, didn't I?" I asked, but I already knew the answer.

"I don't know. Maybe," Esther said. I hated to hear it. It made me feel unworthy of friends, but it was good to get an honest opinion.

"What am I going to do?" I tried to keep the despair from my voice and failed.

She hugged me and I awkwardly patted her back. Then she leaped to her feet and grabbed my arm, pulling me up. "You're going to do what I'm going to do. Get psyched about having an awesome prom dress, and look so seriously hot that everyone wishes they were you."

"I don't know how to be hot." Maybe I should just let the win of the promposal be as far as it went. Theo could get another date in a second.

"You do so know how. If you look hot, you feel hot, and you got yourself a confidence feedback loop. And that has to be true because you are always going on about it. You and me are gonna mesmerize the entire junior-senior class." She pinched my cheeks.

I swatted her hands away. "Maybe you will, but I'm not going to be mesmerizing anyone," I said.

"Yes, you are," she said. "Listen to me, when you are on Theo's arm tomorrow night, the entire cheerleading squad is going to be jealous. Squeak will be too, I'm sure of it. Best of all, you will be the alter female."

"Alpha female," I corrected.

"Whatever." She dismissed her error with a wave. "It's going to be a night you'll never forget."

That's what I was afraid of.

# CHAPTER TWENTY-SEVEN

## Saturday—Prom
## Days to Prom: 0

Theo drove a black Mustang. I'd always thought it was a nice car, but was never necessarily impressed by it in any way. I certainly didn't recognize the year or the engine size or any other details. However, as clueless as I was about cars, I understood a male would further ensure his ranking by making various displays the other males would recognize as proof of his alpha status. An expensive, impressive-looking, powerful car would shame the others who didn't have such a vehicle, and attract high-ranking partners.

So even though I should have expected it, I was nonetheless surprised and somewhat disconcerted as my heart sped when I heard it pull up to the house. I ducked back behind the curtain when he opened his door and stepped out of the Mustang. Making sure he wouldn't be able to see me, I peeked through the tiny opening between the curtain and the window. He sprinted up the walk, and my father answered the door. Theo, in a black-on-black tuxedo, came into the house. He shook my father's hand and then handed me a long-stemmed red rose. He looked incredibly attractive, and the rose was a nice touch, if not terribly clichéd. Still, I felt myself blushing as I accepted it. "It's beautiful, thank you."

Theo smiled and offered me his arm. I lightly placed my hand on his forearm near the bend of his elbow.

He then looked at my parents and in a casual way said, "Oh, Mr. and Mrs. Oxtabee, I forgot to tell Iris. Everyone is getting together at Isabelle Tate's house before we head off to prom. You know, so they can get pictures and have a drink." He laughed.

"But I sent you a text saying that Esther and Darren were meeting with some of his friends at Olive Garden before prom. They are expecting us." I was uncomfortable with the social norms I was going to have to navigate to begin with, but the thought of letting down Esther made everything worse.

"Just text them. Darren's chill. He knows about the other party. He's probably already told what's her name—"

"Esther," I managed despite the kernel of anxiety that was rapidly expanding and headed toward a full-blown panic attack.

He turned to me and took my hand, lifting it to brush a kiss across my knuckles. "Esther will understand. She's your friend, right?" I nodded and pulled my hand from his. My anxiety lessened as soon as he let go.

He turned back to my parents and casually wrapped his arm around my waist. I stiffened. He didn't seem to notice. He gave them a warm smile. He was much more charming than he was at school, being polite by fulfilling the social expectations and norms of such an occasion, and it made me wary.

However, both of my parents chuckled and looked pleased. I tried to dismiss the feeling, as my people radar was hardly accurate. There was no doubt the churning of adrenaline, cortisol, and likely excess stomach acid was the reason for my weird mix of emotions that swung from excited to anxious to nauseous and back.

"How wonderful! I still have some of my chocolate chip cookies, which are delicious—if not addictive, according to Iris—and a bottle of wine I can bring." There was a very real chance that my mother was going to have a much better time than I would tonight.

"I know the Tates. We'll see you there shortly," my father said with a warm smile.

It wouldn't be long before I entered the much wider society of the world, and there was no better time than the present to learn how to function in a setting of small talk and cheese cubes. My father would refer to it as learning to swim with the sharks. I took a deep breath and held it, preparing myself for the heretofore unknown waters.

Theo took my arm and leaned in to whisper in my ear. I jumped back a little, his closeness and familiarity catching me off guard. "Are you all right? You look weird. Are you breathing?"

I let the air out in a rush. "Yes. Perfectly fine." I forced myself to drop my shoulders from my ears and take on a relaxed stance, as that might fool my mind into being calmer. I smiled. "Wonderful, in fact."

"Um, okay then, we're off." With a wave to my parents, we walked to his car and he opened the door for me. I carefully held my dress so that I wouldn't close the door on it and then slid into the front seat. I reached for the door and instead hit Theo's ribs, as he had bent down and leaned into the car.

"Oh!" I jumped in my seat and leaned back. "I'm so sorry." Why was he practically in the passenger-side seat with me?

"Hey, relax," he said, and grinned. He carefully took my seat belt and reached across me to buckle it, then straightened. I tried to relax and looked up to give him a smile. It must have come off as forced, because his eyes narrowed briefly and he pursed his lips before somewhat loudly closing my door and moving to the driver's side. He seemed to have forgiven my lack of appreciation for his gentlemanly gesture, because when he got into the driver's side and buckled in, he flashed his extraordinarily white teeth at me before saying, "Let's go have some fun."

* * *

We reached the Tates' only a few minutes before my parents. I stood slightly behind Theo on the patio as a group of eight couples swarmed around us. I knew no one and recognized only a few of the girls from the cheerleading squad and the two that hung around Theo as if they were his loyal subjects.

My mother spotted us and waved. She had her phone in hand to take pictures. My father followed with his centuries-old Canon 35 mm camera. Another father approached him with his own oversize obsolete photography bag. They began comparing lenses, and it occurred to me that it was a social custom that went back to before we developed language. It said, *We are the same*, and, *I am better than you*. Thus creating both a social bond and the opportunity to establish dominance.

I turned to point this out to—Theo. I had been so caught up in my observations that it surprised me to see it was him and not Squeak beside me. His absence had created a far larger hole in my life than I could have imagined.

"Hey, what's up? You've got resting bitch face on."

"What?" Did Theo just say that? I looked at him with wide eyes and open mouth.

"Whoa . . . what's wrong with you?" Theo looked something between disgusted and annoyed. I couldn't blame him. I was hardly a vibrant, fun-loving date, thinking about my ex–best friend instead of taking social-media-worthy "perfect couple" selfies. I shook my head a little to readjust my thoughts. Time to fully embrace William James's theory of "as if." I would act as if I were engaging company, thrilled to be in his presence. Then I would be. It was the malleability of the brain. And the heart? I hoped so.

I put on the warmest smile I could muster and met his eyes. They were icy blue and intimidating, but I stared into them, keeping my expression soft but happy. "Sorry, I was just overwhelmed for a minute. I can't believe I'm here with you."

His face relaxed and he smirked. "Well, you are." He leaned in close. I fought the urge to lean back and away from him. Before he could get any closer or do anything else, someone called his name and he turned away from me.

"Hey, Coop!" he shouted to his friend. He glanced back at me. "I've got some things to discuss with Coop. Be right back." Without waiting for my response, he strolled away with long, confident strides.

"Are you Iris?"

I jumped a little and spun in surprise. One of the pom-poms stood very close to me. Where had she come from? Her eyes were bright and her interest in me was obvious. If not a little creepy.

"Huh? I mean, yes. And you are?" I asked. The way this popular group wound around one another so smoothly, gliding up behind people without signaling their approach, did not bode well for my being able to relax and go with the flow of the evening. I was going to be constantly trying to figure out who was coming up behind me and where the people who had been in front and to the side of me had slid away to. I tripped and bumped into things too often to be able to sneak up on anyone. If only Esther were here to be a safety barrier for me. She'd be at prom, though, and that gave me hope for a less-than-disastrous evening.

"Meagan," she said brightly.

"Nice to meet you." I was sure my smile didn't reach my eyes, but she didn't seem to notice or care. She just kept talking, all the while checking me out, from my hair to my navy-blue satin dress.

"I heard about you! You're the one Taylor was talking about. You're, like, a genius, right? She said you were—ow." She looked down at her arm, where her friend—I assumed she was a friend—had stepped up and aggressively pinched her.

"Shut. Up. Meagan," she said from behind a forced smile.

"Oh! Yeah. Okay." Meagan looked a little frightened, or maybe she was embarrassed. It was hard to tell what her expression really was due to the thick liquid eyeliner that framed her eyes. "Laters, yeah?" her friend said without really looking at me.

"Sure, laters," I said. I wasn't sure what that had been about, but I guessed I was of interest since I was there with Theo and was unknown in their social group. An interloper from another pack who could be mistaken as a threat. My safest move was to stay close to Theo.

As I walked down to where he was now standing with a small group of males, one of the fathers whistled loudly and shouted, "Group picture time!"

I was briefly overrun with everyone moving toward the front of the house. Theo motioned for me to join him, and I managed not to fall or twist my ankle as I made my way over. The potential for an enjoyable evening was increasing. So far so good. I could do this.

It was a grueling ten minutes of parents shouting things from "Say cheese" to "Okay, nobody fart," followed by groans.

One of the mothers said, "The food is served!" Part of the group broke off and made their way to the back of the house, where I assumed some tables had been set up. The remaining females, almost simultaneously, held up their own phones and began taking selfies of themselves or with their friends and dates.

If Esther were here, we would be doing the same. She was the one in charge of taking selfies. And Squeak had always been in charge of making sure I smiled in pictures. I found myself feeling lonely despite being around so many people.

Theo elbowed me, none too gently. "Get your phone."

"Oh yeah," I said as I grabbed my small purse, which hung over my shoulder by a long, thin navy-blue silk strap. My mom had made it in less than an hour so it would match my dress and I could safely carry my phone. Because, "You know you'll want to take pictures." Which really meant, "You better take a lot of pictures."

I fumbled with my phone, not ever having taken selfies myself, and I couldn't find the right symbol to touch to get the front lens. Theo finally took it from me, pressed one of the upper corners of the screen, and handed it back. I held it up and pursed my lips as everyone else seemed to be doing.

Theo pressed his lips together in a half scowl as he stood just over my shoulder. He pointed a finger sideways at me. I took the picture. His expression seemed to indicate he was not overly thrilled or impressed with being with me. It was a little disturbing, but he seemed to think it was hysterical.

My mother ran up to me and gave me a hug. Her cheeks were flushed pink, probably from wine, and her eyes shone. "Have fun, sweetie. Theo, take good care of her and get her home safe."

He gave my mother a small bow and smiled. “It will be my pleasure.”

“Glad to hear it.” My mom smiled at us and kissed my cheek. She turned to join my father, who waved to us. When my mother reached him, he put his arm around her and they walked toward their car.

As my parents pulled away, another car—a limousine, actually—pulled up behind them and managed to fit into the now-empty space. Everyone’s attention was of course on the bright white luxury car. The back door opened, and Squeak stepped out.

Squeak was here? In a limo? I stepped instinctively behind Theo to hide. The thought of actually facing him had my heart racing and my mouth dry.

Theo reached back and took my arm, pulling me beside him. He was frowning and his eyes were slits. “Let’s go,” he growled. Pom-Pom was now exiting the car, and Squeak was closing the door for her. Her dress was much as I had imagined it—a deep-wine, formfitting gown that came just below her knees. Her chestnut hair fell down her back in big, bouncy barrel curls, much how I had worn mine for the one and only day I could manage it. It was no surprise she had hair skills. Although it was perfectly done—probably salon. Maybe she wasn’t as perfect as I imagined.

All I could manage was, “A limo?”

“Taylor’s asshole dad has a limo rental business. She’s just trying to show me up.”

He pulled me down the hill toward his car, which was unfortunately parked very near to the limo. There would be no avoiding Squeak now. I couldn’t help but stare at him. He wasn’t wearing a tuxedo. Not many of the boys were. He was dressed in a very nice navy-blue suit with a wine-colored tie that matched Pom-Pom's dress. He looked mature and polished. Fit and all. Handsome.

As we got a little closer, he looked up, scanning the large yard. Was he looking for me? Did he know I would be here?

Taylor leaned over and whispered in his ear. He gave her a little smile as he took her arm and began walking up to the party. I thought I heard Theo growl. Worried less about what would happen when Squeak and I met up, and more about the pending confrontation, I tried to subtly steer Theo away from their path, but his stance and steps were quick and determined.

As we grew closer, Squeak looked up from Pom-Pom and nearly stumbled when he saw me. He gaped as he looked me up and down, and a soft smile lit his face. I could only assume his stunned expression was due to the makeup and dress I wore. He'd never seen me like this. On the one hand, it was a tiny bit insulting that it seemed to shock him so much, but on the other, I told myself, he must have thought I looked beautiful. My involuntary blush and smile gave away my pleasure at his reaction. He met my eyes and his smile faded. Then he focused on Theo and his face was stony. Whatever pleasant feelings I had experienced drained away and my stomach twisted.

Neither Squeak nor Pom-Pom spoke as they neared. Everything about Theo felt flexed and ready for a fight. His pace quickened. The boys' shoulders collided just as Pom-Pom and I tugged in opposite directions with enough force to keep them from crashing full on into each other. They were only able to hit shoulders as they pushed past each other, Pom-Pom and I pulling them farther away from each other as best we could.

Theo's hair was messed up, and his tuxedo jacket had unbuttoned and was rumpled from the impact with Squeak's shoulder. He was breathing hard, and his breath seemed slow to return to normal from his surge of aggression.

Pack members of social mammals normally groom in order to placate and reassure a leader. The physical touch and concerned attention decrease aggression and agitation. But I assumed any grooming behavior I might attempt would be somehow misinterpreted and only serve to further antagonize him.

Nevertheless, I reached up to brush his hair back from his face. He jerked away. "What the hell?"

"Sorry," I said quietly, and looked away from him. He smiled then and shrugged. "Don't worry about it."

I was relieved he wasn't as angry as he had seemed at first. I must have surprised him. Despite the fact that he was making what seemed like an effort to be nice to me, I was beginning to feel that this night was headed for disaster, and tried to think of something that I could do to salvage what was likely the only prom I would ever attend. It would be difficult seeing Squeak with Pom-Pom, but it was a large room, and a large percentage of the junior and senior classes would be there. It shouldn't be too hard to avoid him. I would focus on my date and try to keep his focus on me. And besides, I would get a chance to be with Esther and Darren.

Theo looked briefly behind us, getting a last look at his competitor. I had no doubt that Theo saw Squeak's coming here with Pom-Pom on his arm as a direct challenge to his alpha status. He said nothing as we arrived at the car. Without opening the door for me, he stalked over to the driver's side and jerked his door open. "Let's go," he grumbled.

I got in without a word and fastened my seat belt, preparing myself for what I expected would be a grand exit. He revved the engine and then threw it into gear. The tires squealed as we pulled out and turned the corner. Gripping the door handle, I stared out the windshield, trying not to be too concerned about his rather rapid mood swings, which, given his obvious negative and competitive feelings toward Squeak, were to be expected. I glanced over at him and saw that his stiff body language was beginning to soften and relax as we sped toward Sunnylake Ballroom and Restaurant.

# CHAPTER TWENTY-EIGHT

When Theo and I entered the venue—newly remodeled to attract corporate events, weddings, and obviously proms—I was in a haze brought about by the stress of riding in an extremely fast car next to Theo the Track Star, who was a very well-dressed but nevertheless reckless driver.

As he handed over the tickets at the door, I was preparing myself for another panic—this was prom, after all. But surprisingly, the adrenaline rush from the ride here was having a positive effect on my outlook. As we walked beneath the arched trellis of green vines and nicely realistic silk flowers, Theo wrapped his arm around my waist and bent his head close to my ear. "You look beautiful."

"Oh! Um, you do too," I said. Theo laughed. I examined my rose in great detail until we stepped up onto a small platform decorated with a dark, glittery background to get our picture taken. In the time it took for the photographer to pose us and for the bright flash to snap, I realized that until then I hadn't thought of this as a real date. I had simply considered Theo as not much more than a lab rat most of the time.

Something sour crept back into my mood. I had been taking advantage of his vulnerability, and despite our earlier run-in with Squeak and Pom-Pom, his actions suggested he might actually have feelings for me. It would seem *he* thought this was a real date.

Theo leaned down to whisper in my ear as we stepped off the

footprints drawn on the floor, marking the spot to stand for portraits. A small shiver ran through me. I wasn't sure if it was in response to his warm breath against the nape of my neck as he spoke, or if I'd had a chill.

"Looks like they decorated just for you."

I smiled, but I wasn't really sure what he meant—until we entered the ballroom.

Fairy lights were draped in groupings that looked like countless glimmering stars. The space was otherwise barely lit, so that the candles on the tables added to the feeling that we were walking through the night sky among the stars.

I glanced down at my dress. The room really did look as if it had been decorated to match. My rational mind knew that wasn't the truth of the matter, but it felt quite nice, and I decided to go along with my subconscious reactions and enjoy it. It was clear, however, that I'd become just as much of a lab rat in my experiment as Theo. There was a long tradition of scientists experimenting on themselves, but they usually did so intentionally.

I could, at least, intentionally act as if I was having a good time and enjoy myself. Act as if and your mind can be fooled it is the reality of the situation. I had never imagined I'd ever do something like go to prom, and certainly never with what was arguably one of the most coveted popular students. I would accept my success not only in my experiments, but also in this evening's attempt to enjoy a normal high school experience.

The vague hollow feeling and twinge of guilt I'd had a moment ago dissipated. It was all so interesting. Even being cognizant of my brain's chemical reactions to this sort of stimuli did nothing to temper or lessen my uplifting physical reactions. Even more proof.

Theo took my hand, interrupting my thoughts. He led me toward a table in front of the stage, where the DJ was. And the speakers. I tottered on my heels for a moment before getting my balance back. I had never endorsed the whole high-heels-are-attractive thing. They're supposed to make a woman's body appear more proportioned to the Western ideal of sexy—which is really absurd when you think about it. What they actually do is make you walk on your toes with your chest thrust forward and your butt up. A primate in heat.

On top of the ridiculousness of the stance they require, the more a girl has to jerk around to keep her balance, the more vulnerable she is, once again firing off the more basic male instincts. To hell with the Darwinian imperative and heels that cost a fortune—they're a serious disadvantage in a fight. There is a reason why all the detective shows and movies have hot, tall, leggy actresses who can run in heels. The ones who can fight back while still being hindered by their mate-attracting ornamentation are strong, healthy, in-demand, desired mates. In real life, though, the struggle to survive would immediately have me kicking these off and running like hell.

The DJ started his loud mash-up of music I'd heard on the radio, or in other words, background noise I'd learned ways to block out. Music didn't matter much to me, and I never paid attention to what was popular or a "hit." Mostly because it did little for me except cause me great discomfort and, sometimes, actual pain. The only reason I even knew any of these musicians, and I use the term lightly, was because Squeak would talk me into listening to whichever boy band Esther was enamored with at the time so I could help him effectively tease her. Squeak had also tried to keep me up to date on the latest musical trends. By explaining certain styles, he had helped me learn to listen to music and find intellectual enjoyment. He had said that knowing something about popular music significantly raised my chances of having a successful conversation with someone other than Esther or him.

Squeak.

I didn't want to have conversations about music with anyone who wasn't Squeak or Esther. I scanned the room for him, but it was early and everyone was moving, talking, and preening. Between the liberal use of hair spray and styling gel, body glitter on every bare-shouldered girl, and guys in well-fitting suits and tuxes, I didn't recognize anyone. Which was a good thing. It meant no one would recognize me, except those who had been staring at me at the preprom gathering. I hadn't recognized me after my mom finished my hair and makeup. Theo's eyes had lit up when he first saw me, and so had Squeak's, for that matter, so the makeup and the bright plumage must be creating the intended effect.

It would be best if I stopped looking for Squeak and resumed what was turning out to be a very interesting evening of observing people's behavior.

Theo was shouting to his friends, a group of tall, muscled boys who had just been at the Tates' house. Regardless, I still didn't know their names. Theo had failed to introduce me to anyone. That was surprising, given his command over social niceties, but no one was perfect.

They were shouting back, having something that looked like a conversation and already ignoring their dates. I pulled out a chair and sat down. I probably should have waited for Theo to pull the chair out for me, but I didn't have the patience for the adoring-and-submissive-female act. My feet hurt.

The girl next to me was obviously annoyed at her date. I had an urge to point out to her that all the boys were shouting, laughing, and ignoring us equally. And they were quite obviously checking out every girl in the room with a slit up the side of her dress, accentuated breasts, and a minimum two-and-a-half-inch heel. Chimps, the whole lot of them. Predictable chimps. But maybe that was the very reason why I was beginning to have a good time. I understood chimps.

The girl next to me smiled in what was supposed to pass for a friendly greeting, but it was definitely not a Duchenne smile. I felt like I should watch my back in case she had a knife handy to put in it.

When the girl across from me stood halfway up and leaned onto the table to talk to someone on the other side, her breasts nearly spilled out of her dress. The metallic confetti stars tossed over the tabletop immediately adhered to her bared flesh. Who knew? Maybe she'd meant to do that. Men liked sparkly things. All things considered, the competition in the room was pretty stiff. If it helped draw her date's eyes away from some of the other girls, who no doubt would be attracted to the high-ranking males at this table, more power to her.

The DJ was now talking over the music, his words garbled by the volume and our closeness to the amplifiers. He was completely unintelligible, at least to me. Theo seemed to know what he said, because he stepped over to me and leaned down to yell into my ear. "Let's go. First slow dance."

One of his large, very strong hands took my right hand. He pressed his other hand firmly against my lower back. I put my left hand on his shoulder and prayed I didn't step on his feet or trip. But as it turned out, he actually knew how to dance. I did not. Sure, that was no secret, at least to my family and Esther—and Squeak.

But Theo! He seemed to be able to carry me along, and as silly as it seemed, I felt almost graceful.

His scent, emanating from his jacket in the warm room—his scent was . . . well . . . nice. But nowhere near as compelling as Squeak's. I felt the dulling effects of sadness brought on by the absence of dopamine and serotonin—and Squeak. Thankfully, the song ended. Theo took my hand and led me back to the table. He then pulled out the chair for me before going to get us some punch.

When he returned, he handed me a clear plastic cup. I forced myself to smile up at him. I mouthed, "Thanks."

When Theo sat down next to me and pulled his chair so close to mine that our sides were pressed together, the girls at the table glared at me. I glanced up to give him another smile, in order to appear like the attentive date, and a dark look passed over his features. But almost instantly he was smiling and playing with my hair.

I sat up to put a tiny bit of distance between us and put a stop to him fondling my hair. I might have been wrong. There were always subtle things I missed or misinterpreted, especially with people I didn't know well, or when there was a crowd of people, that made it hard to concentrate on what one person was saying and meaning. However, the strange moment left me with a sense of unease.

Given the number of people trying to talk over the loud music, and my sudden doubt about Theo's true feelings toward me, my defenses were down, and my senses were becoming overloaded. It was getting more difficult to attempt to trigger happy feelings about being there with Theo by acting as if I were happy. It had almost worked. The dance had been enjoyable, even the physical closeness hadn't been difficult, but I could feel some of the control I'd managed to have on my often off-putting responses slipping.

I looked away from the table and tried to ground myself. Glancing around the room, I looked for anyone I recognized. Honestly, I would have rushed off to the restroom to get a break if I had been at all certain I wouldn't trip on my heels and land flat on my face.

I saw Esther just in time, and with my luck still holding, she noticed me. She waved frantically from across the room. She and Darren were all smiles. Darren dragged her laughing onto the dance floor, where Esther started writhing, I mean, dancing. I laughed. Esther was here. It was a good thing, too. She was one of two people who knew how to get me out of wiki mode. Given my increasingly confusing mood, I was in danger of slipping into an explanation of who knew what. But luckily, it was hard to start spouting facts when it was too loud to hear anyone. I suddenly wanted to be away from the head table and instead with Esther and Darren.

"THEO," I shouted into his ear.

"Yeah?" he shouted back into mine.

"Let's go dance with Esther and Darren." I pointed to where they were dancing.

He smirked and shook his head. He stood, took my elbow, and led me to another table.

"But . . . ," I tried, but he didn't hear me. I guess Darren wasn't part of Theo's crowd. I had assumed since they were all part of the track team, they were all friends. But I hadn't paid enough attention to the pack mentality. He was alpha and Darren was definitely beta. And no alpha would cross a crowded dance floor to hang out with a beta.

# CHAPTER TWENTY-NINE

The DJ mumbled into his microphone and started a fast song. The bass was so loud my head pounded along with the beat. A male who obviously knew Theo came up and motioned for him to lean in. It seemed impossible that Theo could hear and understand him, but he must have, because he nodded, laughed, and held up a finger to tell him to wait.

He wrapped his hand around my hip and quickly pulled me against him. I involuntarily squeaked and then followed up with a gasp when he pressed even closer. I tried to replace what had to be my shocked look with a cool *whatever* smirk. He likely hadn't noticed either, because he wasn't looking at me, he was shouting in my ear.

"I'm going out back with the guys for a minute," all the while pantomiming. *I*—pointing to his chest. *Going out back*—pointing to the back door and then pointing at a couple of the guys, who'd now gathered in a huddle. *Meet you*—pointing at the refreshment table. *Five minutes*—holding five fingers up.

I nodded, perhaps too vigorously, but I needed some physical space. A minute alone. *Five minutes*—I held up five fingers and then moved my index finger to my thumb to give the okay sign.

I somehow made my way to the refreshment table without tripping or having any other incident. I accepted a cup from a young man who must have drawn the short straw among the waitstaff and was stuck behind the punch bowl.

The drink was a cold relief in the increasing heat of the room. I drank the entire thing and handed it back to him for a refill before he had even put the ladle back in the bowl. With all the dancing and Theo distractions, I hadn't felt the full physical effects of the heat and crowded bodies. Standing alone and outside of the frantic pack, I was covered in four yards of blue, somewhat sweat-stained satin and having difficulty catching my breath.

People were grinding and twerking and some other things no one from a small midwestern town should attempt. It was all mating behavior, and very primitive at that. I found it quite interesting.

I was so caught up in watching the subtle and not-so-subtle interactions playing out in front of me that I wasn't prepared for suddenly seeing Squeak on the dance floor. Pom-Pom was there. With Squeak. Of course, she was. He had asked her. He'd bought flowers. It was a fast dance, and her hands were tightly laced with Squeak's. She reached forward with her chin and put her mouth onto Squeak's ear. Was she saying something or was she sticking her tongue into his ear? Maybe saliva could coat and protect the cilia in his ear canal. She was being unnecessarily demonstrative, but if she saved Squeak's hearing—

I saw Squeak wrap his arms tightly around her and lift his head. Pom-Pom unexpectedly turned her head and met my eyes. She didn't look dismissive or unhappy when she saw me. She looked interested, thoughtful, maybe even curious. Honestly, I wasn't quite sure what her expression meant. She looked away from me and back to Squeak as she put her hand on the back of his neck. When she pulled his head down so she could say something in his ear, I panicked and turned away.

I'd been staring at them like some creeper. Seeing them together made my overall sadness settle in the pit of my stomach. I searched the perimeter as best I could, not wanting to accidentally look at Squeak again. Theo was nowhere to be seen. I turned to make my way to the restrooms to hide and was suddenly nose to nose with Esther. I jumped, and my hand flew to my chest and covered my now-pounding heart. If the evening continued on with such surprises, I was going to need a week in a sensory deprivation chamber just to get my central nervous system out of its fight-or-flight setting.

She grabbed me by the arm and shouted in my ear. The volume of all the noise was likely causing irreversible damage to my hearing. "Iris, I—"

"What?" I screamed back, trying to be loud enough for her to hear me. If I was going to suffer noise-induced hearing loss, so was she. Shared experiences only strengthen friendships, right?

"Dance with us!" She pointed to Darren, who smiled and waved in a very nonthreatening way. How could I be afraid of dancing with them? They would protect me, just as Esther and Squeak always had. A hopeful thought occurred to me. There would be other, new friends. It wasn't like anyone would ever replace Squeak, but they could create new safe spaces in my life.

I nodded after some hesitation, and reassuring looks and gestures from Esther. I followed a dancing Esther and an awkwardly dancing Darren onto the floor.

As soon as we were midcrowd, Esther took my hands and spun us around until I started laughing. When she dropped my hands, Darren took her place. At first I backed up, shocked that he would start dancing with me. For being an athlete, he was a rather stiff dancer. I scanned the room nervously. We must have looked ridiculous dancing together. But no one even seemed to notice us. Perhaps Esther's overenthusiastic movements drew attention away from Darren and me. If no one was watching, I was going to follow Esther and Darren's lead and dance without fear.

I closed my eyes and shimmied a little, trying to move to the music. It was easier to find the beat and rhythm with my eyes closed. I could pretend I was alone with no one watching. My body relaxed, and I began to speed up to match the rising momentum of the music. I didn't even stumble and or crash into anyone. My heart rate increased, I could feel the effect of the endorphins, and dancing, for the first time in my life, was not just anxiety-free but fun.

I opened my eyes when the music stopped. Squeak was standing right in front of me. I froze. Neither of us said anything. We just stood there staring at each other. Then a slow song started, and over his shoulder I saw Pom-Pom smile before turning and walking away. Leaving Squeak and me, together, on the dance floor.

I was befuddled and lost trying to piece together an explanation for her behavior. Was there some survival or success strategy that involved leaving your partner with another female? How did this benefit her?

Squeak looked at me intently, bent his head, and held out his hands. I couldn't move and quickly looked around for Esther and Darren, but like Pom-Pom, they had slipped away. When I didn't take his hands, he moved forward and gently pulled me closer to him. He lifted my hand and placed it on his shoulder and then put his arm around my waist. He took my other hand and held it against his chest. Near his heart. At first we didn't look at each other. "Are you sure?" I couldn't help asking.

"Yes."

I felt his pulse speed despite the slowness of our movements. He looked down at me and . . . were his pupils dilated? The lighting *was* a bit dim, but his pupils—they looked much larger than would seem necessary to let in adequate light. Why had he asked me to dance? Was this his way of telling me we could be friends again? Did that mean he was attracted to me? That the dance was affecting him? Was it affecting me? It was.

I don't know how long we looked at each other. Then he guided me into a turn and we came closer. I forced myself to break our gaze. Closing my eyes, I breathed in his scent. He smelled so good that I couldn't help resting my cheek on his shoulder. His chin rested on top of my head. Then his head bent and I felt his cheek press against my hair. We danced silently until the song ended. He held me tightly for a moment before letting me go. His eyes were moist and I hiccuped a breath. Before either of us could say anything, Theo was beside me, wrapping his hand around my upper arm. He put his face close to Squeak's and then spoke in a deep, threatening tone. "Back off." He pulled me from the dance floor toward the back of the room near the refreshments. I went with him. For both their sakes, I wanted as much distance between them as possible.

When we reached the bar filled with sodas and iced tea, I looked back over my shoulder, but Squeak was gone. Then Esther rushed over.

". . . talk to you!" I thought Esther said.

"You want to talk to me?" Was this about Squeak?

"Yes." She nodded. Then I thought she said something about Taylor. Not Squeak.

"Theo," Esther shouted into my ear.

And then Theo was beside me, shouting in my other ear.

*Yes.* I nodded and pointed to Theo and then looked at Esther. *Here he is.* I pointed again.

I glanced again at the dance floor and saw *them*. Pom-Pom ran her fingers up Squeak's arms and slid her hands around his neck. After our dance, how could he let her hang on him like that? And look so happy about it? We'd felt so—connected. Had I missed my chance? I should have apologized while we were dancing. I watched as she said something to him that made him smile. She then stood on her toes and kissed his cheek. Had he just danced with me to get back at me? No, that couldn't be his motivation. After all, his pulse . . . his pupils—

Esther tugged hard on my arm.

*What?* I mimed, throwing my hands up. Theo immediately put a cup in my hand. I glanced at him. At least someone was unambiguously being thoughtful and kind, unlike Squeak. I was more confused than I had ever been. Why had Squeak danced with me? I said, "Thanks," and quickly drank it.

It was like pouring propane from a Bunsen burner down my throat. I coughed, gasping. Theo pounded my back.

Esther's face was ashen, and she gave me a pleading look I didn't understand. Granted, things were becoming a little fuzzy. I straightened and coughed once more.

*What?* I mimed again. Esther didn't have to worry so much about me. I knew she'd had a drink or two at football bonfires. Why shouldn't I start having typical adolescent rebellious behavior? More than anyone in the room, I understood how the body metabolized alcohol. The effects of one drink would burn off in one dance. Well, given my size and lack of acquired alcohol tolerance, it might take two very enthusiastic dances. But so what? Did anything matter anymore?

Theo shouted in my ear, "Wanna dance?"

"I'm fine!" I shouted at Esther as Theo took my hand and started walking. I looked around the dance floor and saw Squeak and Pom-Pom were still dancing. Together. As if nothing had happened between Squeak and me.

Suddenly my body ached. I couldn't go back out there. I tugged Theo back. "Air," I shouted into Theo's ear. "Outside." My head was beginning to feel fuzzy, likely from the high alcoholic content of the drink he'd given me. Nothing and no one were making any sense. I just needed some air. He raised his eyebrows and then gave me a slow smile before taking my arm, intending to lead me to the rear door.

I chanced a look over his shoulder to see if Squeak was there. He wasn't, at least as far as I could see. If he was somewhere close by, he would see me being whisked away, out into the night, by a tall, handsome man in a slick, expensive tuxedo. Not that he'd give it a second thought if he did.

Theo held the door open just enough for me to slip through and then followed. The cool night air washed over me, and I shuddered a little with surprise from the unexpected chill. Perspiration's main purpose is, after all, to cool down the body so it won't become overheated. Not perspiring will only lead to damaged organs and, potentially, death.

Nevertheless, I would really have liked to have a sweater. Despite shivering, my body's way of warming up, I managed to catch my breath for what felt like the first time since walking into prom.

"Thanks," I said.

"Hey, no problem. You okay?" Theo wasn't looking at me.

"I'm fine," I said.

"You look fine." Now he was looking at me. His smirk made it sound like a pickup line.

That in and of itself was such a textbook move that I laughed. "Thanks." I somehow managed to trip while standing still. Theo held my arm to keep me from falling. The world spun a little. "What was in that drink?"

Before Theo could answer my question, Squeak stepped out onto the path behind us.

# CHAPTER THIRTY

Theo's eyes narrowed and his now-familiar smirk returned. When Pom-Pom appeared beside Squeak, Theo wasted no time. He wrapped his arm around my waist and pulled me tight against him. His face was so close we might as well as have been kissing.

I pulled my head back as much as I could, but it just made the angle of my head even more uncomfortable.

"Don't move. Make this look good." He grinned. It contorted his face and gave me an unsettling chill.

Then Theo lifted his head and looked to the side. I turned my head and followed his gaze. Squeak and Pom-Pom were gone. Before I could look to see if they were still outside, Theo took my hand and began pulling me down the path toward the parking lot. "Ha! They obviously didn't want to stick around to watch us go at it. Hope you're not disappointed, but I don't want to waste any more time."

Disappointed? Did he mean because he didn't kiss me? I puffed out a breath in relief. That was a close call. "Where are we going?"

"Where the real party is," he said.

I stumbled along after Theo. He nearly dragged me, as I was unable to match his long, confident stride while tottering on my heels. When we came near the edge of the parking lot, he took a sharp right turn, slipping between two tall and overgrown hedges.

There were what looked like three or four couples gathered near the chain-link fence separating the parking lot from some other rather uninspired landscaping. A high-pitched squeal of laughter rose from the group. Theo came to an abrupt stop when we reached them. I clutched his arm with my free hand to keep from falling.

"Coop, pour me and my lovely date some punch, will you?" Theo said, as if issuing an order instead of requesting a favor.

"Comin' your way," said Coop as he handed two empty red plastic cups to his date. She held them while he opened a can of soda, poured half into each cup, and then pulled a bottle of vodka from a backpack at his feet. He finished filling the cups with the vodka. His date, the earlier-met Meagan, came over and handed one to Theo. He winked at her as he took it. She brushed her hand over the top of his leg as she held out the hand holding the other cup to me.

"Here you go, genius. Drink up," she said in a self-satisfied if not smug tone, finally turning her gaze from Theo to me. I took the cup and said, "Thank you." I was feeling light-headed from the first drink, and any concerns I might have had about consuming another highly alcoholic drink were suspiciously absent. And then someone who looked a lot like Meagan, same hair, same dangerously long acrylic nails, began talking about Squeak.

"Taylor really likes her new guy. He looks pretty into her—you're not jealous, are you, Theo?"

Theo snorted. "Let the freak have the bitch."

How could he say that about Squeak? Not only was it mean, but it wasn't true. There was nothing freaky about him. I turned to Theo, ready to defend Squeak. No matter how things stood between us, or didn't, no one deserved to be talked about that way.

Before I could say anything, one of his friends stepped up and punched his shoulder. "Dude, you sure you're okay with that? They'll probably be hooking up in a closet before the DJ takes a break."

Hooking up? Did they mean what I thought they meant? Were they talking about sexual intercourse? The image of the two of them together, half-dressed, in a closet flashed through my mind. My hands shook as I lifted the cup, tilted my head back, and nearly poured the entire drink down my throat in one go. Cup empty, I took a long breath.

"Nice!" said one of the other guys who usually shadowed Theo around school and had been at the earlier gathering.

Who knew? This might be more fun than I thought. Then my once-thoughtful, kind prom date grabbed my butt, causing me to jump in surprise and drop my empty cup. One of the girls who'd been at the table at the start of prom grabbed the cup as it rolled away. She handed it to her date beside her, and he handed it to Coop along with his own cup. Coop repeated his bartending movements as before.

"What was that?" I asked.

Theo took a drink from his cup and then calmly asked, "What was what?"

"That display of dominance and objectification."

"So I grabbed your ass," he said with a smirk. He cast his eyes downward, "checking me out," as Esther would say.

I considered him. Things were becoming a little blurred, and the group's laughter seemed to circle me before receding into the background, mixing with the muffled sounds of dance music.

"Oh, lighten up. Just means I like you." He shrugged and then took a slow drink from his red cup.

"Maybe, sort of—but . . . it can also be a show of aggressa-i-sion—aggression." I had to stop and try to focus. But was he correct in some way? Was that right? Something about it rang true, but I knew there were reasons that it was actually sexual assault. Although, I was having problems putting together the reasons. Words ran past and tangled in my head. Paragraphs suddenly formed and flew out of my mouth. Wiki mode slipped free from my hard-earned filters as my intoxicated brain lost control. "Vodka is a central nervous system depressant. Not only—it increases production of beta-endorphins in the hypothalamus, which is lighting up your nucleus accumbens . . . ," I said, or at least I think that's what I said. My words sounded a little slushy.

"Uh-huh." He leaned over, reaching for me. I ducked and moved away from him, stumbling a little.

"You're not really attracted to me. It's the alcohol; it's the physical contact with a female showing bare skin. . . . Your left anterior cingulate cortex doesn't know I'm just a prom date. . . . It's directing blood to your, uh . . .

"And buttock grabbing, slapping . . . that might be because monkeys and people who have social bonds have unspoken—well, monkeys don't speak, but you know what I mean—signs, signals, like it's okay in sports, it is often construed as homoerotic behavior among the football or baseball players, towel snapping, butt slapping, and such, but really it is a way of building come-rad . . . comrads . . . no, camaraderie—"

Laughter erupted, and I put up my hands and shook my head, perhaps a little too vigorously, because I stumbled sideways a bit before one of boys near me caught my arm and steadied me.

"No, guys, we're monkeys—you know, apes, primates, really cousins—but even they know it's an assault if it isn't obviously a welcomed behavior. I don't welcome ownership, so you can knock off any ideas of mating probability. Did you know that alcohol affects the mid region of the brain, your baser, more primitive lizard brain, well, it just reacts and you do things that a rational person with higher cognitive functions is able to understand and not act out, especially when it comes to relations among the sexes.

"Of course, our secondary sexual characteristics do present us visually as different, we are still mammals and react to those visual cues," I continued. I thought, confidently, I must be making wonderful arguments, based on the rapt attention they seemed to be paying to me. I was certain that despite my somewhat drunken state, I was amazingly not slurring my words. Or was I? It certainly didn't sound that way to me.

"Like boobs! Here's to boobs!"

"Aren't bigger better?"

"Iris, how big are yours? Does the size of your boobs have anything to do with the size of your brain? You know, like Theo has huge feet," a feminine voice said, "so he must have a huge d—"

These people knew nothing. Theo's feet were big, but he was also tall, and that indicated his general anatomy would be sized accordingly, so his penis could be larger than average, but it certainly didn't guarantee it. The optimal size for mating precludes penises that are too large or too small, so genetically as a species we would tend to perpetuate and therefore reward a moderately sized penis in males. They would likely be more successful.

"Hear that, dude? Step up, let's see some proof!"

I said all of that out loud? And then I heard myself say more, much more, but I couldn't be sure what, exactly.

"Okay, that's enough. Let's go. The chaperones are gonna start snooping around soon," said Theo.

"Theo, I don't think I could dance much, maybe we could sit at the table for a while?" I needed to stop talking. And stop spinning. But I wasn't spinning, I was walking, with Theo mostly holding me up. When I looked up, we were back inside and walking onto the dance floor.

I was immediately surrounded.

"Iris, right? You like experiments?"

"She's the penis expert."

People were laughing and pointing, asking very rude questions, but I was having trouble concentrating on the words. I wasn't able to separate individual people out from the crowd and noise. I wanted to answer them. This was important information they needed to know. The room came into focus, so many people laughing, staring at their phones, watching. A girl came close and held her phone out for me to see. I couldn't see it well. Was she showing me some funny video?

Theo then turned me around and held me facing out in front of him. He hissed into my ear, "I know about your little brain tricks. You thought you'd, what, trick me, fuck with my head? Well, now you're the one that's fucked."

"What? How?" I was scared. Things were making less and less sense. My big grown-up brain started to lose control, and my little lizard brain woke up. I wanted to run away through the underbrush as fast as I could. First Squeak, had he danced with me to hurt me too?

No, I'd felt his pulse race, heard his heart and breath quicken. You can't fake that. He still had some feelings for me. And I was starting to realize I had a lot more feelings for him than I'd thought I could ever have for anyone.

But none of that mattered now. It was fifth grade all over again, and this time Squeak wasn't coming to my rescue.

"Oh, all the little girls came running to tell me. They probably hoped they'd win some points and I'd take one of them to prom."

"I wasn't—I didn't mean—"

He held up his phone in front of my face. On the small screen was a girl in a blue dress, slurring her words, swaying, clutching Theo and jabbing him in the chest, pointing to his groin, saying words like "penis," "testicles," "breasts," "amygdala." Me. It was me.

Theo knew what I'd done, and he was getting revenge. Someone had recorded my drunk wiki leaking, spewing. My toes tapping, my hands gesturing wildly, and—I gasped and felt a sob trying to escape. Tears were starting. I turned away and tried to run.

I barely got anywhere before my ankles bent, and I fell forward, one high-heeled shoe falling off, the other twisting on the floor with my foot firmly in it. Pain shot up my leg. I lay there, unable to stand, not being strong enough to face any of it. Plus, I was very, very drunk.

Someone was lifting me to sitting.

"Hush, Iris, it's okay." Esther was gently holding my arm and tucking my hair back and behind my ear, now tangled and falling in front of my face. Before I could even focus and make sense of the sudden appearance of Esther, Taylor was speaking. She was very calm and very much in charge.

"I've got her. Let's get her out of here," she said. Then they were lifting me to standing. My arm slung over Taylor's shoulders.

Theo was suddenly in my face. "You think I'm brainless, don't you? You—"

And he was gone. Squeak had him by the lapels, fists bunched. "Get away from her. STAY away from her."

Darren ran over to us and stopped short behind Esther. "I got one of the chaperones, Officer Wilken, Ben and Zach's dad. He's coming."

"You're a freak. You and your freaky freak asshole friends," Theo yelled, and tried to shake Seth off.

"Seth, forget him. Come help Iris," Taylor said as I leaned against her to keep the weight off my twisted ankle.

"Taylor?" I hadn't acknowledged her and honestly wasn't even sure it really was her.

"Yes, Iris, it's me. I'm so sorry this got out of control and we didn't find you sooner. Seth was upset when we saw you outside, and then I didn't know about any of this until someone on the squad told me.... I'm really sorry." She actually hugged me.

"But . . ." My head was really spinning and I felt horrible, but I managed to get out, "You guys hate me."

"Oh, Iris, no. Well, maybe at first. But Seth is so sweet, and it broke my heart to see him so sad and torn up over you." She gave one of my hands a squeeze. "I thought maybe—but he wasn't the same without you. I've been trying to cheer him up for days. I mean, I like him a lot, but we're just friends."

"This isn't over," Seth said to Theo.

"Yes, it is," Officer Wilken said as he strode up. Dressed in a suit rather than his police uniform. He was here not as law enforcement but as a chaperone, since his sons were here and part of the prom committee. But he was still an adult in charge, and I was relieved to see him.

"Fuck you, Fynne," Theo said.

“Mr. Fynne, go help your friend. You’re lucky you didn’t throw any punches. As far as Miss Oxtabee is concerned, I have a pretty good idea what the situation is, and I’m willing to look the other way if you get her out of here, right now.

“As for you, Mr. Grant, it’s clear you and your friends have been drinking. . . .”

“Come on, let’s get that ankle iced and then see about getting you home,” Taylor said.

“I’ll take Bee home,” Seth said.

He was going to take me home? He’d called me Bee?

Taylor nodded. “We’ll all take her home.” I was standing on one foot and began to lose my balance and fall forward. Taylor put her arm around my waist and held me up. “You’ll need help.”

Seth nodded. “I’ll be right there,” he said, and turned to say something to Officer Wilken.

Taylor began to lead me out of the ballroom. I leaned on her and got ready to limp toward the main doors. Esther followed close behind. The room started to spin and my mouth turned sour.

“Oh, look out, I know that look. She’s gonna puke,” Esther warned.

We stopped, Taylor looking from side to side for something or someone to help. We were now standing next to Theo as he talked to Officer Wilken. He turned to me. When he saw me still there and standing so close to him, his face grew instantly furious. He took a step forward before Officer Wilken could stop him.

But Esther was by my side. “Stand back!” She pulled her phone from her bra, where she usually stashed it—always said that she liked to keep it handy.

I was going to ask her whom she was going to call when, I couldn’t stop myself, I leaned forward and vomited—all over Theo's chest and then, before he could move away, his shoes.

"Taylor, Esther, grab some wet paper towels. I'll get her to a table to sit down until we can get her cleaned up a little. Then I'll take her home."

Seth. It was Seth. I tried to look up at him, opening my mouth to apologize for everything I'd ever done or would do, but my mouth soured and I squeezed my eyes and mouth closed.

"Take a deep breath," Seth said.

"I'll find somebody who works here and see if I can get an ice pack for her ankle," someone said. Taylor?

"Good idea, I'm on the cleanup supplies," I heard Esther say.

Then Seth slowly guided me to a chair and lowered me onto it. I felt him sit down beside me and gently rub my back.

"How are you feeling?"

"Not good."

He laughed a little. "Yeah, guess not."

My head was still spinning and I didn't dare open my eyes. Besides, I needed to say some things, and it would be easier if I didn't have to look at him when I said them.

"Seth?"

"Yeah?" His hand stilled on my back.

"I'm so sorry. I didn't mean to hurt anyone. You know that, right? I mean, I really didn't mean to hurt you. I mean, I think I love you."

Everything got quiet and then dark. If he responded, I didn't hear it. I passed out.

# CHAPTER THIRTY-ONE

## Sunday

Ow. I woke with my hands pressed against my temples. My head was throbbing. What had happened? I felt like I'd fallen off a building.

Still holding my head with both hands, I slowly sat up. Pain shot up my leg as I tried to bend my knee and rest my foot flat against the mattress. If my ankle could scream, it would have. Then I remembered everything. Well, mostly everything. The vodka, the video—what I said to Seth.

I lay back down with a groan as my mother came into my room.

"You're up?"

"Depends on your definition of 'up.' I don't think I'll ever get up again." I moaned an extremely pitiful moan.

"Oh, you'll get up. Think of it as a teachable moment. A lesson learned."

Based on that comment, it was clear she knew what had happened last night, or at least the drinking part. She sat on the edge of the bed and laid her cool hand on my forehead. "You should take something. Do you want a few ibuprofens?"

"Yes, please."

She got up and went into the hall bathroom and came back a second later with a glass of water and two capsules. I cautiously sat up on my elbows and allowed my mother to slip the pills into my mouth and hold the glass while I drank.

"You're not mad?" I asked.

She carefully set the glass on my beside table before answering. "I'm disappointed. I'm furious at Theo Grant for giving you those drinks and treating you like that. As terrible as the whole situation was—is—I'm thankful that it happened here instead of when you're away at school, where it could be even more dangerous.

"What I really hope you learned, other than hangovers aren't worth the crime, is that . . . everyone is a person first and deserves to be treated as such," she said solemnly.

Since I didn't remember much from after I vomited all over Theo, Esther or Seth must have brought me home and told my mother everything, including what I had done by making Theo the unknowing participant in an experiment.

"And not like lab rats," I said. While my poor attempts to influence his behavior didn't excuse Theo's actions, I was feeling horribly guilty about what I'd done, to Theo and to Seth.

"No, people aren't lab rats. Except, of course, if they sign up for it. Which he didn't. What he did was inexcusable and definitely cruel; however . . ." She frowned but leaned over and lightly kissed my forehead. Her lips were smooth and warm.

"What you did crossed a serious line. That doesn't excuse what Theo did, but anytime you treat people as just subjects in an experiment, you are on a very slippery slope. Please promise me you won't ever do anything like this again to anyone." Her disappointment showed in her expression, and I was ashamed.

I reached out for her hand. "I promise."

She reached up and briefly cupped my cheek with her other

hand. "Good." She paused and gave me a small smile. "Now, drink lots of water today. I also had your father run out for sports drink. Unfortunately, he won't be back until later this afternoon, since he had to run some more-complicated errands. Your electrolytes are going to be seriously out of balance."

"I think maybe I take after you more than I thought." I rested my head on her shoulder.

"Maybe I've just learned a few things from you," she said softly as she ran her hand lightly over my hair.

The well-worn cotton of her MAKE ART, NOT WAR T-shirt was comforting and familiar. I was beginning to feel more comforted than uncomfortable with being held. I wasn't sure what had shifted in my brain to quiet my easily overloaded senses.

I wanted to get out of my room and into the sunlight. Maybe sitting outside would help speed my recovery. Something about sunshine was healthy, right? My head started hurting. I had to stop trying to think. "I think I want to go downstairs. Maybe go out and lie in the hammock or something. It might make me feel better. Nature and whatever."

I sat up and tried to swing my legs over the side of the bed without my ankle hitting anything. I tested putting pressure on it before attempting to stand.

"Okay. But slow down. Let me help you get dressed, at least. Seth is downstairs waiting for you to feel better so he can see you."

Seth, I couldn't see Seth. Not after what I'd done. Not after what I'd said to him. Not after that dance. Plus, he'd seen me out of control and intoxicated. I was ashamed and embarrassed. Who knew what he thought of me now? If our friendship had had any hope of healing, I'd probably permanently ended it with my behavior last night.

"No, I can't see him." I groaned as I fell backward onto my bed and put a pillow over my face. "I'll never be able to go to school. Everyone knows who I am now. Is it too late to let me finish my classes at home or online this year? I might even be able to do my senior year online, or transfer to the Catholic school. Almost no one knows me there." My voice was muffled beneath the pillow, but I was certain my mother heard every word.

Then I thought of something else. I pulled the pillow from my face and threw it across the room as I sat up. "What if it goes viral? I won't be able to hide. I'll have to get one of those online college degrees. I'll never get into grad school, much less a PhD program. It's over. My life is over."

"Iris Jane Oxtabee, I'm almost speechless. I never knew you had such a dramatic flair. Now, my lovely flower, get a grip. Your life is not over. I think you need to get up, get a shower, and go down to have at least a cup of coffee with Seth. He's on his third cup and is waiting patiently for you."

"NO! I can't, I can't, ever." I pulled the duvet over my head as I lay back down.

"You can and you will. He's your best friend. You'll feel much better and be able to put things into perspective once you talk to him. Now come on."

She pulled the duvet off me. I was wearing an unfamiliar pair of sweatpants and a bright pink T-shirt with sparkly letters that spelled out JUICY.

"Uh, Mom?" I pointed at the T-shirt.

"You were wearing that when you came home. Don't you remember? Esther and that nice girl Taylor had wrapped and iced your ankle and found something for you to change into from one of the girls who had clothes for the after-prom party. Your dress was a bit smelly, to say the least."

"I remember the vomiting part," I muttered.

"Well, that's a plus. It will certainly give you pause next time someone hands you a big red cup. That's a memory that generally takes a while to fade."

"It's called aversion therapy," I said.

She carefully pulled me to standing and helped me limp to the bathroom. "It sounds like you're almost back to your old self. You'll feel nearly normal after a nice hot shower."

My hair was still wet, but I pulled it back anyway. I hopped down the stairs on one foot while holding on to the bannister. When I reached the bottom, I could see Seth sitting on a stool at the kitchen island. He spun to the side, one hand still resting on a coffee cup.

"Good morning, Sunshine," I heard my mother call out from somewhere else in the kitchen. Seth laughed and smiled. I couldn't remember the last time I'd seen him smile like that at me. Why was he smiling at me?

"Stop," I said to my mother as I hobbled into the kitchen and dared to slide up onto a stool next to Seth.

"Nope," she said while pouring a cup of coffee.

She brought it to the island and put it down in front of me. "I'll be up in my studio." Not waiting for a reply, she left the kitchen and quickly stepped up the stairs.

I glanced at Seth. The shame and guilt I felt made me mute. I looked quickly at my coffee and took a few quiet sips without even adding milk or sugar.

"Bee? Look at me."

I couldn't meet his eyes. Had I really told him I loved him last night? Maybe I'd just thought it and I'd passed out before I could say it.

"Bee, come on," he said gently.

I reluctantly turned my head and met his eyes. He didn't look like he wanted to break the news that he didn't love me too. So maybe he hadn't heard me if I had said it out loud. I wasn't exactly coherent last night. He looked like . . . like him. Like my best friend. Well, even if we were never more than friends, I'd take what I could get. Because while I knew I wasn't thinking straight yet, I also knew I didn't want to be without him ever again, whatever that meant. Then suddenly it all came pouring out.

"I'm embarrassed and ashamed and so, so sorry. Can you forgive me? I understand if you never want to be seen in public with me or if you're still angry or disappointed, but please, please, be my friend again."

"Bee, stop. I forgive you. I started to tell you last night, but well, you know, you sort of passed out. But we'll get to that in a minute. First, I need to catch you up on what happened after we brought you home."

"We?" Had he brought me home with Taylor and Esther? Of course he did. He wouldn't have abandoned his date. Wait, Taylor had offered to help. I was starting to remember a little more.

"Yes. Taylor, Esther, and I all brought you home. I would have taken you alone, but those two would have none of it. Taylor was really freaked out and wanted to make sure I could pay attention to driving instead of you. She was right. Even with those two in the car taking care of you, all I wanted to do was climb into the backseat and hold you until we got back." He sat back and sucked in a big breath. "Anyway, then, of course, we had to explain everything to your parents. Not something I ever want to relive. Man, you owe me for that one." He shook his head with a small laugh.

"Oh." I didn't know what to say. I wasn't sure how to react, either. Seth acted as if we had already made up and the past had been forgiven if not forgotten.

"Now, where to start?" Seth said.

I wasn't sure I wanted to hear anything more about the evening. I remembered nothing after . . . well, I'd rather not remember that part. Either I'd been so drunk that I somehow blacked out, or what followed had been so horrific I was protecting myself by suppressing the memory. "Well, Mom did say that Esther and Taylor took care of my ankle and got me cleaned up."

At this he raised his eyebrows. "Taylor?"

I blushed. "I may not remember much, but I do remember her helping me get up from the floor when I twisted my ankle. She was kind to me. I didn't expect that. Did she really yell at Theo?"

"Yeah, she did. Before and after you puked on him," Seth said with a laugh.

I leaned forward and rested my forehead on the cool countertop.

"Hey, he deserved it. Besides, turnabout is fair play."

"Don't tell me any more," I said, not lifting my head. The cool surface felt nice against the front of my throbbing skull. It still ached with the insistent reminder of the follies of underage drinking. My mother was right. Just the thought of vodka—or any alcohol, for that matter—made my stomach churn and threatened to bring up what little coffee I had drunk.

"Oh, I think you are going to want to hear the rest of the story."

Still keeping my head on the counter, I rolled my head so I was resting on my temple and could look at Seth.

"You sure?"

"I'm sure."

"Okay." I gingerly sat up.

"Your folks were somewhere between horrified and worried, and probably mad, too. But we were quick to fill them in on the experiment, and then Theo setting you up and getting you drunk. We also told them about the video and the crappy, childish response of all of Theo's group as well as some other losers."

I thought I was going to cry. Everything hurt, and I felt sick. It was a different kind of physical pain and reaction than from the hangover. That would at least get better. I was pretty sure this pain would never go away. Not trusting myself to say anything without bursting into tears, I simply nodded.

"So this is the good part," Seth said as he leaned in.

That got me. "The good part! There's nothing good about last night!"

"Ah, see, there you're wrong. Esther knew you were going to spew. She saw it coming and was at the ready with her phone and got it on video—Theo covered in puke and freaking out."

I would have jumped off the stool if my ankle hadn't been throbbing with a constant reminder of the sprain. "I thought you said this was the good part. How could she do this to me? Please, please, tell me she didn't post it."

"Can't do that, 'cause she did." He looked so pleased it was killing me.

"No!" I said.

"Calm down." He took both my hands. "You weren't in the shot. Far more of the school is entertained by him covered with vomit than by his shitty stunt. In fact, a lot of people are pissed at what he did and what he's done to other people in the past. His video has twice the views yours does. Come Monday, everyone will be talking about that a hell of a lot more than about you.

"I can't promise you won't get teased, but it won't be too bad. We have less than a month of school left. We'll get you through it. We've got your back. Man, Esther really made a masterful move. She might be in competition for your title of genius."

"Really, are you sure? I wasn't in the shot, people aren't talking about me?" I asked, still not believing this was true or he could be so kind so soon after everything.

"People are still going to talk about you, but Theo is the one who's got the serious humiliation to live down. He has a lot farther to fall than you do."

"Thanks."

"Hey, I didn't mean it like that. You know what I mean," he said with a kind smile.

Maybe we were friends again. He really did have a point—the more popular you were, the more people you stepped on to get that way. There would be a lot of underclassmen thrilled with his public setdown.

"Look, by next year it will all be forgotten. Someone else will do something more scandalous and tastier, I'm sure. Fifteen minutes of fame and all that. Social media stars are fleeting."

"A star, huh?" I felt some of my headache recede. My shoulders relaxed and dropped down from where I'd had them tensed by my ears. Seth was back where he should be and having the calming effect on me I'd come to count on. What scared me the most was the possibility that this reconciliation was only temporary.

Seth stood and took my hand. "Come on, let's go outside, it will do you good. It's a gorgeous day."

We moved out to the front porch, where the warm sun was helping to relieve some of the hangover symptoms, especially after Seth handed me his sunglasses to wear.

"Taylor went out of her mind when she heard the squad talking about how pissed off Theo was when he heard what you'd been trying to do to him." His voice was barely above a whisper.

"So you knew the experiment was, um, compromised?" I said, resting my head on his shoulder. I sensed that things had shifted between us, but in a good way. I no longer felt the dull ache in my chest that had settled there after the fight and hadn't lessened until now. Things were going to be different. I wasn't scared of that anymore. This must be what hope felt like.

"Only after we'd danced. Oh God, Bee," he said, and then shook his head. Here his tone changed and he turned to hug me.

I gently pushed him away. I needed to see his eyes, his familiar, warm eyes. With everyone and everything so radically different from the day before, it felt good to see something that hadn't and wouldn't change. "Why did you ask Taylor to prom?"

"I was hurt and she is really a good person. We're friends."

"But she was all over you on the dance floor," I said, sounding a bit too jealous.

Seth caught my tone and grinned. "She's touchy-feely, with all her friends. She's been a good friend to me, really made me talk about how I felt about you, especially after she saw how upset I got when Theo kissed you," he said.

He seemed embarrassed admitting that seeing Theo kiss me had upset him, but I was mortified that I'd even kissed the jerk. "Don't remind me. It was awful."

We both sat silently for a moment. There was only one way this conversation was going to go, and I don't think either of us knew how to approach it. The silence got to me first. "How *do* you feel about me? You don't still hate me, do you?"

"I won't lie, it's going to take some time to get past some of the things you've done. But I think I want to—get over it, I mean." He lightly placed his hand on my arm.

I put my hand over his. Relief rushed through me. It wasn't perfect, but we were still friends. "Thank you. I want you to too. I want to tell you things, like, ten times a day, and you're not there. Poor Esther is exhausted." I half laughed over the lump in my throat. I was dangerously close to crying. "Seth, I've missed you, and I'll never be able to say I'm sorry enough."

He pulled his hand out from under mine and moved closer to me. "I don't think we have a choice but to figure this out. You need to tell me things. I need to have you tell me things. I've been bored without you."

I wanted to feel relieved. I had him back as a friend. But I'd discovered that I really wanted to be closer than that, despite all the reasons, neurological and sociological, that said I shouldn't.

We sat quietly for a moment. There was so much more to say. I didn't know how to start. Luckily, Seth found a way to get past the awkwardness.

"So, I'm Seth now?" He looked at me, managing to insert both teasing and genuine curiosity into his question.

I nodded. "Squeak doesn't fit anymore."

"Bee, I haven't squeaked in years." He looked as if he couldn't believe I'd been so unaware of the changes in him since grade school.

"I didn't notice. I mean, I noticed when we were fighting in the lab. No, that's not true. I noticed before then. I just didn't want to—I don't know, it confused me . . . about how I felt about you." I looked down and away from his face. It felt good to be telling him how I felt, but at the same time I was terrified. Everything would change after this. Change wasn't something I was good at. But maybe it was time I learned how to be.

"I thought you were never going to notice, and then . . ." He removed his hand from my face and reached down to hold mine.

"And then," I repeated. We both grew quiet. I watched as he played with my fingers. "It doesn't make sense. You're like my brother. I think I'd been thinking about you more than I used to, and I couldn't admit it because it didn't fit the normal pattern of human development of attachment or the research. . . . There's nothing about us that translates into passion," I said.

"Really?" The corner of Seth's mouth quirked up in a half grin.

"I'm serious. There's a sound reason for the sibling effect. It's in our wiring. If you grow up around someone, your brain just thinks 'sibling' and there's no attraction. It helps prevent inbreeding and—no, that's not what I meant. I mean, I don't want you to think of me that way if you don't, but—"

He held up his hand to interrupt me. "But I've never been comfortable with anyone like I am with you. I've never wanted to be around anyone else all day, every day. You're a part of me, and I can't imagine it any other way."

I put my head back on his shoulder. "And you're the only one I've ever felt comfortable touching," I admitted. We sat there for a few minutes, not saying anything. It was . . . good. I didn't feel like I needed space or that his shirt was going to make my face itch. And then I started thinking about things that did make me itch.

"I should have asked you to prom before you even started the experiment. I just thought maybe you'd see that you had some sort of real feelings for me before I asked. I didn't want you to say no," he said.

"Why didn't you ask me after I started the experiment?" I asked.

"Well, you made it a little difficult when you started on about how easily you could control the male heart and were going to nab the alpha male for a prom date. Nice. How the hell was I supposed to step up and say, 'How about me? Can I ask you to consider settling for a beta?'"

"Well, if you hadn't waited until the last minute to ask me, I wouldn't have come up with the whole terrible plan."

He moved to stand up. I panicked. He was going to leave. Why couldn't I ever say the right thing?

"I'm sorry, I just—there's so much previously unknown data. It just clouds everything I thought I was beginning to understand. I'm so used to being right," I said.

He sat down next to me again, this time holding both my hands. "You're right a lot of the time, but people aren't robots and they're not apes. All the fMRI research you love so much is guesswork at best, at least right now. People are fluid and unpredictable in some horrible and terrifying ways, but that unpredictability and the ability to change are what makes everyday life fascinating."

I nodded. "Neuroplasticity."

He just looked at me.

"Sorry," I said. Desperate to change the subject, I pulled one of my hands from his and reached up to lightly run my finger down the length of his nose, noting the small bump and slight bend to the left.

"I remember when this happened." I let my hand drift away. The past injury was barely noticeable. But it gave his face character. Symmetrical features are supposed to be attractive, but really? They may make someone beautiful but not very interesting.

He laughed lightly. "I do too. It ended what could have been a historic baseball career."

I scowled. "Baseball career? You were eight."

"I was nine and you were eight. When that pitch broke my nose, I abandoned my plans for going pro." He gingerly touched the bridge of his nose and winced. A bit too dramatically to be sincere.

"I'm sure the world wept," I said.

"No, probably not. However, the universe is another matter. The universe mourned my abandoning my one true calling." He reached up again to feel the crookedly healed bit of bone. "When I am a rich and famous physics teacher, I'll get that fixed."

"No, don't," I said with an urgency that surprised me.

"Why? I mean, if it means that much to you—"

"I mean it's you, you wouldn't be you without it," I insisted.

Seth shrugged. "Okay, if you say so. I never cared much one way or another, until you went off about symmetrical features."

"I was wrong."

"And that's a good thing, right?" he asked quietly.

I laughed and rested my hand on his shoulder. "Yes. It's a good thing and I'm really sorry about your nose."

"Yeah, you suck at pitching; you still can't throw a ball straight," he said.

"Thanks, way to compliment a girl," I said.

"You're not a girl, you're Bee," he said. And for the first time in more than a week, he grabbed my ponytail and lightly tugged.

A quiet, almost desperate whimper escaped me, and I threw my arms around him and buried my face in the strong curve of his neck and shoulder.

He wrapped his arms around me. "Bee?"

He was so warm and he smelled so good. I was ashamed, and . . . This was Seth. My best friend in the entire world. I tried to get even closer.

"Seth?" I asked. My voice was muffled. I still had my head buried against him, pinning him to the spot. I wasn't about to let him move, not yet anyway. "I was so wrong about everything. I thought I'd lost you for good and then you would move away, go to college, be gone forever, and I didn't know what to do."

He unwrapped his arms from around me and sat back.

"I made a decision last week and accepted a financial aid deal. And I managed to get a few small scholarships that will cover most of my first year's expenses."

I was afraid of the answer, but I had to ask. I had to face the facts and the future. I'd done so much damage by trying to avoid them. "Where?"

"Claremont College."

"Ten miles from Hillcrest? One town over? You're staying?"

"Well, I'll be living at school, but yeah. I wasn't ready to leave you, even if I never wanted to talk to you again. To be honest, I don't think I'll ever be ready." He shrugged his Squeak shrug and smiled his mature Seth smile.

"People aren't just concoctions of hormones and enzymes. I know you don't always see that. I don't know if you ever see it. But I think you do. Sometimes. There's a layer of the world we can't see, we can't chart, can't predict. We try, and just by luck sometimes we get the right answer, or at least the answer we think is right. The one we're looking for, anyway . . . Listen to me, I'm here and I will always be here for you. You're my bestest Bee. And I love you." He paused and took my hand, lifting it to his mouth, and lightly kissed the palm of my hand.

I wanted to kiss him. So I did.

I covered his smile with my own. His lips were warm and full, easy to kiss and be kissed by. I wrapped my arms around his neck and held on. Everything about the kiss was what the researchers said it would be when attraction was mutual and the participants had strong immune systems.

Seth pulled back and looked at me for a second before leaning in close. "You know, I've been waiting for that kiss since I was fourteen."

I kissed him again. He tasted good. He smelled wonderful. I couldn't get close enough. It was safe here and at the same time completely unknown.

There were a lot of things we had waiting for us, most of which had hard answers, especially in the next few months. I had to trust everything would work out. So I let go of holding on to only what I could see and prove. And then it was all there, all the answers, all of life, all of *us*, in that kiss. A kiss that felt like it was starting new in every moment. A kiss I never wanted to end. A kiss that, at least for the unknowable moment, made everything okay.

# ACKNOWLEDGMENTS

I am blessed with friends and family who have unending support for my whims and writings. I could have never persisted without all of you.

I want to acknowledge my agent Lisa Rodgers from JABberwocky for her belief in and love for Iris and Squeak from the rough draft to the final story.

Thank you to my early readers Bronwyn Gagne and Julia Lipkowitz for the editing suggestions and cheerleading.

Thank you to my critique partners Judi Fennell, Cathy Pritchard, Stephanie Julian, Beth Long, and Lisa Stone Hardt.

Thank you to Valley Forge Romance writers for over fifteen years of support and knowledge.

Thank you to my wonderful editor Jessica Smith for the enormous amount of time and attention she gave to this manuscript. Iris couldn't have made it through this long process without you.

Many thanks to Dr. Amy Margolis for her time, knowledge, and willingness to write such a wonderful addition to Prom Theory. I am humbled.

I can't thank the cover designers and copy editors enough for all their extraordinary talent and for their help in polishing Prom Theory both inside and out.

And finally, thank you to Robert Sapolsky for inspiring Iris with his amazing books, research, and humor.

# AUTHOR'S NOTE

While my oldest child shares many traits, experiences, and social difficulties with Iris Oxtabee, Iris is a unique person, although fictional. Aspects of Iris's character I wanted to focus on were her determination and successes. Simply because a child has a learning disability or an Autism Spectrum Disorder, does not mean everything in life is difficult, nor does it mean some things can't be overcome once coping mechanisms and life skills are learned. This takes knowledgeable support from friends, family, and professionals. It also takes understanding, patience, and acknowledgment of the gifts that often accompany these disorders.

Nonverbal Learning Disability is not a condition many know much about, unlike Autism Spectrum Disorders, which have gotten more attention in the media, including movies and television shows. NVLD and ASD do share a lot of traits such as: motor skill problems, unawareness of personal space, trouble interpreting social cues (body language, tone of voice, facial expressions), poor organization and time management, sensory issues, and mood regulation.

Some of the main differences between the two disorders arethat teens with NVLD have visual-spacial issues (difficulty with directions and sometimes learning to read), are auditory learners, have early language development, and in general are very good with language, and share information in socially inappropriate ways. They can also be very literal and miss sarcasm in conversations. ASD students can also have learning disabilities but NVLD, as it is understood now, is a learning disorder, and although it might look like it sometimes, it isn't an Autism Spectrum Disorder.

As a parent of a now-adult child with NVLD, my worries that the big wide world will break their spirit or drown them in the anxiety and depression that often accompanies NVLD or ASD are still with me. But so is my amazement of their gifts. Their vast knowledge of birds and other wildlife, ancient civilizations, languages, and artistic ability has at times, (and perhaps to their dismay) drawn groups of both adults and children to them with questions and wonder.

They have learned to drive when at times it seemed like that would be something out of their reach. They have excelled academically, even at math, though the effort was intense and real. They overcame significantly delayed fine motor skills due to a nearly obsessive desire and focus on learning to draw. This too came at a cost as teachers would have to insist they did not draw in class, and much of the time this behavior was seen as disruptive. But as the school district psychologist told me after the final testing was completed their junior year of high school for their IEP, "That fine motor difficulty? They've 'fixed' it." A kid for whom it seemed they would need to learn keyboarding in elementary school because using a pencil was a struggle, now gets compliments for their beautiful handwriting.

I wrote Prom Theory because I wanted Iris, and every child, no matter their difficulties, to have understanding friends, a strong community of supportive educators, andloving parents who try their best to understand how and why things that come so easily to many children seem to elude theirs. Through this story, I hope I've shown a little bit of what a world like that might look like. I also hope this story helps readers better understand classmates who act and react differently from others, and that I've brought some attention to a disability that can go unrecognized or misdiagnosed so that students might have more of a chance to get the assistance and skills to be successful in life. We need to support and lift up the neurodiverse. They often are the ones who make the big discoveries, create the never-before imagined, and change the world.

Ann LaBar
October 2020